My Fair Highlander

My Fair Highlander

Mary Wine

BRAVA

KENSINGTON PUBLISHING CORP.
www.kensingtonbooks.com

Chapter One

"Tell me you did not tell that barbarian Scot that he could court me."

Jemma Ramsden was a beautiful woman, even when her lips were pinched into a frown. She glared at her brother, uncaring of the fact that most of the men in England wouldn't have dared to use the same tone with Curan Ramsden, Lord Ryppon.

Jemma didn't appreciate the way her brother held his silence. He was brooding, deciding just how much to tell her. She had seen such before, watched her brother hold command of the border property that was his by royal decree with his iron-strong personality. Knights waited on his words, and that made her impatient.

"Well, I will not have it."

"Then what will you have, Sister?" Curan kept his voice controlled, which doubled her frustration with him. It was not right that he could find the topic so mild when it was something that meant so much to her.

But that was a man for you. They controlled the world and didn't quibble over the fact that women often had to bend beneath their whims.

Curan watched her, his eyes narrowing. "Your temper is misplaced, Jemma."

"I would expect you to think so. Men do not have to suffer having their futures decided without any concern for their wishes as women do."

Her brother's eyes narrowed. She drew in her breath because it was a truth that she was being shrewish. She was well past the age for marriage, and many would accuse her brother of being remiss in his duty if he did not arrange a match for her. Such was being said of her father for certain.

Curan pointed at the chair behind her. There was hard authority etched into his face. She could see that his temper was being tested. She sat down, not out of fear. No, something much worse than that. Jemma did as her brother indicated because she knew that she was behaving poorly.

Like a brat.

It was harsh yet true. Guilt rained down on her without mercy, bringing to mind how many times she had staged such arguments since her father died. It was a hard thing to recall now that he was gone.

Her brother watched her sit and maintained his silence for a long moment. That was Curan's way. He was every inch a hardened knight. The barony he held had been earned in battle, not inherited. He was not a man who allowed emotion to rule him, and that made them night and day unto each other.

"Lord Barras went to a great deal of effort to ask me for permission to court you, Jemma."

"Your bride ran into his hands. That is not effort; it is a stroke of luck."

Her brother's eyes glittered with his rising temper. She should leave well enough alone, but having always spoken her mind, it seemed very difficult to begin holding her tongue.

"Barras could have kept Bridget locked behind his walls if that was his objective. He came outside to meet me because of you."

"But—"

Curan held up a single finger to silence her. "And to speak to me of possible coordinated efforts between us, yes, but an offer from the man should not raise your ire so much, Sister."

The reprimand was swift and solid, delivered in a hard tone that made her fight off the urge to flinch. Her brother was used to being in command. His tone was such that not a single one of his men would argue with even if she often did. But that trait was not enhancing her reputation. She noticed the way his knights looked at her with disgust in their eyes. When they didn't think she could hear them, they called her a shrew. She would like to say it did not matter to her, but it did leave tracks like claw marks down the back of her pride. Knowing that she had earned that slur against her name made her stomach twist this morning. Somehow, she'd not noticed until now, not really taken the time to recognize how often she quarreled with her brother. He was a just man.

"You are right, Brother."

Curan grunted. "You admit it, but you make no apology."

Her chin rose and her hands tightened on the arms of the chair as the impulse to rise took command of her.

"Remain in that chair, Jemma."

Her brother's voice cracked like a leather whip. She had never heard such a tone directed at her before. It shocked her into compliance, wounding the trust she had in her brother, allowing her to do anything that she wished. The guilt returned, this time thick and clogging in her throat.

"Has Bridget complained of me?" Her voice was quiet, but she needed to know if her brother's wife was behind her sibling's lack of tolerance.

"She has not, but I am finished having my morning meal ruined by your abrasive comments on matters concerning your future. You may thank the fact that my wife has been at this table every day for the past six months as the reason for this conversation not happening before this."

Bridget, her new sister-in-law, had taken one look at the morning meal and turned as white as snow. No doubt her brother was on edge with concern for the wife who had told him to leave her alone in one of the very rare times Bridget raised her voice in public to her husband. Curan had slumped back down in his chair, chewing on his need to follow his bride when Jemma had begun to berate him.

Her timing could not have been worse. But hindsight was always far clearer.

"I will not speak against our father and his ways with you, Jemma. However, you will not continue as you have. You were educated well, just as my wife, and yet you spend your days doing nothing save pleasing your whims. You have refused to see Barras every time he has called upon me as though the match is beneath you; it is not." Her brother paused, making his displeasure clear. "Well, madam, I believe a few duties will help you place some of your spirit to good use." Curan drew in a stiff breath. "I will not force you to wed, because that was our father's wish. Yet I will not tolerate anyone living in this castle who does nothing to help maintain it. You may have the day to decide what you prefer to do, or on the morrow I will have a list of duties given to you. Food does not appear from thin air, and you shall help make this fortress a decent place to reside."

Her brother stood up and strode away, several of his knights standing up the moment their lord did to follow him. Conversation died in the hall, and the sounds of dishes being gathered up for washing took over. Jemma watched the maids and cringed. Shame turned her face red, for she noticed more than one satisfied smile decorating their lips.

Standing up, she left the hall, seeking out the only living creature she could trust not to lecture her.

But that was only because a horse could not talk even if she often whispered her laments against its velvety neck.

In the dim light of the stable, she moved down the stalls until she found her mare. The horse snorted with welcome, bringing a smile to her face, but it was a sad one. Jemma reached out to stroke the light gray muzzle, the velvety hairs tickling her hand. Storm had been her constant companion since her father's death, and she realized that she had never really dealt with that parting. Instead she'd refused to admit that her sire's departure from this life had cut her to the bone.

Instead of grieving, she had become a shrew, irritating everyone around her and escaping to ride across her father's land while the rest of the inhabitants toiled at all the tasks required to maintain a castle keep.

Curan and the others labeled it selfish, but in truth it was running. She had swung up onto the back of her horse and ridden out to avoid facing the fact that her father was dead. It had never been about escaping her chores or thinking the match with Barras beneath her; she had sought out the bliss of not thinking at all, which removed the need to grieve from her mind. She simply ignored the fact that time was passing, choosing to remain locked in a few hours that never progressed. That way, she didn't have to face the sadness that threatened to reduce her to a pile of ashes.

Barras . . .

The burly Scot was something else she liked to avoid thinking about, yet for a far different reason. He looked at her as though he wanted to touch her. Even now, a shiver rippled down her spine at just the memory of the way his eyes traveled over her curves, tracing them, lingering on them while his eyes narrowed and his lips thinned with hunger. Some manner of sensation twisted in her belly, and it set her heart to moving faster, but she was unable to decide just what it was. Or maybe she had merely avoided naming it to remain locked in her fairy bubble where she didn't have to face the grieve that wanted to assault her.

She was shameful to do so.

There was no other way to describe herself. Guilt cut through the façade she'd built to convince herself that she was doing nothing wrong. Well, she had the nothing part correct. It was a lacking that needed her attention. Storm pawed at the ground with rising excitement. The horse was used to her coming every morning to ride.

"Not today, my friend. At least not until later."

Turning around, Jemma squared her shoulders. The staff stared at her with confusion on their faces, but she walked smoothly toward the back of the castle. Autumn was in the air now, the harvest being brought in. There was work aplenty for every set of hands from the young to the old. The storage rooms were being carefully stocked with nuts, roots, and new grain. Barley was bundled in the fields and brought up to the castle yard for thrashing once the seeds were beaten from the chaff; women sewed them into bags for the winter. Girls mostly attended to the chore of sewing because it gave them practice with plying their needles on rough cloth.

Edible roots such as carrots and leaks were being carried up in baskets strapped to the backs of men. Squash would ripen last, but the children would be sent into the countryside to pick berries while the day was bright. The sun was up, and everyone worked to fill the storerooms before winter arrived.

"My eyes must be so old that I cannot trust what they show me."

Maitland Mitchell had been serving Amber Hill since she

learned to walk. Jemma felt her cheeks brighten with a scarlet blush for the way the woman looked at her. Maitland aimed a hard stare at her while wiping her hands on her apron. The piece of fabric bore several splotches and smears, attesting to the fact that Maitland was still an early riser. Jemma knew that that apron had been clean at dawn.

"You may trust your eyes if not my ability to learn self-discipline from you."

The woman's expression softened, her eyes sparkling with welcome.

"Well, you appear to have come to your senses, so no more talk about it. You are not the first one to discover they have no defense against grief. I never doubted that you would see that it was time to move on. 'Tis glad I am to see a pair of willing hands. We've much to do; there was frost spotted on the hills last night."

That meant that winter was beginning to return. The days would slowly shorten now, which meant that getting the last of the harvest in was on everyone's mind. Jemma pulled an apron off a hook that was set into the wall of the work rooms. Approval shone in Maitland's eyes, and that was something that warmed Jemma's heart. Maitland had helped to raise her, taking over when her mother died. The woman didn't hold any great position, but she had experience that made every person serving Amber Hill give her deference. It was respect she had earned and something Jemma realized she longed for.

"I've got soap cooking in the yard. Give it a turn and check the fires and make sure those children are staying well away from the embers."

"Aye." Jemma turned and moved quickly toward the yard. Huge cast-iron kettles were sending steam into the morning sky. She could smell the lye as it was being heated with the vegetable fat. Wheelbarrows of black, sooty ash stood near

large screens formed from fabric. The ash was shoveled into
the screens and water poured through it to bring the lye out.

Picking up a long-handled paddle, Jemma began turning
the thickening mixture away from the sides of the cauldrons
where it was cooking faster. They would keep it boiling until
the entire pot was soft and gel-like. Wooden boxes sat nearby
to be filled once Maitland decided the soap was ready. It
would be left to dry before being cut into pieces. The steam
made her head itch, and the scent tickled her nose. Her shoulders began to ache, but she smiled.

She had finally stopped running.

How was it possible to not see what she was doing? Her father had been her best friend. She sighed. Grief was a powerful thing. Riding along the edge of her family property was
very foolish in such uncertain times. Maybe she had been
seeking a way to join her father without realizing that was her
goal.

He wouldn't want that; she didn't truly long for it, either.

It was a truth that her father would be very unhappy to hear
of her unwise behavior. Riding the border land between England and Scotland was never a good choice, but now that
Henry Tudor, the eighth king to be named Henry, was so close
to his death, relations between Scotland and England were
worse than ever. Scotland didn't even have a king anymore,
but a tiny baby queen named Mary who'd been crowned at
nine months of age. Henry the Eighth had negotiated a be-
trothal of the baby girl for his son Edward, but there were
many in England who wanted Mary Queen of Scots raised in
England so that she would be Protestant instead of Catholic
like her mother.

A war of rough wooing had commenced, and the border
was not safe. Her own brother was one of the men sent to the
border to hold the land for England. The future king Edward

would need all his subjects to help him maintain his hold on his country while he was still a youth. All the crowned heads of Europe were watching to see if England would crumble when the mighty Henry the Eighth died.

Her brother Curan kept peace with his Scottish neighbors by more than just the army under his command. He and Laird Barras combined their wits for the sake of business ventures that were bringing good profits to both men. Happy, well-fed people had little to rebel against.

But that didn't mean she was interested in the Scot courting her.

Yes, you are . . .

It was a whisper that was born somewhere in the darkest part of her mind. Some manner of longing to see just what the Scot did when no one else was near enough to see them. Her lips tingled as she imagined what it might be like to have his against them. Would his kiss be forceful or gentle? She shivered in spite of the heat bubbling in the cauldrons.

Wedding her was just another way for Laird Barras to get what he wanted from her brother, but that didn't keep her from thinking about the way he looked at her. She wouldn't be the first woman married off to her brother's business partners, but that didn't mean the match would be a cold one, the looks the man sent her were very warm indeed.

Is it what I desire?

That question brought another sigh to her lips. It was a truth that she didn't know what she wanted. She was twenty-four years old, and the time for saying nay to any offer for her hand was past. Where had the time gone? She had simply stopped thinking about anything save for her father when he began showing signs of illness. How long had it lasted? Jemma struggled to think about how many years her sire had battled that invading weakness of his limbs. She had tried everything to restore him to health, reading every available book that offered insight into the condition. But in the end, her sire had lost even the ability to speak, blinking his eyes being the only way to communicate with her.

How long?

It had been years, seasons blurring in her memory, and during that time she had never taken time to think about marrying. Curan had been off earning his title with the king, leaving only her to comfort their dying father and care for him. She refused to leave it to servants; he was her father. The man who had chased her through spring fields when she was a girl and laughed when he caught her. The proud man who had allowed his daughter to crown his head with flowers and worn them with a level chin past his knights. Tears stung her eyes as memories, rich with love and tenderness, rose up from her mind to remind her why she had thrust the entire world away in favor of being at her father's side. She did not regret her choice.

If there had been offers for her, they had gone unread. She scoffed beneath her breath; there must have been some offers. There was nothing wrong with her. In fact she was devoted to her family, and that would never be questioned since she had tended her father with so much love. An odd feeling crept over her. It was almost a sensation of desperation. She didn't want to think that no family had offered for her.

Well, except for Gordon Dwyre, Laird Barras.

She bit her lower lip because she wasn't being very kind in her thoughts toward the man. He was Scots, but that was something he could not change any more than she might alter the fact that she was English. There was more than one match across the much disputed border. Besides, if Edward did wed Mary, then England and Scotland would be one nation. Thinking such a thing brought a sense of peace to her, too, even if she doubted that being united beneath one monarch would have the power to remove all the differences between English and Scot. A small smile curved her lips; she could not picture her brother donning a kilt,, and the plaid Barras wore added something untamed to him. Deep down, her insides twisted once again as she considered the way the man moved.

However, many a royal match had been broken before the wedding ever took place. There was pressure from the French to see the little Queen of Scots married to their prince. Such a union was what fueled the war of rough wooing that saw the English trying to kidnap the baby queen and take her into England where she would grow up happily anticipating her wedding date with Edward.

The games of the royals set the tone for uncertainty among their subjects. Jemma cast a look toward the green hills of Scotland. What sort of man was he—Gordon Dwyre? She should agree to meet him—quick glances were one thing, but she knew nothing else because she had never allowed the man to converse with her. Meeting him was the logical choice, the well-mannered one, and marriage was after all a matter for logical thinking not contemplation of hot glances.

But that was what her mind dwelled on.

She would tell Curan at supper that she had thought the matter through and decided to be introduced to the Scot. Many noble daughters never had the opportunity to even speak their opinions of their intended grooms; her brother was being kind.

So why did she feel so torn?

He was spending far too much time waiting on her.

Gordon Dwyre, Laird Barras, reined his stallion in and

scanned the edge of his land. His retainers were fanned out behind him. They knew their places well, blending in with the land formations to make it look as though he was alone.

Today, there was no taper of dust rising up into the afternoon air. He moved his gaze off the hills and felt disappointment sour his disposition.

That was annoying. He'd never formally met the woman, at least not beyond watching her race across the land that was so close he might almost call it his own, or ducking into the hallways beyond the great hall where he had met her brother. His lips curved up with the memories. The woman rode with a wild abandon that drew his attention when there was much he should be investing his time in that did nae involve riding out onto the ridge to watch her. When she discovered him sitting at her father's table, her eyes turned dark, snaring his attention in a far different manner. It was almost if the woman was daring him to come after her.

That was something he had a great deal of difficulty ignoring. Much like coming out to see her riding in the early morning.

There was something fascinating about the way she leaned low over the neck of her horse and let the animal surge forward with every bit of its strength.

It also drew a frown from him. He'd admit that freely enough. The woman didn't seem to have any fear of breaking her neck. But that idea only took him back to being enchanted with her and why she took to the hills so often. It was almost as if she was running away from something. There were times he swore he could feel her pain on the wind.

"Well, lads, it looks like we're going to be left wanting today."

Maybe that was for the better. He had a clan to look after and several smaller lairds who surrounded his land to maintain friendships with. Sitting on his stallion and watching for his English neighbor's sister wasn't going to accomplish any good. However much he might be fascinated by her, he needed a wife who would be his partner, not a girl who did nothing with her time but ride. That was a hard fact, and he was accustomed to facing such; he wouldn't have lasted two months as laird if he couldn't choose the best things for his clan. It was more logical to seek a wife other than Jemma.

But knowing it was the best choice, the one rooted in logic, didn't keep him from nursing disappointment all the way back to his castle.

Jemma was late to supper. Curan narrowed his eyes until he noticed the way she walked. Her brother processed a keen sense of sight, one he'd developed while riding across hostile territory in France at the side of the king.

"Is Bridget feeling better?"

Her brother's face reflected his frustration. "My wife claims that she is well and balanced, yet she cannot enter this hall without her belly heaving."

Jemma froze with one hand on a round of bread. "Oh . . . I see . . . oh, how wonderful. That is welcome news. Amber Hill needs a baby." She smiled, joy filling her.

But Curan looked far from feeling wonderful, deep concern etched into his face.

"It is the way of it. You should take one thing at a time to her and see what does not cause her stomach upset. Then we shall know what it is that does not agree with her. I understand that all women have something that they cannot bear to smell while they are with child."

One of her brother's eyebrows rose. "Is that so?" His gaze went to the table, scanning the dishes that were laid out for their supper.

"Father's constitution was very delicate . . . when he was ill . . ." Her voice trailed off, and she broke a piece of bread off the round in her hands but discovered she had no appetite. Grief renewed its grip on her, making her ache with loneliness. "I shall take this bread to her now and see if it pleases or not."

Her brother caught her wrist before she rose from her chair. "I am sorry I was not here to share in the duties, Jemma."

She shook off his grip and picked up a wooden plate holding warm bread. Snapping a cloth, she covered the bread with it. "It was a daughter's place, Curan, and I do not regret a moment of it, only that I seemed to be unable to resume my life once father had gone. You were correct to take issue with me this morning. I didn't realize that I had turned my back on everything until you forced me to see it. It is time to move on with my own life. I will meet Lord Barras if you still wish to consider a union between our houses." She lifted the plate up and offered her brother a steady look. "But I do know a bit about soothing unsettled bellies. Let us see if Bridget finds my methods of any comfort. It is time for Amber Hill to have new life again."

Approval shone in her brother's eyes along with relief. For all his strength, there was a good heart buried deep inside his hardened exterior. Turning her back on him, she made her way through the corridors of Amber Hill. It was a modern fortress, one of the towers being completed even now. Her brother hoped to have the roof in place before the weather turned foul. That would allow the builders to finish the inside of the tower during the frozen months when building furniture and finishing window shutters might be done.

Bridget Newbury was sound asleep in the huge bed she shared with her new husband. Her hair was flowing across the pillow, but her face had a pinched look that betrayed how her condition was needling her. Jemma knew well how to keep her steps light and silent. She placed the bread on the table, pulling back the cloth cover enough so that her sister-in-law might see it when she awoke. She would eat at some point and her belly would ripen.

That was a pleasant thought.

Jemma walked back down the stairs and turned to go toward the stable. The sun was beginning to set, the horizon turning scarlet. But there was still an hour of light, and today she had earned her riding time. That fact gave her satisfaction, and she realized that she had not felt so in a very long time. There had been nothing save worry and dread filling her, but it was beginning to drain away now, allowing her relief. She noticed the beauty of the evening sky, the manner in which the sun illuminated the drying plants covering the ground. Even the air smelled sweeter.

Her mare let out an eager snort, dancing from side to side in the stall. There was no one about, because supper was on the table in the hall. Jemma saddled the mare herself and led her out into the yard.

"Hold, Mistress," Synclair bellowed at her from the battlements. He was the senior knight among her brother's men and heir to a title as well. But he seemed to have a liking for earning his place. With expert agility, he came down the stone stairs that were set into the back side of the curtain wall, one hand on the pommel of his sword to keep the weapon steady where it hung from his hip. Synclair aimed his blue eyes at her.

"Where are you heading, Mistress?"

This knight always did the unexpected. While everyone supped, he was the one walking the curtain wall.

"Just taking a short ride."

"The sun will be gone soon, Mistress. Best you plan to do

your riding when the morning has broken." His eyes suddenly darted to something past her, and his expression tightened.

Jemma turned to see Lady Justina making a rare appearance on the walkway that was attached to her tower-top chamber. Or what it should be called was a prison, for the lady was not free to go where she wished. Synclair was captivated by her, yet she seemed to avoid the knight to the point of secluding herself within her chamber; that was the one place Synclair would not venture. To do so would be to infringe upon the code of chivalry. But the lady was making her way along the curtain wall now, walking where she might be intercepted without honor being tarnished. Synclair began moving toward her without any further protests, drawn to her with a light in his eyes that made Jemma slightly jealous.

No man had ever looked at her in such a manner, and it was the truth that she was partially to blame for such. She watched the way the knight took to the stairs that would connect with the wall Lady Justina was moving across. Silently but with firm purpose, he climbed those steps with hard motions of his legs.

Jemma mounted her horse, taking the chance to leave the yard before one of the other knights worked up the courage to challenge her. She had done what she should, performed to everyone's satisfaction, but there was part of her that still ached for her father. She needed a ride, even a short one, even if she knew that she had been using her riding to escape from harsh reality. Tonight, she would use the ride to soak up the life about her.

She wasn't escaping today, simply tempering the feelings of loss that still lived inside her. Her mare took to the open land quickly, stretching her legs out after being kept inside most of the day. Above Jemma the sky was afire with gold and crimson, the night breeze beginning to whip up around her. It turned her cheeks cold, but she only laughed. Her dress was good English wool, and on her feet was a sturdy pair of boots that kept her ankles warm even when her skirts flipped up and away from her legs.

She crested a hill and gasped when she found herself galloping toward a body of armor-clad men. The mare let out a frightened squeal before rearing up. Fear making her skittish, the horse pawed at the unexpected arrival. Jemma battled to remain in the saddle, but it proved impossible with the mare so far up on her hind legs. Jemma's thighs lost their grip, and she fell to the ground while the horse landed on her front feet and charged off, away from the men who had frightened her.

Jemma lost every bit of breath in her when she hit the ground. Pain speared through her from the side of her hip where she landed first and then all the way through her body, right up into her mouth. Her teeth slammed together so fast, every tooth hurt from the impact. All the pain felt trapped inside her, building and burning while she struggled to draw in one single breath. She was powerless to do anything but suffer. Her heart felt as if it might burst, and her lungs burned for want of air. Dark spots danced in front of her eyes before she managed to force her jaw open and suck in a breath. It wasn't large enough, but it kept her vision from darkening further. Pushing it out, she drew another one in, this time succeeding in filling her aching lungs.

"Well now, what have we here? A wild Scot woman off to meet with her lover?"

Men snickered all around her, the sound frightening beyond belief.

Jemma drew in another breath and narrowed her eyes at the one who had spoken. The sound of their laughter might be frightening to someone who was easily scared, which she was not.

I dare not fall into panic's grasp . . .

The men halted their horses, ringing her while they stared down at her from beneath the visors of their helmets. There were at least thirty of them, and not a single one offered to help her off the ground. Pain still maintained its grip. Her hips became numb, or there was simply too much pain for her mind to feel it all. Dragging in a few more breaths, she succeeded in restoring her sight. What she viewed wasn't pleasant. Smirks decorated the lips of those men watching her. They were unkempt, their faces sporting several days' worth of whiskers. The armor they wore was darkened from lack of polish, and their behavior further attested to their lawless nature.

"I believe our fortune is looking up. Here's a treat for us all to sample. I hear these Scottish bitches like their men rough and randy."

"You have no right to wear the plumes of a knight with immodest speech such as that." Jemma pushed herself up and winced at the new pain that resulted. Her hips were no longer blissfully numb. Red-hot pain pierced them when she forced her body to stand.

"Mind your tongue, wench, or I'll cut it out." He even pulled a small dagger from the top of his boot to threaten her with. The blade was dark, and a shiver raced down her spine when she realized that it was dried blood that made it so. "I don't take orders from women."

"I am Jemma Ramsden, sister of the Barron Ryppon."

The man with the dagger spat on the ground in front of her. "You are what I say you are, and listen to me well—claiming to be noble-blooded carries a high punishment." He swung one leg over the back of his horse and hit the ground with a thud. His gaze settled on her chest, and the tip of his tongue appeared to take a swipe along his lower lip. He reached out and struck her across her face. It was a vicious blow, one that sent her tumbling away from him.

"Listen to me, lads, these Scots will stop at nothing to protect their thieving way of life. I have heard of Lord Ryppon, just like the rest of you, and I tell you this. No border baron would allow his gently bred sister to ride across the border land with her thighs spread over the saddle. She lies."

"I do not. I am Curan Ramsden's sister. The border land is no place for weak-kneed daughters, and that is why I was never taught to shiver at the sight of my own shadow." Jemma wiped a hand across her mouth, removing the blood trickling out of the corner. "You will keep your hands off me, sir."

"Hands?" He snickered again and reached down to cup his crotch with one of his mail-gloved gauntlets. "I'm planning on putting more than my hands on you. I've got a thick English cock for your lying Scottish flesh to entertain. We've been charged with finding your queen, and it has been too long since me and my men have had any fun. Ryppon would never let his sister out of his fortress this late in the day. You're riding out to meet your lover, and I plan to help you get the tumble you came out here looking for. Get on your back if you want it without pain."

There were a few low grumbles of agreement that sent a chill down her back. It was icy cold and full of dread, but Jemma held her chin steady.

"You'll keep your hands from me, sir, and that is the last time I will tell you so."

"Good. I'm sick of your talking."

He reached for her, and she lifted her leg to plant her foot squarely on top of the crotch he'd so blatantly tried to threaten her with. Her boot pressed down on top of soft flesh before the knight let out a strangled cry. He stumbled backward a few paces, sending a surge of hope through her, but it was short-lived. With a vicious snarl he turned to glare at her. Fury lit his eyes, and he let out a foul curse while rubbing his injured flesh. Lust mingled with that anger, making her fight against the urge to back away from him. It was instinct, but Jemma forced her feet to stand firm. She refused to crumple at his feet; doing so would only seal her fate because he was the sort of man that preyed on those less powerful than himself.

"You'll pay for that, bitch! I'm going to enjoy watching you bleed when I'm finished with your cunt."

He lunged toward her, his comrades cheering him on. But his grasping hands never touched her. Instead, she heard the pounding of hooves so close she knew the horse was going to trample her beneath its deadly hooves. She stood still, accepting that fate instead of the one the unkempt knight had planned for her. Jemma actually smiled, taking in a deep breath in anticipation of the horse crushing her body beneath it.

But no pain punctured her body. In its place a hard arm scooped her off her feet, pulling her up and on top of the beast that had galloped into the ring of Englishmen. The sudden appearance of that rider sent the English into a frenzy of panic. Their horses reared, and she heard the sound of their armor shifting. There were cries and curses, but most of it was drowned out by the sound of the horse she'd been tossed across. Her head went over the saddle to hang down on one side. She gained a crazy view of the ground and hooves all moving too quickly to make sense of from upside down. The fact that she had declined to eat supper suddenly served her very well, for there was nothing in her stomach to sicken her.

A hard hand pressed her down, helping to keep her on top

of the horse. A new sound rang out around her; it was a solid chanting in Gaelic.

It looked as if the English knights had found what they were searching for—the Scots they so arrogantly believed themselves better than.

For the moment, she prayed that the Scots won.

Chapter Two

The Scots didn't need divine intervention.

They took the English by surprise, which gave them the advantage. Streams of tartan-wearing men surged over the hill, the horses following close behind each other. The English had been ringed around her, their attention on what their leader was doing. Now their horses reared up, fear in their eyes. With no warning, the Scots chanted again, and their deep voices boomed around the startled English like thunder breaking above their heads. The fading light lent more strength to their attack for it seemed as if they materialized out of the night.

"Hold this for me, Bryon."

Whoever had pulled her off the ground tossed her once more. This time she landed in a tangle of her own clothing on the ground at the feet of a small group of younger boys. Jemma snarled as she tried to get her head upright, but the bouncing of her head upside down had muddled her senses. It took several moments for her sight to stop spinning, and still more time to gain control of her body again. She kicked at her skirts because they seemed to be stuck, trapping her feet where she could not use them. A soft male chuckle drifted over her ears before she was hooked beneath her arms and lifted up.

"Is that better now, lass?"

The voice was young but hinted at approaching manhood. Jemma lifted her face to stare at a youth with shoulder-length hair and a round knitted bonnet tilted off to one side. He couldn't be more than fifteen, but the boy was a full head taller than her and there were several more standing near him. They looked down the hill with eagerness shining in their eyes. Most of them failed to keep their feet still, but they remained where they were and strained to watch what was happening below them.

Jemma turned and gasped. The sound of men clashing against men was horrific, far more so than any description might have prepared her for. She saw nothing noble about it, only the brutality. Most of the English failed to pull their swords. The Scots closed in on them with clubs, striking them off their horses. In the close quarter of the battle, the crude wooden weapons proved more effective than the swords hanging in their scabbards. Several of the English found themselves thrown by their frightened mounts. Men strained to stand beneath the weight of breastplate armor, some of them falling beneath the hooves of their own comrades' horses. Screams filled the night, and it was impossible to tell whose cries came from which man because the fight was in such close quarters. Her mind tried to sort it all into understanding and had difficulty making sense of it.

But she did notice the lack of slaughter. Those clubs, although painful when they struck, did not spill enough blood to kill because they had been aimed at unseating the English. The Scots swung low, to catch the men below where their breastplates offered protection, knocking the English off their mounts like melons. She'd witnessed her brother teaching his younger charges just such a task and never understood how brutal it might be when employed. A shiver raced over her skin as she watched, too stunned to turn away.

The Scots herded their enemy into the center of them, riding around them to keep the fallen English contained. The youths behind her suddenly began to run after the horses that had left their English masters to the mercy of the Scots. The boys mounted and then began to tie the reins of the other horses together until they had a chain of riderless horses trailing behind them. They leaned over to catch the dragging reins but maintained their seat in the saddle using legs with an amazing amount of strength. Her eyes strayed back to the men who had rescued her; they were stronger still, hard men who appeared undefeatable in spite of their lack of armor.

"This is an act of war upon England," roared the knight who had so recently tried to assault her. He'd been knocked to his knees.

"I'll agree with ye there, man, but Scots who just committed the act of war." The man talking was clearly the leader of the Celts. His voice was edged with solid authority, and his men became quiet while he spoke. He sat tall atop a huge stallion that was as black as midnight. His sword was held in a confident grip, but it was his expression that sent a shiver down her spine. Hard and edged with fury, he glared at his captives while pointing the deadly tip of his sword at their leader.

"This is Barras land and yer in Scotland, which makes ye the invaders."

"We are sent on the king's business to bring his son's bride to where she can be raised well and protected."

The Scots grumbled, their words muffled, but it was clear that they were not friendly. Their leader chuckled, drawing Jemma's attention back to him.

"Ye're here to try and steal my queen, man, and that is something that I'll not be having."

The English knight spat on the ground. "We will not be allowing you savages to raise the future queen of England. She will be raised away from the pope's grasp."

The amusement that had coated the Scotsman's face faded until there wasn't any hint left.

"Dinna call me a savage, man, no when I just had to stop ye from raping the first woman ye came across like some horde of bastards straight out of hell." The sword point reflected the rising moonlight. "You're on my land, and ye will nae be raping any woman here, be she peasant or noble."

His land? Jemma stared at the Scot, shock holding her in its grasp. Laird Barras didn't look at her, his attention directed at the English knight, but it felt like he was conscious of her. It was the oddest feeling, but she would have sworn that he was angry on her behalf.

"The bitch needs to be taught her place."

"You English have no place calling us Scots savages. We do nae teach by using the back of our hands across a woman's face."

The English knight succeeded in rising to his feet. He sneered at Laird Barras. "You just want the bitch for yourself."

"What I want is to run ye through and spare this world of having to tolerate ye. But I believe I'll leave ye here to face her brother when he hears of what ye have been doing with his sister. From what I hear, Lord Ryppon is nae a man to be crossed."

The English knights shifted, and many of them cursed. They looked as though they wanted to panic once more, but the Scots allowed them no space to escape through their ranks.

"She's a lying whore."

Laird Barras grinned. "Nae, man, she spoke the truth, and I would not care to be wearing yer boots when the sun rises. That's the only reason I'm going to leave ye alive, to be eaten by one of yer own kind. I find that idea just a little bit more appealing than ridding my land of yer stench myself. But only a wee bit so if yer a smart man, ye'll get off my land before I change me mind."

He slid his sword back into the sheath strapped across his back. The movement highlighted arms thick with muscle. Lifting the sword above his head caused him no strain. One hand held the reins, and he wheeled the stallion around to face her. She felt his attention settle on her more than she saw it. The last of the sun was gone, night closing around them like a curtain. But she still witnessed the relief that passed over the Englishmen's faces. They helped one another to their feet and looked at the Scot with relief shimmering in their eyes. Many of them crossed themselves with thanks because it was a relief they had not expected to feel. The reason was harsh—hatred. It radiated from the Celts who sat on their horses watching their leader. Allowing these Englishmen to live only meant that they might kill their relatives sometime in the days ahead. Armed Englishmen riding across Scottish land only meant one thing, and it had nothing to do with friendship.

As she had just learned. The English would use violence to gain what they wished without any remorse. She looked at the dirty plumes crowning the knight's helmet and decided that they fit him well.

"If ye've any sense, ye'd start for the border before Ryppon discovers what ye were about with his sister." Laird Barras leaned down over the neck of his horse. "And if I see ye again on my land, I'll not leave ye drawing breath to test my goodwill again."

His voice was hard as stone, leaving no doubt that he was a man who would not hesitate to kill. He looked every inch the warrior, but Jemma discovered herself grateful for his harshness, even drawing comfort from it. The man was saving her life and sparing her a painful death, too. The English didn't wait but began walking toward England. It was humbling to set armored men on their way without their horses, but to return the animals would see the men becoming a force to be reckoned with once more. Laird Barras proved to be merciful by sparing their lives, but he was no fool.

He turned to look at her. The night sky was beginning to fill with tiny points of light, and that starshine cast him in white light, making him appear unearthly, like a god from legends past. A Norseman Viking who swept across the land, unstoppable because of his sheer brawn.

A ripple of sensation moved over her skin, awakening every inch of her flesh. It should have been impossible to be so aware of any single person's stare, but she was of his. His stallion snorted and pawed at the ground a moment before he pressed his knees into the sides of the beast. Lament surged through her, thick and choking as she anticipated his leaving.

He pulled the stallion up alongside her, a grin of approval curling his lips when she remained in place without a single sound passing her lips. Jemma found herself too fascinated to speak. Too absorbed in the moment to ruin it by allowing sounds to intrude.

"Up with ye, lass. This is not the sort of company ye should be keeping."

He leaned down, his thighs gripping the sides of his horse to keep him steady. Her gaze strayed to his thighs, and she stared at the bare skin that was cut with ridges of muscle, testifying to how much strength was in him.

"Take my hand, lass. I'd prefer not to have to pull ye off the ground again."

But he would. She heard that clearly in his voice. That tone of command that spoke of a man who expected his word to be heeded no matter what her opinion might be.

Of course, staying was not something she craved. She lifted

her hand and placed it in his outstretched one, only to pull it away when his warm flesh met her own. That touch jolted her, braking through the disbelief that had held her in its grasp. Her body began to shake while her face throbbed incessantly from the blow that had been laid across it. She suddenly felt every bruise and scrape, her knees feeling weak as the horror of what she had just faced sunk in deep to torment her mind with grisly details. Details of what the English had been intent on doing to her. The idea of touching any man was suddenly repulsive, and she clasped her hands tightly together.

"I thank you for your . . . assistance . . . but I will return to . . . Amber Hill."

Jemma looked around for her mare, but in the darkness it was difficult to determine which horse was hers. The younger boys had several horses each, and she couldn't decide which one belonged to her. She suddenly noticed how cold it had become, and the darkness seemed to be increasing, too, clouds moving over the sky to block out even the star shine.

"Give me yer hand, lass. 'Tis time to make our way from this place."

His voice was low now and hypnotic. Lifting her face, she found his attention on her, his eyes reflecting the starlight back down on her. Jemma lifted her hand but stopped when she felt her arm shaking. The motion annoyed her, but there seemed to be nothing she might do to banish it.

"Do it now, lass. This is nae a safe place to linger."

"But is going with you a safe thing to do?" She truly wondered because he looked so at ease surrounded by the night. All his men sat in their saddles without any outward sign of misgivings or dread for the deepening darkness. Her words didn't please him. His expression tightened, and something flashed in his eyes that looked like pride. A soft grumbling rippled through his waiting men.

"I will nae strike ye."

Which was better than she might expect from the horseless Englishmen standing nearby. For all that they were her countrymen, she discovered more trust inside her for the Scots. There was no real choice; she hungered for life, and the Scot's offer was her only way to hold on to that precious thing.

Lifting her hand, she placed it firmly against the one offered. Barras closed his hand around her wrist, and she jumped to help gain the saddle. He lifted her up and off the ground to sit behind him.

"Hold on to me, lass."

There was no other choice. She had to cling to him, press her body up against his in order to share his saddle. Her thighs rested against his, and the motion of the horse made their hips move in unison. The thick scabbard strapped to his back was the only barrier between them. She actually welcomed the hard edges of the leather scabbard because it kept her from being completely immersed in his body. There were several things she should have been dwelling on—the English left behind in the night, or the way her brother was most likely going to have her flogged for riding so late in the day. There was also Synclair to consider. The knight was going to be far more than unhappy with her for slipping out the moment his attention was taken away from her. He was not a man who made the same mistake twice.

Instead she was completely focused on the man she clung to. Her arms reached around his slim waist. It was amazing how much warmth his body generated. Holding so tightly against him kept the chill of the autumn night from tormenting her. The wind chilled her hands on top where the skin was exposed, but her palms were warmed by the man she held on to.

Her head was tucked along one of his shoulders, one cheek

pressing against the wool of his doublet. His sword was strapped at an angle across his back, the length of his plaid pulled up over his right shoulder helping to cushion the weapon. Suddenly, the Celtic fashion of dressing was not so odd. Instead it was quite logical and useful. That bit of thinking made him seem less of a barbarian and more of a very efficient warrior.

Her heart accelerated, which increased the tempo of her breathing. She drew in his scent and shivered. It was dark and musky, touching off a strange reaction deep inside her belly, a quivering that became a throbbing at the top of her sex. Each motion of the horse sent her clitoris sliding against the leather of the saddle, and the scent of his skin intensified the sensation somehow. It was unnerving, and she licked her lower lip because it felt as dry as a barley stalk. Every hot glance he had ever aimed at her rose from her memory to needle her with a longing she hadn't truly admitted she had for the man. Now that she was pressed against him, part of her chastised herself for not jumping at him. No matter how often she had listened to other women talk of their sweethearts, it had never been something she had longed for. Now, her body refused to be ignored any longer and enjoyed being against him.

If Barras noticed, he made no comment, which she felt herself being grateful for. Sensation was rushing through her, filling every limb and flooding her mind with intoxicating feelings that seemed impossible to control. Her fingers opened up, just because she failed to squash the urge to see what his body felt like. Tight ridges of hard muscles met her fingers, covering his midsection, and even his clothing did not disguise them.

His men closed around them, the sound of horses' hooves drumming out everything else. But a slight turn of her head and her ear was pressed against his shoulder, allowing her to hear his heartbeat. Another shiver raced through her, rushing down to her stomach where a strange sort of excitement was brewing. Her mouth was dry and her arms tightened around him because she feared she might lose her hold on him due to the quivering that seemed to be growing stronger along her limbs. It was a strange weakness, like too much wine. Even her thoughts felt muddled.

A rough hand landed on top of hers. Jemma flinched, her entire body reacting to the touch. His fingers curled around hers, completely covering her smaller hand in his. But it was his thumb that she noticed the most because it slid around her wrist to the delicate skin on the underside. That tender spot felt the rougher skin of his thumb stroking across it before pressing against the place where her pulse throbbed. It was a strangely intimate touch, and she yanked her hand away from beneath his and curled her fingers around the wide leather belt that kept his kilt in place. She felt his chest vibrate and knew that he was chuckling, even if the wind carried the sound away before she heard it.

Jemma snorted, enjoying the fact that she could make whatever sounds she wanted. But his head turned to cast a sidelong glance at her, and she realized that he'd felt the sound just as she had felt his. Jemma was startled to discover that she was communicating with him on some deeper level . . . a much more turbulent one. Her thoughts returned to the way he'd looked at her in the past.

They rounded a hill, and a fortress came into view. It was almost black against the night sky, with thick towers that rose up against the hills behind it. A wicked-looking gate began to rise, the grinding of metal chain cutting through the pounding of the horse's hooves. Her breath froze as fear tapped its icy fingertips against her.

This was not Amber Hill.

It was not even England.

She shuddered, unable to contain the dread creeping through her. It stole away the excitement that had been making her so warm, leaving her to the mercy of the night chill. Indeed life might become very frigid if she awoke in a Scottish fortress without there being any marriage agreement. The gossips would declare it her own fault for riding out without an escort.

Laird Barras rode straight under the gate and into the courtyard without hesitation, his stallion knowing the way well. But he had to rein the horse toward the front steps instead of the stable. The animal had not even fully stopped when he turned and locked stares with her.

"Welcome to Barras Castle, lass." His voice was rich with enjoyment. Jemma pushed away from his back, trying to force enough breath past her shock to reply without betraying her unsettled state.

He jumped down from the horse and still seemed to be able to meet her gaze far too easily from where she sat atop the horse. Somehow, viewing him from across a hall had failed to impact just how large a man he was. Jemma reached for the reins, an urge to place distance between them needling her almost beyond the fact that she knew the night held far worse dangers than the man watching her.

There was something about his gaze that cut down to the deepest part of her. She had never felt such a thing before, never endured her belly fluttering with excitement as it was right then. It shouldn't be so simple a thing to do to her. They had been nothing but the simplest of touches, and yet she quivered.

"You should have taken me to Amber Hill."

He reached up and closed his hands around her waist. There was amazing strength in those hands, and he pulled her from the saddle in spite of the way her thighs gripped it, attempting to remain on the horse. He set her down next to him, his hands taking far too long to slide off her. His lips curved just a minute amount, telling her that he was indeed taking advantage of the moment.

"The night is full of dangers, lass. Why do you think men build castles? It is nae because we enjoy the labor."

The gate was lowering, and the sound drew her attention. It groaned and the metal chain reflected the starlight as it set the gate back into position. She felt like a trap was closing about her, choking her so that breathing was nearly impossible.

"But—I can't remain here . . ."

"What would ye have of me, Jemma? Should I ride up the path toward yer brother's fortress and hope that his archers refrain from emptying their quivers until they see our faces and not just our Scottish clothing?"

"You might have sent me up that path once we were close enough."

His lips curved slightly. The doors to the first tower opened, allowing light to illuminate him from a lantern held aloft in the hand of a servant. Gordon Dwyre stared at her face for a long moment, his expression turning dark.

"I find that there is a certain satisfaction in knowing that ye are not unattended and getting yerself into harm's way, madam. The men that ride the border land are often intent on foul business."

She raised one hand without thinking to touch the side of her face. Pain shot through her the moment her fingers braised it. Laird Barras's lips became a hard line of disapproval. She had to tilt her chin up to keep her gaze locked with his. The man was large, and for some odd reason she was very aware of it. Sensation prickled all over her skin, that flutter of excitement returning.

"Inside with ye, Jemma. My housekeeper will make ye welcome. I need to see to my walls in case those English marauders have any comrades out there set on harming me people now that they no longer have ye to torment."

"I cannot stay here."

Jemma learned one thing about Gordon Dwyre in the next moment. He was not a man who discussed matters he felt fell beneath his authority. The man stepped forward and swept her off her feet before she realized he was bold enough to handle her. Too accustomed to Synclair, she failed to bring her hands up fast enough to ward off the huge Scot. Barras had her cradled in his arms in the blink of an eye, against his chest with one arm beneath her knees and another behind her back. Her breath hissed through her teeth with surprise.

"You must not."

Her voice was too high pitched, but that didn't even slow the man down. He climbed the stairs and carried her right over the threshold while his arms bound her to him. He spun her loose, and she retreated from his larger frame. Her cheeks flamed with temper.

"I have and I am nae sorry for it. Fate already gave you more luck tonight than ye have any right to expect. If me men hadn't discovered yer mare, you'd be lying dead out there." His voice tightened, and he stepped closer to narrow the gap between them. Once again he moved with a lightning quickness that took her by surprise, his hand latching on to the fabric of her skirt near her waistband where the cartridge pleats were deepest.

"And it would nae have been an easy death, Jemma. Be very sure of that. For all that they are yer own countrymen, they would have raped ye until ye bleed and then kept at ye until ye died beneath them, shivering and helpless. Ye will stay in this tower where the walls can offer you protection."

His eyes flashed with emotion so powerful, she stepped

away from it. But her unconscious motion carried her back into the tower, so he released her and grunted softly before turning around. His kilt fell in longer pleats in back, and they swayed with the motion of his walking. Beyond the open doors she could hear men working to unsaddle the horses. There was low conversation and the sharp sounds of the hooves hitting the stones of the courtyard. A hush fell when their laird appeared, proving that the man was not one of the lazy nobles who enjoyed his title while sending others to do the tasks his position required. Gordon Dwyre moved without hesitation back into the night while the doors were shut and the lanterns remained inside with her.

"I do suggest ye mind the laird."

"Is that so?"

The woman holding the lantern didn't take offense. Jemma blushed deeper when she heard her own tone, because it was surly and the woman standing in front of her was Jemma's elder. It didn't matter if the servant was peasant born or not, age was worthy of respect. Instead of frowning or shooting her a cutting look designed to instill some manners in her, the woman's lips curved into a smile.

"I am named Ula, and ye would not be the first woman to discover herself placed exactly where the laird wants ye. If ye are in fact Lord Ryppon's sister, yer sister-in-law should have told ye a thing or two about our laird when it comes to following a course that he's set on."

Jemma stiffened, but her temper did her little good. Bridget hadn't needed to tell her about her time in Barras Castle. Her brother had been enraged when his bride fled across the border to her kin before celebrating her marriage. Her kin had promptly gifted her to Gordon Dwyre because the man was their overlord. As far as Scotland went, he was a very powerful man. With a baby wearing the crown here, lairds were more powerful than ever. On their own land, their word was law. She shivered because instead of being frightened by that fact, she took solace in it. His words echoed inside her head as the expression on the English knight's face rose up to sicken her with just how correct Barras was.

"My apologies for being ungrateful. I seem to have forgotten how to be polite."

Ula nodded her head. It was a small reminder that the woman did expect respect even if she was a servant in the castle. That was only right and something that brought shame to Jemma again. Her father would not have approved.

Jemma sighed, suddenly feeling lost. She didn't recognize a single face or wall; even the clothing was foreign to her gaze. Coupled with the fact that she had nothing to call her own but what she wore, the feeling of being misplaced grew until it threatened to overwhelm her.

"Come along, lass. Let us see if yer face can't be cleaned up a wee bit."

Jemma stared at the woman but nodded because it was something to do besides standing in the door frame.

But her misgivings grew with every step that saw her going deeper into the Scottish fortress. The stories told around the winter hearth whispered across her mind with tales of women who never returned from such places.

Gordon couldn't recall the last time he'd felt his temper burn so hot. He was a man who knew full well that controlling his impulses was wise, but tonight he was being tested beyond everything he'd ever known.

"Ye look ready to kill." Beacon Barras spoke softly, but he knew that Gordon would hear him. The man was his friend, but Gordon still snarled at him. Beacon shrugged, unconcerned.

"No one would think ill of ye if ye did. That was a right nasty bit of doing that we interrupted."

"I daresay the English would consider it ill if I ran those piti-ful excuses for men through. 'Tis a worry we do nae need with the winter creeping down from the mountains."

"Is that truly Ryppon's sister?" Beacon was watching the darkness beyond the curtain wall, keeping his gaze moving because he wasn't as at ease as his words might make a person think.

"Aye, and much as I like the man, I had more respect for him this morning. What manner of fool allows any woman out so late in the day? She didna go riding this morning and 'tis my thinking that she should have waited until the sun rose on the morrow."

Gordon clamped his mouth shut. He'd spent too much time watching Jemma. Rumors were already making the rounds that he lacked the courage to approach the lass. It might sound innocent, but any hint that he wasn't bold enough to take what he wanted was an invitation for some clan to think his borders were easy pickings. There would be raids if that happened and blood flowing when he rode out to protect his people.

"Well now, she's nae a timid thing. I'd wager her brother didna give her leave to ride out."

That posed a very good question, one Gordon felt begin-ning to burn in his mind. Was the lass truly so foolish as to ride out on her own without considering that the night held dangers? Her sister-in-law had fled across the border, so maybe Englishwomen were being reared in ignorance these days.

He hoped not.

He'd thought the lass spirited, not foolish. The last thing he needed was a marzipan bride—a woman who was nothing but pride and pretty features. He needed a woman who could use her wits when the time called for it.

"It seems that ye have gotten yer wish to meet the lass after all." Beacon offered him a slight nod of his head. "So I'll bid ye good luck, Laird."

Luck indeed. Gordon frowned because his hope was strangling on a rope made of facts. He'd allowed his fascination to lead him astray. A bride was chosen for her family connection and gain it brought to the clan. Not because he'd become infatuated with an idea spun from his own imagination.

It would be better to not see the lass again.

He ground his teeth together and lost the battle to resist the urge to discover exactly what sort of female she was. Girl or woman? God help him if she was the woman he'd imagined her to be.

Because he didn't think he'd be able to give up such a prize now that he'd managed to bring it home.

Jemma sat still, listening to the sounds of the tower. It was strange and yet familiar. Ula had left her while muttering about fetching warmed porridge. Jemma found herself scanning the room and noticing where the glow of the lantern ended and the shadows took control. The shapes of the walls were different, but the feeling of the stone around her one that she was accustomed to.

Or should be.

Yet she still felt ill at ease. Standing up, she paced to the end of the large chamber, stopping when she reached a window. The shutters were still open, allowing in the night breeze. The air smelled fresh and full of winter. But what she felt most of all was the presence of the master of the castle. Gordon Dwyre, Laird Barras. Her rescuer and captor. It was truly a strange combination, one her mind toyed with while she turned to pace back across the floor.

She gasped, her heart freezing when she discovered him standing behind her, without a sound, as though he'd been summoned by her own thoughts. Sensation rippled across her skin, leaving gooseflesh behind.

"Evening, lass. I trust ye are comfortable in me castle."

Chapter Three

The man moved too silently; there had to be something unnatural about him.

Jemma felt frustrated with her own thoughts, finding them too somber for her liking. Men such as Gordon Dwyre were still only men; she'd felt his heart beat and his breath filling his chest. He was as real as she.

Instead of comforting her, that thought only blew across the coals of longing that were left from being pressed up against him.

Her gaze swept the Scot from head to toe, picking out all the details that made him so silent when he moved. Strength was etched into his body, proving that he was more a man of action than words. He still wore his kilt, but the pommel of his sword was no longer sitting above his right shoulder. She didn't make the mistake of thinking that he was now less dangerous.

The man embodied the idea. It was in the way he moved and the manner that he held his arms. Ever so slightly away from his body, his fingers hooked into the wide leather belt he wore. A simple wool doublet was unbuttoned to the middle of his chest. A little ripple of awareness crossed her skin, and she bit her lower lip to dispel it.

"Ula knows her craft well. She'll not leave ye wanting beneath me roof."

Jemma realized that she'd been struck silent by her desire to look at him. That annoyed her because such had never happened before. It shouldn't be troubling her now, especially when she needed her wits to convince the burly Scot to return her home. She had freedom of choice there. Here she was subject to Gordon's will, and that knowledge sat uneasy on her. For all that her life had been a simple country one, she realized that she had never lacked freedom.

"Yes, Ula was most kind."

He stepped farther into the room, his kilt swaying slightly. She noticed the garment because it was so different from everything she was accustomed to. In fact, Gordon Dwyre was unlike anything she knew, which must explain why she had difficulty mastering her thoughts when he was near.

Of course. That made sense, and understanding would lead her to logical thinking. That was what she needed.

"I shall remember her fondly."

A soft chuckle filled the room. Gordon closed more of the gap between them. "Are ye in a hurry to depart, lass? The sun will nae be rising for some time."

"Of course I am eager to return home. I mean no insult by such. However grateful I am for your assistance, returning to Amber Hill is my first priority."

His expression tightened. "Well now, lass, ye see there is our conflict. Returning ye to any place that can nae keep ye from harm."

"I told you, it was my own doing."

Laird Barras folded his arms over his chest. "I recall that very well, lass, which is why I hesitate to take ye back where ye are clearly able to work yer will over those who should be doing their duty to keep ye from harm."

"I made a mistake in leaving so late in the day."

"Ye did that, sure enough, and it nearly cost ye yer life."

There was no mistaking the judgment in his tone. Jemma bristled beneath its cutting edge.

"It is not my normal way to challenge the rules set down by my brother."

"I disagree, lass. I've watched ye riding across that section of land too many times to count."

Watched me riding?

Jemma twisted her hands in the fabric of her skirt while pacing a few steps away from him. Her belly twisted with sensation.

He'd watched her, *too many times* to count?

"You shouldn't have done that." There were only the candles on the table, and as she moved, she left their light behind her. The shadows felt more secure with their darkness to help conceal her emotions.

"Nae, lass, ye should not have been out where me men and I could watch ye."

His voice rang with heavy judgment. It needled her pride, setting a spark to her temper.

"I am not your concern, sir, and I was always on my father's land."

He followed her, and she stood torn between the urge to retreat farther or stand fast to remain in the glow from the candles. Something flickered in his eyes that looked like approval.

"At the moment ye are, because it was my men that I just risked to save ye. Be very sure that I do nae place me men in jeopardy for just any reason, even if ye are too foolish to be allowed the freedom yer brother has given ye."

Jemma gasped, caught somewhere between pride and astonishment that he would consider it his right to decide what was best for her. That desire struck her as oddly intimate, rippling over her skin like a caress.

"Making an offer for me does not grant you the right to dictate to me, sir."

He uncrossed his arms and she shivered, her memory filling with how it felt to be pressed against him. A flicker of excitement returned to her so quickly she chewed on her lower lip, needing some outlet for all the churning sensations trapped within her.

"No, lass, pulling ye off the ground before ye were raped does." His voice cut through the air like a hot knife. There was nothing friendly in his expression, only harsh judgment.

"I asked yer brother for the right to court ye only, I never offered for ye and I'm thinking that a wise thing at the moment. I do nae need a wife that has nae got the sense of a child."

His rejection stung.

Jemma felt it traveling through her like a lash from a whip. She'd only felt leather bite into her flesh once and for the very same reason. Lack of attention to what was happening around her.

She had been a mere ten years old and walked into a section of the training yard she had no place being. A thick, braided leather whip sliced down across her back before the men noticed that their space had been invaded. It had been her mistake to go there, and her father had made that clear with a lecture witnessed by every man training in that yard. It had been her sire's place to reprimand her. It was a lesson she had never forgotten until her father died.

That made Gordon Dwyre's judgment sting even more. She was not perfect, but that did not mean she needed another man attempting to act as her parent.

"Well then, it seems we are in agreement. I do not belong here, Lord Barras." She pronounced his title with an English accent to drive home just how different they were.

The man snorted at her.

One direct sound that communicated just how much he disagreed with her. Jemma felt her chin rise—just a tiny amount—but his attention lowered to it, noticing the stubborn motion. His eyes flashed with an equal amount of determination to see her accept his will.

Which she would not do.

"I will look forward to sunrise and my departure."

He didn't care for her telling him what would be. Jemma witnessed the flare of resistance that lit his eyes, but he drew in a sharp breath, battling against the urge to argue with her. Jemma turned her back on him. It was a bold thing to do, possibly as foolish as riding out of Amber Hill against Synclair's wishes.

But the tension was becoming unbearable. She had to move, do something to force the moment to pass before she buckled beneath the strain.

It was more than that . . .

She dug her fingernails into her palms while time felt as though it was frozen. She could still feel Gordon behind her.

Gordon?

When had she begun thinking of the Scot with his first name? To be sure that was going to bring her nothing but lament. The man wasn't interested in her, far from it. He considered her foolish and a nuisance. His judgment stung in spite of her determination to cast it aside by reminding herself that she shouldn't care a bit what he thought. Just because she enjoyed his glances.

And being pressed against his hard body . . .

She stiffened, trying to force the memory aside, but it was a battle that her body wasn't willing to lose. The tension became too much, and she turned her head to look back at him.

The spot where the large Scot had stood was empty. Jemma turned and scanned the dark corners of the room but found them empty of anything except furniture.

He did move silently. It was a pity that it was not so simple to remove his memory from her mind. Disappointment flowed through her, prickling her with a sense of loss that she cursed.

"Men do not always grasp what drives a woman to do the things she does."

Ula spoke in a quiet tone that drew a snarl from her laird. But the sound did not disturb the housekeeper. She kept moving on even steps that never faltered. The woman walked right up to him and offered him a wooden mug with no fear of his temper.

"It does nae matter. I'm going to take her home and let her brother have the pleasure of dealing with her. I see why she's uncontracted now."

Gordon took the mug of ale and drew off a long swallow. Ula didn't agree with him. He could see it in the woman's eyes, and it annoyed him because it was the sort of look that women often gave men. One that suggested they felt that whatever was on their minds, men were incapable of understanding.

"The lass was riding out on the border land without a care for any harm that might befall her. 'Tis clear that she is nae married because she's spoilt."

Ula stiffened and Gordon grunted. "Speak yer mind, Ula. I have never dictated that ye must hold yer tongue. That is an English trait."

"Ye have never needed to because I know when to keep my lips from flapping, Laird."

Gordon shrugged and took another swallow from his mug.

"Aye, ye are wiser than many that I've met. But I see that ye disagree with me on the girl. Why? Yer own son was riding with me. I didna think ye would care to hear that he was run through because of some English noble lass that does nae have the sense to remain inside her home when the sun is setting."

"I would nae care for such news, 'tis true."

"But?" Gordon pressed her, for some reason craving to know why the housekeeper disagreed with him when it came to Jemma Ramsden.

"But I have heard from Lilly who is the daughter of the blacksmith and has a sister married over on the Ramsden land to their cobbler Samuel Jerkins, that the girl was nursing her father for the last four years." Ula tilted her head to the side, obviously considering her thoughts before speaking. She lifted one finger. "She could have left it to the maids, but Lilly said the lass tended her father with her own hands, even sleeping in the manservant lodgings alongside the master chamber. That is nae a spoilt child but one who loves their parent."

"She was still riding along the border land with the sun sinking on the horizon. Maybe ye have nae heard, but we rescued her from a band of English rogues who were moments away from raping her."

Gordon felt a prickle of relief cross his skin to settle into his bones. It surprised him because it was not the first time he'd intervened in foul plans. None of those times had made his knees feel weak or lingered in his thoughts much beyond a good mug of ale. He finished off what remained in his grasp, hoping to be done with the entire event.

It persisted, though, and Ula refilled his mug as though the housekeeper knew that he would not dispense with this bit of business easily.

"Fine, she is nae spoilt. At least no when it comes to being devoted to her family. But that does nae change the fact that the woman is senseless. She would require a great deal of effort to protect."

"She would no be the first to make mistakes while her heart was full of grief. The talk is that the girl only took to riding when her father died. That is a powerful blow that many buckle beneath." Ula lowered herself before turning to face the hallway. The housekeeper walked down the length of it and entered the room that Jemma was in. A moment later she emerged without the pitcher.

Gordon had to force the ale in his mouth down his throat or risk choking on it.

Grief . . . aye. There was something that sent more than one person off to doing things they normally never would have. Things that they regretted when the pain had dulled enough for them to resume thinking clearly.

Of course, the more strength the person had, the more insane the recklessness. His fellow laird, Deverell Lachlan, was grieving hard for his lost bride and riding the night like a highlander. The man's face was covered in a beard that grew longer every time Gordon saw him, and there seemed to be no easing of the pain etched into his friend's eyes.

Aye, grief was a powerful thing.

He turned around to look back down the hallway from where he'd left Jemma. He was suddenly not so disgusted with her, part of him longing to go back into the room where Ula had placed her.

It was a bedchamber, even if the bed was all the way across the room from where they had been talking. Still, there would be plenty of people who condemned him for being alone with a maiden in there.

Jemma was a maiden. He'd stake his stallion on that fact.

She'd shivered against his back, her heart racing while she tried to keep that knowledge from being noticed. A woman with experience wouldn't have been so flustered. A knowing gleam would have entered her eyes. Maybe she would have lowered her lashes to conceal such, but only maidens looked back with such wide-eyed surprise when they met a man who drew their interest.

Jemma had cast those looks at him when he walked into her home to meet with her brother. She was drawn to him as surely as he was to her despite the fact that she was virgin still. He should call Ula back to stand as witness to what transpired between them, but he was finished with watching while surrounded by others. He'd done the chivalrous thing and visited her brother, and all that had done was allow Jemma to hide from him.

That knowledge did not stop him from moving back down the hallway. With his firm belief that she was nothing but a spoilt nuisance removed, there was nothing to keep him from seeking her out.

Jemma sniffed at the ale and wrinkled her nose. She had never cared for it, which was almost considered a sin because ale was a staple of English food. She liked all grains well enough, but once they were fermented with yeast, she found them sour. Hot porridge was her preferred way of taking in her barley and wheat.

"We've cider if ale does not please ye."

Jemma jumped and then muttered a word that her brother didn't think she knew. Of course she'd learned it from his men, but like all males, Curan liked to think that the women of the house were deaf anytime the men were cursing.

"I do not need anything save for the sun to rise."

"Which will nae happen for many hours."

Gordon Dwyre strode back into the room, his hand wrapped around a mug. She suddenly noticed the bed in the room, which sat some twenty paces across the floor. The Barras tower was built in the older fashion, without walls to divide the floor. Newer construction afforded a receiving chamber separated by a wall from the actual bedchamber. She was strangely aware of that bed and the way her body had responded to Gordon's while they were pressed together.

"I thought you were gone from me. Disgusted by my lack of forethought." She walked away from the ale and the bed, moving off into the semidarkness just beyond the candles' glow.

"Why do ye ride as ye do?"

Jemma felt her eyes widen and took another step into the darkness to cover her expression. Gordon placed his mug on the table and watched her from beneath lowered eyebrows. He had dark hair. Like midnight, but his eyes were blue.

"It doesn't matter what sent me out, only that I realize now that it was foolish."

One of those dark eyebrows rose. "I hear ye started riding when yer father died. Do ye think that I can nae understand what grief does to a person?"

"I can't fathom why you would think I might share such a personal thing with you. We are strangers, sir."

He chuckled, crossing his arms over his chest. The motion made his arms bulge, the muscles pressing against the fitted sleeve of his doublet. "Strangers, aye we are but that does nae mean that I have never done something I regretted while in the midst of grief."

"Fine. As you will, sir. If that pleases you and softens your judgment of me then so be it." She discovered that her hands had planted themselves on her hips like an angry wife, and she jerked them off only to fumble with them while she attempted to compose herself. "Somehow I doubt that riding is an escape for you since you do it so often."

His face transformed into something that was wickedly handsome. His lips curved, and his eyes held a gleam that was full of male satisfaction.

"Well now, there's riding and then there is riding that pleases a man. I admit to enjoying a good, hard ride. Often."

He was talking about bed sport. His eyes shimmered with mischief, and his lips curved in mocking display.

Her cheeks heated and her jaw dropped open. She snapped it shut with a click of her teeth. But she had to fight the urge to look at the bed. Her mind was suddenly full of just what the Scot might look like in it.

What might it feel like to have those lips touch my own . . . ?

"You have no place judging my actions, sir."

"You mean, I should nae be handing out my opinion when I'm nae perfect myself?" He crossed the room, closing the distance between them with a stride that held her fascinated. He grew larger and more imposing with each step, but she was frozen in place, too hypnotized to move. He had to angle his head down to keep their eyes connected now that he was so much closer.

"Well now, lass, aren't ye judging my riding habits right now, too?"

Jemma slapped her hands down on her skirts, unable to remain still any longer. "I wouldn't be if you weren't so coarse as to bring up the subject. I do assure you of that, sir."

"Ye assure me? Is that so?" He reached out and captured one of her hands in the blink of an eye, his larger fingers curling and turning her wrist up so that he could see its delicate skin.

"Release me and go, we should not be alone."

"No just yet. I'm thinking that it's high time we did more than look at each other across a distance."

Her breath froze in her throat, and her jaw dropped open once more in shock. "You . . . you are behaving abominably. Release me now, I tell you."

"Well now, lass, and that takes me right back to pointing out to you how reckless riding out near sunset is." His fingers tightened on her wrist just enough to give her pain, but only for a brief moment. When her eyes widened with the discomfort, his grip eased, giving her release. It was strangely intimate, the way he read her emotions off her face. Such knowledge sent uncertainty surging through her.

"Ye see, now that ye have left the sanctuary of yer brother's protection, ye have to deal with whatever comes yer way. The rules and etiquette of proper behavior often crumble when ye ignore them first."

"So I am to blame for whatever you choose to do with me?" She pulled on her wrist, but it was a wasted motion because he held her securely.

"Aye, lass." His voice held a rich tone that made her heart increase its pace. In his eyes was more heat than she struggled to ignore within herself. It shone there, staring at her while tempting her. But there was something else about him that she noticed, the difference between him and the English knight that had done nothing to temper his grip.

Trust me . . . Jemma heard the words rise from her memory, and she realized that she did in fact have faith in him.

"You are not so coarse."

Her words affected him. She witnessed the flare of pride that lit his eyes, almost as if he enjoyed knowing that she did trust in him. But his lips also curved in a sensual motion that sent a shiver down her back. There was a promise lurking in his eyes, too, one that assured her he was not a man who would let conversation deter him from gaining what he truly desired. He would not hurt her, but that did not mean that he would not follow his desires.

"If I was coarse as ye say, lass, I'd not bother to temper my grip."

"I know that."

Jemma felt her eyes narrow. The man was teasing her. Well, he was not the only one who knew how to annoy another. Lifting her foot, she aimed for his toes and stomped down as hard as possible. She felt the leather of his boot give beneath the force of her strike, but the man only laughed one moment before he lifted her arm and twisted it behind her, binding her against his body.

"You rogue." Jemma sneered her insult into his face, wanting to make sure he heard her. But Gordon stared right back at her, his eyes snapping with fire.

"Ye are a wildcat, and a man is wise to keep yer claws contained when he's close enough to be reached."

Her throat felt as if it were clogged and that even a single breath might not pass through it. She was pressed against him from thighs to breast and only managed to keep her shoulders separated from his wide chest by arching her back away from him. Her muscles ached from the strain, but Gordon granted her no mercy. He kept her bound against him.

"This is completely indecent."

His lips twitched up once more. "Aye, it is, lass, but I find it rather enjoyable."

She used her free hand to shove against his chest. "Of course you do. You enjoy riding, as you so shamelessly informed me. Well, I have no such fondness for carnal activities, sir, so unhand me this moment."

Before I go insane from the urge to stop struggling and allow you to show me what a man's embrace feels like . . .

"Are ye sure about that, lass?" His voice had deepened, becoming husky and alluring. "Or is it possibly more a fact that ye have never had a man who rode out after ye and tried his hand at seeing if ye enjoyed his kiss?"

She looked back into his eyes and gasped when he angled his face to press a kiss against her startled lips.

It lasted only a moment before she jerked her head away. But he followed her, releasing her hand so that he might frame her face with his hands and hold her steady for a longer kiss. His mouth settled on top of hers, hot and soft while she heard a moan rise from her chest. She couldn't help it, there seemed to be no way to contain all the sensation inside her. It was bubbling over like a too-hot pot. Only removing it from the fire would stop the contents from escaping over the sides, and Gordon wasn't releasing her.

Jemma pressed her hands against his chest, but that became more of a reason to remain when she discovered she liked the way his chest felt beneath her fingers. His lips closed over hers, gently at first, teasing her with a delicate press of his mouth against her own, only applying enough strength to keep her head in place while his lips began to slip along her own.

Slowly, softly, in a motion that sent trickles of delight down her body. The sensation was not confined to her lips; it flowed down her torso and into her belly where that flutter of excitement fed off it. Another moan rose up from inside her, and her hands slid up to his collarbones and over the top of his wide shoulders where she gripped him. The kiss changed immediately. Increasing the pressure against her mouth, Gordon pressed her lips apart wider with his. But instead of finding it harsh, she enjoyed feeling his strength. There was something perfect about knowing that she was soft compared to his hardness. Behind her stays, her breasts felt very delicate, and she noticed how simple it might be to press them against him and have them give way to his firmer form. Her nipples tingled before drawing into tiny pebbles.

"Well now, lass, it seems that ye will have to be rethinking yer opinion of riding, for it sounds like ye just might find it to yer liking." His hands gently massaged the sides of her face, carefully avoiding where she had been struck. She saw his gaze touch on the bruise darkening her skin, rage flickering in his eyes for just a moment before his attention returned to her face. "Even if it is a carnal enjoyment, between a man and woman, that is no necessarily a bad thing. It can make for a very warm winter, I'm thinking."

Jemma gasped and shoved him away with every bit of strength she had. He released her but chuckled, letting her know that her freedom was only hers because he granted it to her.

That knowledge stung her pride.

"Between strangers such as us, it is a sinful thing, sir. So stop thinking about such."

One of those dark eyebrows arched in arrogant display. "Well now, lass, I've asked yer brother for permission to court ye. A thing I did long before tonight, so do nae be calling me sinful just because ye enjoyed running yer hands across me chest."

Jemma snarled. "You kissed me first."

Gordon shrugged. "Aye, I did. Does that mean that ye would like the opportunity to touch me first? I'm ready to stand steady while ye do with me as ye please, lass." His eyes sparkled like a boy's. "I feel the weather growing warmer at just the idea of ye reaching for me."

Her hand flew out before she thought about it. She balled up her fingers and punched him on the side of his mocking jaw just as she'd seen the men doing in the training yard. Pain snaked up her arm and into her shoulder, drawing another profane word from her lips.

Gordon laughed, full volume, and the man actually leaned over to brace his hands on the top of his thighs while he continued to roar with amusement. In spite of the pain, Jemma pulled her hand back for another swing. Gordon ducked when she came at him this time, his body lowering so that the force of her strike carried her over his wide shoulder. He took full advantage of her inexperience with fighting and surged up so that she ended up bent over his shoulder. One hard hand connected with her unprotected bottom with a smack that echoed off the chamber walls.

"Put me down!"

"As ye like." He slapped her unprotected bottom another time before dumping her off his shoulder. Jemma shrieked as she felt her body falling through the air. A vision of her slamming into the floor made her cringe, but her body bounced on the soft surface of the bed instead. Her skirts flew up and came down in a tangled mess that knotted around her legs.

"You beast!" She flipped onto her stomach and felt the night air brush against her bare thighs above the top of her knee-high stockings. She jerked her face up to discover Gordon admiring the view her tussled skirts afforded him. Kicking at the fabric, she rose up onto her knees but stopped because the man stood in front of the bed, blocking the path she would have taken off it.

He looked for all the world like some Viking from winter stories. The ones that were told near the end of winter when all the better stories were exhausted. Sitting back down,

Jemma rolled over, intent on leaving the bed from the opposite side. But something large and heavy landed on the bed. She snarled and tried to swing her legs off the bed only to discover that her dress held her back. Turning her head, she found Gordon lying across the foot of the bed with one elbow propped against its surface and his head resting in his hand while the beast smirked at her.

His heavier body lay across her skirts, trapping her with only her chemise to guard her modesty.

"Ye hit me, wildcat, so do nae be crying when it was you that set the tone of our conversation."

Jemma grabbed her skirt and gave it a yank, but the fabric remained lodged beneath his weight. "You earned it for behaving like such a blackguard and stealing a kiss from me."

"Hmmm . . . possibly."

"There is no question about it. Now get off my dress, we should not be in . . . in—"

"In bed together?"

Jemma felt her face burn with a blush. "Exactly."

"With yer skirts tossed?" His lips were curving up in a grin while his tone mocked her.

"Stop it. This is cruel. Riding out was foolish, but I am not a slut, and you should not be looking at my thighs. No one has ever looked at . . ." She couldn't help how pitiful she sounded. Helplessness was closing around her with an icy grip. There was nothing to stop him from doing what he would. Even her own body seemed to have a liking for his touch. She looked away from him, unable to prevent two tears easing from her eyes. She may have done some foolish things since her father's death, but never had she shamed him.

A soft word muttered in Gaelic drew her attention back to Gordon. He lifted his body so that her skirts were loose. She pulled them toward her and sat up so that her legs were covered once again. Gordon relaxed against the bed once more, lying in a contented pose while he studied her. It was by far the most unusual setting she had ever been in. All her life had been dictated by rules and traditions. The prospect of being in bed with a man she barely knew had never occurred to her. At least, not if that man was not her husband. Brides often had to deal with meeting their spouses for the first time on the their wedding night.

But she had no such comfort as knowing that wedding vows protected her honor and future. Losing her maidenhead tonight would see her facing a harsh reality tomorrow morning. There would be plenty who would point and judge her for not being pure. Gordon wouldn't face such. No, the shame would be hers alone and well deserved for sneaking past Synclair the way she had. There was no one to blame but herself.

She drew in a deep breath and banished the tears from her eyes, better to face what was to come than shiver in dread.

"Well? What do you want now, Gordon Dwyre?"

His lips twitched, but they didn't curve. The man appeared to be watching her, studying her.

"I shouldn't have looked at yer thighs, lass."

Jemma nodded agreement.

"But I enjoyed it full well." He smiled with arrogant confirmation of that enjoyment.

She offered him a short huff. "If you think I'll thank you for that compliment, you are mistaken."

He lifted one thick finger. "Maybe not, but I see that ye find me as interesting as I find you."

"I do not."

His lips parted as his smile became larger. "Ye undress me with yer eyes, Jemma; 'tis a fact that I find it hard to resist."

"Try harder." She would, she had to.

He shook his head. "But ye did hit me, so—" His gaze lowered to her lips and passion flared to life in his eyes. "Ye owe me one sweet kiss to relieve the pain."

"Trust a man to believe kisses relieve pain."

One of those eyebrows rose once more. "Do ye deny that many a mother has offered a kiss to soothe the discomfort of her child?"

"You are not a child." And she was far too aware of it for her own sanity. Her nipples were still hard, begging for the touch of his skin against them. The idea of kissing him was threatening to cast every scrap of self-discipline aside.

"If I roll onto me back and allow ye to tickle me belly, will ye offer me a sweet kiss, Jemma?"

Her mouth went dry. "I shall not." Jemma forced the words past the wicked urgings that were emerging from the excitement flickering inside her. Part of her did want to touch him, almost too much to ignore.

"Well, that's a pity. I think I would have enjoyed it full well." He winked at her before rolling over his shoulder and off the edge of the bed. His kilt went flying, but he landed on his feet in a balanced stance before straightening up, and all she gained was a flash of his trim backside.

A pity . . .

Her cheeks flamed scarlet.

"I must admit that I did enjoy putting ye to bed, lass. I hope I get the chance to do it more often."

She gasped and snarled as she struggled to crawl off the bed, but her dress hampered her progress.

"Why do women wear such stupid clothing?"

Jemma didn't realize that she had voiced her thought until she heard Gordon laughing once again. This time it was husky and sweet, sounding far too enticing for her frayed self-control.

"Well now, lass, I admit that the idea of seeing ye in a kilt would be pleasing indeed." His face became a mask of sensuous intent, shocking her how much she noticed his emotions. "But that would put yer thighs on display to everyone, and I think that I'm not liking that part of it at all." He plucked at the edge of the rust and orange wool that formed his kilt, lifting it a few inches to show his own thigh that was cut with powerful muscle. Her gaze lowered to it, remaining there until the wool pleats of his plaid fell back down to cover his bare skin.

"No one will disturb ye in this chamber. Ula will knock."

"So I may feel at ease, is that what you suggest?"

He shrugged. "I could stay and do me best to help ye settle in. We do seem to find things to talk about." His eyes narrowed. "And do."

"The chamber is very nice. Thank you for your kindness, but I have all that I require." She fired off her retort rapidly. "Pray, do not let me keep you from more important matters."

He chuckled at her, his lips flashing an arrogant grin. "Very well, lass, although I confess to being just a wee bit disappointed in yer choice."

He considered her with one more long look before turning and quitting the room. Jemma relaxed, her body sagging on her knees in the middle of the bed with her skirts puddled about her. Her heart was beating fast as though she had been running. The night air felt good against her skin because she was warm, just like on a summer day. Her corset felt abnormally tight, and her nipples were still hard behind them. She felt drained now that he was gone, as though her emotions had returned to normal. But she now understood how little she felt during her everyday life.

Jemma gasped at the horror of the moment, raising a hand to cover her mouth. Horror, torment, and longing. Shock held her in its grasp so tightly, all she could do was sit there while the events of the night replayed themselves across her mind. She trembled at the recollection of how close she had come to her own death, but that paled when compared to the way she quivered when she thought about the kiss Gordon Dwyre had pressed against her lips. The darkness around her suddenly became more friend than enemy because it shrouded her and her blush. Try as she might, there was no way to banish Gordon from her mind.

No, there was only the night and the man who had kissed her beneath its velvet curtain.

His cock was hard.

Gordon made his way down the hallway, forcing his feet to carry him away from the woman who had awakened his flesh. Her kiss had been sweet, so much so he felt drunk on it.

"I heard that ye rode back in." Anyon leaned against the wall with her skirt raised up to show him one long leg. She was a well-shaped woman and knew how to use what nature had blessed her with.

Used it to bring a great deal of pleasure, too. She offered him a sultry look from beneath lowered lashes before sending her hand over her own thigh. One slow rub that normally captivated him. She lifted her eyelashes and stared at him with invitation burning brightly in her eyes. Her breasts swelled temptingly above the edge of her bodice that had always been cut just a small amount lower than the other women who served in his house. He'd never lamented that fact, either.

But tonight it wasn't holding his attention. Instead he noticed the knowing gleam in her eyes and the practiced slant to her smile.

And almost coy.

"What keeps you from me, lover? Shall I come to you, like a harem girl in the east?" Her skirt fell down to cover her leg, and her hips swayed with just the right amount of motion while she moved to him. She didn't rush, knowing full well how to draw out the moment to build up the passion.

"Not tonight, Anyon."

She fluttered her eyelashes and ran a knowledgeable hand along the front of his kilt. Just a light caress, but she sighed when she felt his erection.

"If ye are weary, I'll ease the stiffness from yer flesh before ye seek yer bed."

She sent her hand down to the edge of his kilt, her fingertips touching his bare thigh before denial shot through him so hard he jerked away from her. Hurt crossed her face, confusion filling her eyes.

"Ye desire that Englishwoman ye brought back with ye."

Hurt edged her words, and she pressed her lips into a hard line before backing up. "She'll not be able to satisfy ye as I can. She'll cry that ye bruise her. The English are too soft to be good bedsport." Anyon held out her arms. "Come to me, lover. I'll give ye what ye crave as I have before."

"I know ye have, but tonight I have no appetite for ye, Anyon. 'Tis sorry I am to say such to ye."

He kept his voice low, but her eyes still blinked rapidly as she tried to hold off tears. Anger darkened her complexion. "Fine then. See what sort of sleep ye get with that swollen cock keeping ye company."

"Anyon—"

She didn't give him time to try to comfort her. In a swirl of wool she turned and disappeared down the hallway. The night swallowed her up as though she had never been there.

Gordon Dwyre cursed.

Low and deep and he meant every last syllable.

Chapter Four

Jemma fell asleep sometime in the early morning hours. Her body fought against her mind and won, at least for a few hours of much-needed rest. The bed was soft and comfortable, cradling her while her dreams were filled with Gordon Dwyre. Was the man her host? Possibly. She wasn't sure, but she was equally certain that she did not want to label him her captor for fear that it might be so. That left her tossing and kicking most of the night.

Dawn spread its pink fingers over the horizon, and she opened her eyes because she was sensitive to the change in light. Rubbing at her burning eyes, she looked toward the windows and gasped. Rising from the bed, she walked across the floor to stare at the glass-paned windows. Such was an extreme luxury. Something found in a palace where princes and dukes slept. She reached out and fingered the veins of lead that held the small panes of glass together to fill in the entire window.

"Trade with yer brother has brought many good things to Barras land."

It was Ula who spoke. Her tone even and just a tiny bit hushed to reflect the early morning hour. Jemma turned to look at her but became engrossed with gazing at the rest of the chamber. Tapestries hung on the wall. Each one was a work of art, the weaving of threads into depictions of legend or biblical stories. The two that hung in the chamber were eight feet by ten and hung on thick wooden beams. One was a soft-colored representation of the baby Moses being placed into the river by his mother. The other was a bright blending of harvest colors depicting plump pumpkins and rich vegetables hanging on vines while two lads sampled them instead of filling their baskets.

"Those were made by the laird's mother. She had great affection for tapestry weaving." Ula pointed to the rich shade of orange used to make the pumpkin. "This is Barras orange, and here is the rust, but the boys wear the green and mustard colors of the Seton clan that she came from."

The housekeeper smiled with the memory. "There are many stories in each one of her tapestries. I am one of the few who recalls them these days, for she never had a daughter to pass her skill along to. Only sons."

"Many would consider that a blessing and praise her for doing her wifely duty."

Ula turned to look at her. "All children are a blessing. They bring life to the clan and happiness to all. Is yer sister-in-law growing round yet? Yer brother consummated his vows in the old tower."

"Um, well she is sick now and the midwife says her belly will rise soon."

The housekeeper nodded with a gleam in her eyes. "A good time for ye to marry then."

Ula picked up a brush and patted the top of the large chair that sat near the table where the candle had set last night. It was now a small, melted puddle because she had never pinched it out. That was wasteful, and she frowned as she sat down.

"Ye should not have slept in yer dress."

Jemma bit her lip to keep from scoffing at the woman. She certainly had not been willing to take her clothing off. Not even her boots, although that was yet another wasteful thing, for her dress might carry dirt into the bed. She looked at the bed to see that she had only pulled the heavy coverlet over herself during the night. At least she had not soiled the sheets. But her back was stiff from sleeping in her hip roll and cartridge-pleated skirts, her skin itchy from the creases pressed into it by not stripping down to her chemise and allowing the garment to flow about her body.

So much better for Gordon to be able to see my thighs . . .

"Yer hair is a mess, to be sure. I am glad ye rise early, else we might not get it all straightened out before the priest rings the bells for Mass."

"But I am a Protestant."

The hands in Ula's hair froze. "Of course ye are. What with yer King Henry the Eighth setting himself up as the head of the Church and getting himself excommunicated. Ye'd be a poor subject to not obey yer king. Mary of Guise is regent for our little Queen Mary and she is Catholic. 'Course, she was born in France, which means she was following her king, too. That's a woman's lot in this life, we must adjust to follow the whims of men."

Which accounted for the war of rough wooing that had almost cost her so much last night. The room was brightening, warm yellow sunlight spilling through the glass windows like water. In the winter there would be light but no freezing wind. In the yard below a bell began to chime. Slow and steady, the sound rose up in the morning air to touch the ears of everyone who inhabited the towers of Barras Castle.

"Well, 'tis the only service there is here, so ye'd be best to come along and leave the bickering over church policy to the kings and nobles. 'Tis praising the Lord, no matter the manner it is done in."

Jemma couldn't suppress a small sound of amusement that bubbled up from her lips. It was actually quite refreshing to have someone poke a little fun at all the fighting over what service was considered correct. She had read many a letter to her father on the new policies that were sent out from his secretary in London. Always it was little things that were altered, and truthfully she did not see so great a difference. Yet men had died for those changes.

"I agree, but my father warned me often to never say so."

Ula merely shrugged. "At my age, speaking my mind is na so forbidden. At least no when there are no men about to hear me."

There was a truth if ever Jemma had heard one. Men were often power hungry and didn't take kindly to any woman who forgot that they didn't like to share that authority. What was allowed in private was not the same as how she was expected to behave when others might overhear her. Refusing to attend morning Mass might very well see her branded as a heretic. She stood on Scottish ground, and it was a Catholic nation with priests empowered by the crown. Public disobedience would be chastised.

So she followed Ula, lowering her head when she entered the church, but she noticed the looks of approval from the Barras clan members. She found herself listening to the service and noticing the details. So much blood had been spilt over the split between England and Rome. Even now, the English soldiers were intent on capturing Mary, Queen of Scots, just to prevent her from being raised Catholic. There was also a growing pressure from Catholic France to take the girl for their prince and form an alliance against the English because they were Protestant. Scottish and English shared one island, but it was faith that kept them divided. Henry the Eighth had a good idea to unite the two nations.

That would make a marriage between myself and Barras a good match, too . . .

Jemma cringed at her thoughts. They just kept rising up, ignoring her more logical thinking that reminded her she had no control when it came to the man. That was dangerous, very much so.

He kissed well . . .

Her eyes widened while she searched for a counterthought. Aye, but the man was a brute the way he swept her off her feet and carried her inside his tower like some bundle of goods he'd taken as his prize during a raid.

He also smelled good . . .

Her cheeks heated, and she became annoyed with herself as she recalled exactly how much she had enjoyed the scent of his skin. Strong and powerful. It was more than just the fact that he was clean, she had enjoyed the way his scent filled her senses during that kiss. Somehow, it had added to the intoxicating power of his mouth against her own.

She was not applying herself well. Jemma tried to concentrate on the priest, but instead her gaze wandered to the kilt on the man standing on the end of the row on the other side of the sanctuary. His legs were muscular, too, but she still preferred Gordon's. There was a power that radiated from the man, and just thinking about him stirred the excitement that had flared up so brightly, deep in her belly last night.

I had longed to give him that kiss he'd wanted . . .

And just what would that have gotten her? Nothing but dishonor. Jemma used that harsh fact to sober her thoughts. Her insides might have tormented her with how much they craved more of Gordon's touch, but she was still a virgin this morning and that was what she needed to focus her attention on. It was true that there was nothing at all about Gordon Dwyre that was so unique, nothing at all. The change was within herself. Now that she had recognized she needed to stop grieving, her body was telling her it was time to marry.

There was nothing unusual about her host, except his ability to annoy her. She would return to Amber Hill and allow her brother to arrange a good match for her. Obviously there was too much tension between Scotland and England for her to continue to consider Gordon. Henry the Eighth would die soon, leaving his young son Edward to wear his crown. Two children could not bring peace between the two nations. If she married into Scotland, her own brother would have to call her husband his enemy. Even if Curan had given his permission for Barras to court her, that was not permission to wed. Better to leave before her longings gained too much hold on her.

It was logical, but she felt disappointment creeping across her heart. No amount of thinking dispelled it. She needed her virtue, and just because she craved something did not mean it would be hers. There was nothing to do save endure.

That was something she understood well how to do.

The first meal of the day was served soon after Mass. It was a simple offering of porridge topped with the last of the season's fruits. The cereal might be stored and left in large iron pots while the staff attended Mass. The cook used a large ladle to fill wooden bowls with the thick sustenance. Maids brought trays of bowls that gently steamed in the cool morning air. The main hall became crowded and noisy as everyone filled the long tables that ran across the space. Benches skidded on the hard stone floor, and men whistled to their comrades before sitting down to partake of the morning fare. If it hadn't been for the rust and orange tartans they wore, she might have thought she was at Amber Hill.

Except that she didn't recognize a single face. A lump lodged in her throat as she realized how alone she was. There was nothing to force Gordon to return her home. She might never get the chance to stare down those who doubted she was still pure because she was unsure of her host's intentions. He was a difficult man to understand or anticipate. The way he had handled her was clear evidence that he would do exactly as he pleased in spite of her arguments. The lump grew larger and the porridge looked too coarse to force down her throat.

Commotion from the end of the hall drew her attention. Gordon entered with his captains on his heels. Gordon wore a knitted round bonnet tipped to the side of his head. On the right side of the band was a solid gold broach in the form of one rampant lion. The eyes of the animal were set with rubies, telling her that Barras blood was considered noble. Each of the men following him wore a pheasant feather in his cap. It was a mark of their position, and the hall quieted while they passed.

Jemma felt the color drain from her face, for this was not the man who had teased her last night. The man who strode so determinedly down the center aisle, without a doubt or any hint of mercy, was Laird Barras. His stride was purposeful, carrying him quickly toward the table that waited. It was set up on a dais, further reinforcing the authority of the man. Bowls had not been placed on the table yet. A maid lifted a tray and hurried to serve her laird the moment he sat down. Every one of his captains waited until Gordon sat. Women attended the table immediately, bringing tankards and pitchers to fill them with. The morning meal was served to each captain and to the laird. What the men failed to see was the scuffle behind the servers. Girls cut one another off in order to be the ones serving at the high table. One woman actually aimed a silent snarl, her lips curling and her nose wrinkling at another woman when she made the mistake of trying to place a bowl in front of Gordon. But when she leaned over where her laird might see her, she was smiling sweetly as though she were kin to the Virgin Mary. She leaned very far forward, making sure her breasts were displayed for Gordon. His gaze dropped to the creamy swells, and his lips curved just a slight amount.

Jemma felt her cheeks heat with temper. She knew that grin. That curving of his mouth that he'd aimed at her across the bed last night. Her eyes widened when she realized that she was caught in a flash of jealousy.

She looked down at her bowl, silently chiding herself.

"I enjoy riding . . ."

Of course the man did. He knew too much about how to fluster her, how to touch her so that her heart began racing. It should come as no surprise at all that he had women fighting over him. No doubt the man had walked away from her last night and into the arms of another woman who knew more than she did about satisfying him.

Being a maiden had never bothered her before, but for a moment she detested her lack of knowledge. She was ignorant, and she felt the lack keenly. Lifting her face, she looked at the girl lavishing service on Gordon. Her lips were plump and inviting; they glistened as if she'd licked them before leaning over the table where she might be seen. Instead of securely braided hair, tucked beneath a linen cap, her cap hung from her belt and her hair looked tousled or just right for a man to slide his fingers into. Her hips swayed when she crossed in front of the table on her way back toward the hearth. Unlike the other maids, she didn't take the shorter path that ran behind the table; no, she crossed in front and took her time covering the distance. More eyes than just Gordon's watched her, and Jemma stared at the expressions on those faces. Lust was there for certain, but there was also heat and passion. The girl carried herself with supreme confidence, and the cutting glances of the other Barras women didn't gain even a tilt from her head. Instead she smiled at the men watching her, absorbing the attention they lavished on her.

Envy filled Jemma. Bitter and irrational, but she couldn't deny that she wanted what that girl had.

Do I?

That little voice inside her head shocked her, but the question was still a valid one. If she wanted what that girl had, then she would have to be willing to surrender her body to gain it. She'd never questioned remaining pure, it was expected of her, but to be honest she had never even thought about what life might be like if she chose to do otherwise.

Well, it might be very harsh. Jemma watched the woman at the hearth, and things were not so good for her now. The other women sent her cutting glances, and the cook shook her long-handled spoon at her. The girl frowned but pulled her linen cap from her belt and placed it on her head. The cook was not satisfied and reached out to deliver a quick slap. The girl turned red but took her chastisement and snatched a pitcher off the table before turning around to begin filling tankards. Once more she was the center of adoring attention from the men, but the women sent sharp glares at her.

What was worse? Being the virgin bride who gained approval of the females in the house while her husband dallied and everyone knew it, or the woman who was frank enough to flaunt what she enjoyed? Even thinking such a question defied every bit of higher authority that she had been raised with, but Jemma still pondered the idea. When her father became ill, she had stepped out of society and all of its expectations.

There had only been what he needed and the time they had left to share with each other.

"Mistress Jemma."

Gordon's voice sliced through the conversation filling the hall. Everyone near her turned to look at her, and she could feel many, many more staring at her. The woman sitting next to her sent her elbow into her ribs because Jemma hesitated.

Pushing her bench back, she stood up and looked toward the head table. Gordon was watching her with his blue eyes, but his expression revealed nothing of his thoughts.

"I was pleased to hear you attended Mass this morning. You pleased the clergy by doing so."

A murmur of approval rippled across the hall. It made her swallow her response and simply lower herself. Acceptance was not something that anyone gained through challenging the rules that governed life. Besides, no matter if she did disagree with some of the ways that life was dictated to her, order prevented having to live with savageness. Gordon was laird, maintaining order by having expectations for everyone living on his land, including himself. But that did not mean that she would meekly accept the man's rule over her.

"It was most kind of your people to make me welcome, especially since I am to depart so quickly, but I am most appreciative."

He stared at her, his lips curving just the smallest amount while everyone waited to hear what their laird would say. She had never been the center of so much attention and decided that it was not something she enjoyed. Sweat trickled down her back beneath her clothing, and her heart was beating faster. But she held her chin steady, keeping herself looking as if nothing was bothering her at all.

"I consider myself most fortunate to be having yer company here for the next few days."

"Days—" Jemma clamped down on her outburst and watched the beast hide his grin behind his tankard. More than one of his captains was shielding a similar expression. "Forgive me, Lord Barras, but it seems that you were not informed of the fact that I plan to return to my home this morning as my brother would expect me to."

"Unfortunately I can nae be allowing anyone but me men outside the walls until I am certain that the English soldiers I encountered last night are well off me land and no longer a threat. I'm sure ye can understand the need I feel to protect every last soul that the Lord has placed beneath my care." He lowered the tankard and stared at her. "Yer brother would thank me for my concern, I'm very sure of that."

His captains began to agree, nodding their heads and slapping the top of the table, but there was merriment dancing in Gordon's eyes.

"I am very sure that there is no danger while the sun is shining, Lord Barras." She placed emphasis on the word "lord" to make sure everyone heard her English pronunciation of the title. His captains frowned at her, becoming quiet again.

Gordon stood up, and the hall fell completely silent. Not even a spoon scraped against the side of a bowl.

"I am nae so sure, Mistress."

His words were spoken like a judgment. They rang across the hall, making sure no one wearing his colors missed the fact that he wanted her to remain. Jemma felt as if an iron collar were being locked around her neck.

"I am sorry to hear that we disagree, Lord Barras, for neighbors should be friendly whenever possible; yet I must return to my home. That is, of course, the only correct thing to do. My brother will express his gratitude for the service you have shown me, I am certain of that."

Jemma lowered herself, curtsying in a perfect display of

feminine poise and grace. She rose back up smoothly and promptly turned her back on him. There was astonishment on the faces she saw, a few jaws dropping open. Jemma did not stop to consider any of it. She moved at a quick pace through the great hall, the open doors at the far end beckoning to her.

But she never felt the sunlight touch her face. A strong hand latched around her upper arm and pulled her toward a doorway off to the side of the hall. She didn't need to question who that grip belonged to because her body leaped with excitement, recognizing the touch instantly. She waited until the door shut behind them and turned on Gordon with all the pent-up fury her false demeanor had stifled.

"I will not stay here. Best you understand that, sir."

He folded his arms across his chest and placed his body between the door and her. "There will be an understanding here, lass, but no by me. Ye will stay inside this castle until I grant ye leave."

"You have no right to command me so."

"No right?" His voice lowered. "I have every right, Jemma. Ye came so close to being killed by yer own foolishness last night that I have earned the right to enforce my will on ye because following yer whims has been proven so perilous."

She shook her head, unwilling to listen to his words. But he moved forward and cupped her chin in one of his large hands to hold her still.

"Do ye doubt that those English are still out there, or that they have comrades who will help them extract vengeance on anyone they find? Even one of their own?"

"I will be safe at Amber Hill."

"Ye would need an escort of at least fifty men, and I need those same men to safeguard me villages and fields."

"But that leaves me stranded here." Jemma shook off his hand, unable to stomach the touch when she felt as if that iron collar was growing heavier with every sentence he spoke. "I cannot simply live here."

"And why not?" He stiffened. "Barras Castle is a fine place to live, lass."

"That is not my objection to remaining and you know it."

His lips curved up in mocking jest. "Well now, lass, I seem to recall that ye found me to yer liking last night as well. Yer lips moved so sweetly beneath my own—"

"Stop it. Such talk is sinful."

He moved toward her and she retreated, but they were only in a small storage room and a solid wall stopped her within a few paces. Gordon pressed his hands onto that wall, caging her with his thickly muscled arms. He was so close she could smell his skin once more, and she found it more pleasing than she remembered.

"Well then, I suppose that only leaves us action, if ye do nae want any talking about what is between us."

"There is nothing between us—"

His mouth smothered the rest of her denial. Today's kiss was firmer and more demanding. His elbows bent, allowing his body to brush against her own. She jerked, too flooded by sensation to remain still. But Gordon captured the sides of her head once more, his hands spreading wide to hold her face exactly where he wanted it. His mouth continued to demand, pressing against her lips until she opened them. The tip of his tongue teased the soft skin of her lower lip before licking its way along her upper one. It felt as if he was tasting her and savoring every moment. His body kept hers caged against the wall, allowing her no reprieve from the overload of stimulation. It poured into her from the warm scent of his skin to the way his mouth pressed hers to open farther.

"There is a great deal between us, lass, and I am going to enjoy exploring it." He trailed tiny kisses across her cheek and onto the side of her neck. She shivered, never having suspected that her skin might be so sensitive. Delight traveled down her body, touching off renewed excitement in her belly that swirled and leaped into a roaring blaze of need. She gasped, shuddering at the sheer intensity of that need. It clawed at her like some beast in search of nourishment and the only thing it craved was Gordon. She reached for him, her hands unable to remain at her sides in denial of what she desired. It was suddenly clear to her that she was lonely, her body suffering from not being touched. Her hands absorbed the warmth of his body with gratefulness, setting off a quiver behind her knees. She wanted to sink down and press herself completely against him.

The image of them rolling across the surface of a bed shocked her with the carnality of her desires.

"Stop, Gordon . . . *please.*" She was pleading, but desperation was welling up inside her because she knew that her resolve was beginning to be undermined by the flood of physical need.

"The sound of my name on yer lips is sweeter than honey, lass." Gordon straightened his head to lock his gaze with hers. His hands returned to the wall beside her head, and she heard his breathing rasping between his clenched teeth. "Even if I have no liking for what ye are asking me."

"You must stop."

He snorted at her, and his eyes lit with determination that warned her. The man did not care for being told what he must do. He leaned forward, but Jemma raised her hand and covered his lips to prevent him from kissing her again.

"I want you to stop."

He pressed a hand on the center of her chest, his fingers directly over her heart. She gasped, never having felt any man's hand on the soft swells of her breasts. Even her clothing did not prevent her from shivering.

"The racing of yer heart is telling me to keep kissing ye until I find what ye have hidden beneath yer stays."

"Don't you have enough women willing to be ridden because of lust alone? I am a virgin, and your words are misplaced."

"How about me hand? Do ye disagree with where it is, too?"

His fingers pressed a tiny bit harder against her chest. Fear clawed at her as her nipples began to tingle and harden. She couldn't seem to resist the urge to respond to him. It was instantaneous and overwhelming.

"You are toying with me. My brother told me that Scotsmen have honor, even if most of England claims otherwise. Do you plan to show me that or prove the rumors true? There are plenty of English that like to hate men born outside of England, but I have never been one of them. I prefer to judge for myself. Maybe that is a mistake."

His nostrils flared, and she stared at the telltale sign that she had hit him in a soft spot. His hand stayed in place, seeming to grow hotter every moment that it remained against her tender flesh. It should have been impossible to be so aware of a touch, especially when she was so annoyed with him. Everything about their personalities felt as if it was designed to be opposite from the other.

"I deserved that comment." Gordon's tone was tight and his face even more so, but he lifted his hand away from her chest to gently stroke the side of her face with his fingertips. She shivered, drawing in a shuddering breath.

"But I just can't find it in me to say I'm sorry when ye respond so much to my touch, lass." His fingers made it to her hairline where he tugged on one small lock curling in defiance of the braids that held the longer strands and forced them to be neat.

"I am nae sorry, Jemma, and neither are you." His voice was tempting, dark, and full of the promise of more delight should she yield to his will.

"But I am asking you to stop." Because that was the wise choice. One that she detested, and she had to sink her teeth into her own lip to keep from retracting.

His fingers stilled her lips by gliding across them. She quivered and her gaze focused on his mouth, the longing in her belly urging her to gently kiss his fingers in invitation.

"I prefer my name on yer lips."

She reached up and caught his wrist, but pushing it away caused her lips to lament the separation.

"Send me home, Gordon. I am asking you."

Jemma could see the conflict in his eyes. It was the same one she felt prickling along her body. The yearning to touch and be touched in return, warring against the demands of honor. In that moment they were not so different in spite of their genders.

"Nae."

He turned his back on her and moved toward the doorway with purposeful strides.

"Wait."

He didn't stop, didn't even slow down.

"Gordon Dwyre, don't you dare turn your back on me like a coward."

He growled and turned around in a swirl of Barras tartan, pointing a finger at her.

"Do nae ever call me coward, Jemma, unless ye want to experience just how much daring I have inside me."

"Then do not turn your back on me just because you do not

care for the fact that I am correct in saying that honor demands I return home before I am ruined, and you named as the blackguard who did the deed."

He chuckled, but it was not a kind sound. "Ye would enjoy the deed, lass, be very sure of that."

Her throat tightened, forcing her to swallow hard. His eyes filled with enjoyment to see it.

"Exactly why I must remain firm and return home today." Jemma drew in another breath to force her passion to cool. "I will take my mare and do what is proper before this sinfulness has the chance to go any further. It is best for us both. Go and ask your priest if you think otherwise, but I am firm in this decision."

"I can see that." His expression became guarded and his tone too controlled to gain any hint as to his mood.

"Good. We are agreed then. Where is my mare?"

His face remained unreadable. "Where did ye leave her, lass? I'm not accustomed to looking after ye and yer possessions."

"But surely your boys brought my mare back last night . . ." Her eyes widened with the horror of the possibility that she was without a horse. Amber Hill was too far to walk to.

"I surely did bring ye back with me, and that was were my attention was."

A soft gasp betrayed just how disturbing she found the idea of being without her mount.

"Well then, I shall need to have the loan of a horse." Jemma tried to ask nicely, but her voice was sharp with her rising distress.

"I've none to spare."

Jemma felt her cheeks heat. "I watched your men gather up every English horse last night, sir."

Gordon shrugged and closed the distance between them again. She felt his approach keenly, the quiver instantly returning to the back of her knees. Her insides tightened with anticipation, her breath freezing in her throat as she stared at his hand when it stretched out toward her. His hand cupped her cheek, smoothing over the bright spot, and his lips twitched up.

"Well now, lass, those wouldn't be my horses to loan to ye."

"Oh, fye upon you, Gordon Dwyre." She slapped his hand away, unable to play their polite game any further. "You are toying with me yet again."

He chuckled, his eyebrows lowering in smug satisfaction. "Maybe so, lass, but I promise ye that ye'll be locked in the stocks if ye take anything that isna yers by my word."

Her hands curled into fists and she snarled, but the man turned and left the room before she might hurl another insult at him.

Troll!

Black-hearted, muck-dripping troll!

Gordon rode out of the courtyard moments after she emerged from the room he'd taken her into. His men had assembled and were waiting for their laird while he was with her.

While he was kissing me . . .

Jemma wanted to strangle the voice inside her head. Never had she been plagued by such impure thoughts. Well at least she knew exactly who to blame for their uprise.

She watched the source of her disquiet ride down the road that led to the main castle gates. He moved with the stallion in perfect grace, power radiating from him. Her attention was glued to him as fascination renewed its grip. It wasn't that she couldn't tear her eyes away, it was the fact that she failed to think to do so. Finally, Gordon began to blend into the mass of riders in the distance, and she forced herself to investigate her surroundings.

By the light of day, Barras Castle was quite impressive. Four towers rose into the sky, each one amazingly different. They were all built in different styles, standing as a sort of tribute to the longtime prosperity of the Barras clan. Building cost a great deal of money. Many clans used fortresses handed down from the generation before when a noble had brought enough money with him to lay the foundation. Barras Castle was growing, fresh mortar along one portion of the curtain wall proving that this year had been a good one.

The sun shone off the cannons that faced onto the road. Smooth cannon balls were stacked into pyramids nearby, the heavy guns driving home the fact that Gordon backed up his position with blood if necessary.

She sighed, suddenly enduring a surge of longing for home. Amber Hill was very much like Barras Castle. Cannons stood at the ready there, somewhere on the other side of the hills that separated the two fortresses. Shame bit into her for the worry that her absence must be causing, but the row of wooden stocks standing in front of the church confirmed that Gordon had not been teasing her.

His threat stood as firm as those creations of public punishment. There were even flat wooden planks below each one for the writing of the offender's crime in chalk. It wasn't that she feared being clamped into the stock because of the public viewing. What she dreaded was the fact that those wooden racks would ensure that she was waiting for Gordon when he rode back into the yard.

She would prefer to keep their battles private.

Which allows for kissing . . .

She snarled and turned around to find Ula. She needed
something to do before her own thoughts drove her insane
and left her a mindless creature who would happily toss her
skirts for Gordon Dwyre.

Gordon pressed his stallion and his men hard. The stakes
were high, making every mile they covered more important
than the last. His muscles were tight and his senses straining
to capture every detail. Each hill that they crested was climbed
with a care for the fact that there might be hostile English on
the other side. But he headed toward England despite the fact
that he was heading toward the enemy.

He spotted the banners of the Baron Ryppon just after mid-
day. Pulling up on the crest of a hill, he surveyed the lines of
men. They were on his ground, but it was the border land, far
from either fortress. This spot had been disputed for cen-
turies. By night it was haunted with the spirits of the men who
had been marched onto it, only to die for the cause of a
monarch who sat well behind the lines of battle.

"It looks like we found what ye were looking for." Kerry
leaned toward him so that his words would reach him.

"Of the two possibilities, I think this is the least likely to see
us all arriving on Saint Peter's path. But there is still a fair
chance we'll end up a bloody mess."

"Ye could just give the man his sister back."

Gordon didn't answer. He stiffened as rejection of that idea
flooded him. It was immediate and complete. There was no
room for any argument, only the absolute desire to keep
Jemma where he'd put her.

Which meant he'd have to deal with her brother or face being
invaded. Kicking his horse, he moved down the slope toward the
one man who had every right to demand he relinquish Jemma.

* * *

"You cannot expect me to accept that." Curan Ramsden glared at Gordon with barely contained violence showing on his face. The man forced himself to try to reason with him. The afternoon breeze whipped around them while their men watched. It was not a relaxing meeting as they had shared in the past. This time the English glared at the Scots, and every man waited to see if Gordon and Curan might resolve their dispute before the order was given for swords to be employed because diplomacy had failed. More than one man's lips moved in silent prayer just in case a fight was coming.

Curan Ramsden, Baron Ryppon, leveled a hard look at Gordon. "I am grateful for the fact that you saved my sister from her own foolishness, but I must insist that you return her to me now."

"She made that same demand, and I refused."

Curan's face darkened with rage. "Enough, Barras, my patience is wearing very thin with you. No man holds my sister. I won't stand for it. You cannot believe that I would, so explain what you are planning."

"Maybe it's time ye rethought that position, Ryppon. Jemma is a woman, no longer a girl, and it's time ye let her be one." The horses shifted, sensing the tension of the moment.

"What are you saying, man?" Curan pushed his helmet back so that he could aim a hard look toward Gordon. "That I should let her remain with you, because she's a grown woman?"

"She's still a maiden."

Curan drew in a stiff breath, calming down.

"But I wonder if it isna time to be changing that."

"Enough!" Curan made a slashing motion with his hand that drew dark looks from his waiting men.

Barras snorted at Curan. "I do nae think so. I've already

gone to a great deal of effort to ask ye for permission to court her, so do nae insult me by implying that I'd no honor her if I took her to my bed."

"Is that what you plan, Barras?" Curan curled his hand into a fist. "I cannot stand idle while you keep my sister imprisoned."

"Well, it's sure to be better for her if one of us keeps her from riding out without a care for what danger lurks on this land."

Curan drew in a stiff breath. "I concede that you are correct. Jemma cannot be allowed to continue as she has. She was changing her habits, which accounted for how late she went riding yesterday. She is a woman and doesn't know the details of how violent our land has become. Neither my father nor I felt politics a suitable subject for her. I wish I might be so ignorant, for the current policies coming from London do not please me. It was my decision to keep such dark tidings from her."

Gordon felt the tension between them ease. For all that he was Scottish and Curan pure English, they had discovered a common ground between them. Neither felt the need to hate one another simply because they had been raised to do so. They judged each other by their deeds, which was something their countrymen might benefit from learning.

"I want to court her."

Curan narrowed his eyes, and Gordon shrugged. "In my own manner, and mind the way ye are glaring at me, man. I seem to recall ye using a few direct tactics to bring yer bride to yer bed. Ye didna want anyone telling ye how to proceed, either."

"She is my sister."

Gordon couldn't resist grinning at the strained tone that Curan used. "Aye, lad, but the fact is Jemma has grown into a woman who needs to be allowed to deal with a man who wants her. That will never happen beneath yer roof. If I come courting to yer home, she'll discover herself wed to a stranger because she will never see the true side of my nature while everyone is watching us. Besides, I've no more patience for sitting there while she runs away and ye will nae allow me to chase her."

"So you want me to allow her to remain beneath yours? Is that it, Barras?"

Gordon stared straight back at Curan without flinching. "Aye, lad, I do."

The English baron held his thoughts for a long moment, studying him.

"Why? To bed her before wedding her?"

"Why do ye want her returned so quickly, Ryppon? Is there another offer that is better? I'll match it if I bed her."

"If?" Curan raised one eyebrow in question.

Gordon shrugged. "I told ye, Ryppon, I want to court the lass. It may be that I will send her back to ye happily."

"Careful, Barras. Jemma might have made a mistake yesterday, but she took my father's passing very hard, for she tended him for the years that he was ill. A woman's heart is tender, as I am discovering with my own wife. Don't make the mistake of thinking ill of Jemma for loving our father so greatly she faltered under the pain of his passing. That capacity to love is the thing that makes a woman worth more than any treasure on this earth. Women love deeply, and sometimes that sends them into despair when they lose the person they give their heart to."

There was a light in the baron's eyes that made Gordon envious. The emotion surprised him, stealing the heat from his next words.

"I want the chance to discover who yer sister is, and I can

nae do that with ye about." Gordon shrugged. "I've been the master of my own home too long, just as ye did nae take too kindly to anyone telling ye how to treat yer own bride. Ye have been in command too long to sit and perform like an untried lad."

"That is true enough." Curan rubbed his chin. "But if you bring tears to Jemma's eyes, I swear I will smash your face, Barras. Business or no business, and that is my solemn promise to you."

Gordon smiled, the expression cocksure and arrogant, drawing a chuckle from Curan.

"I promise you, Barras, you won't enjoy this fight."

"Neither will you." There was thick promise in his voice but also a good amount of boyish merriment. Curan shook his head but not completely with disgust.

"I'll be back, Barras, and soon."

Curan rode back to join his men, and smiles appeared on their faces when they learned that they would not be ordered into battle. Gordon knew that his own men would be wearing similar expressions. He could feel their relief hitting his back while he maintained his position and watched the English baron turn his men around. There was a single knight who defied his lord's command. Two white plumes were mounted on the back of the man's helmet, signifying his rank. He remained facing the Scots, and Gordon could feel the heat of the man's glare. But his lord jerked his head, and the knight bent beneath the order.

Kerry joined him with an expression that was smooth. But there were questions brimming in the man's eyes.

"Keep yer thoughts to yerself, man. I've enough to think about."

A low whistle was his captain's reply, one that Gordon had heard before when the man was teasing him over something.

Today, Gordon didn't find any humor in the moment, and his captain's whistle irritated him. He sent Kerry a deadly glare, but Kerry only chuckled.

"A wee bit touchy now, aren't ye, Laird?"

It wasn't really a question but a statement of how his man felt about his behavior. Gordon stared at the withdrawing English and felt satisfaction fill him. Too much satisfaction for his mind.

Maybe he should have given Jemma back to her brother.

His body rejected that idea instantly, but he couldn't deny that his pride didn't like the notion that any woman might become so important to him. Love wasn't what he sought. He needed a family and felt that lack in his life more and more lately. That was the only explanation for how often he'd gone out to watch his neighbor riding across the border land. He didn't seek love, only a woman who could give him the family he longed for without boring him.

Jemma had spirit, and her brother would think twice about invading Barras land if his sister was wed to his neighbor. It was a common arrangement along the border land. One that would serve him and his clan well.

It was a good plan, and he'd always followed through with a good plan. Jemma Ramsden would have to understand that.

Ula was a tough taskmaster to satisfy. The housekeeper came looking for Jemma the moment Barras left her. Jemma felt her cheeks heating because she was sure that the woman knew exactly what her laird had been doing with her, too.

"Idleness brings naught but trouble," the older woman declared before beginning to direct Jemma just as she did with the other women that crossed her path. "Besides, winter comes sooner to us here."

"Ula, Amber Hill is not so far from Barras Castle."

"It is nae?"

Jemma shot the woman a glare. "No, it is not."

Ula retaliated with a knowing grin. "Well then, I can see what the laird is thinking in courting ye."

Courting. A misplaced word if ever she had heard one. It was like calling a goat a stallion. They both had four legs and that was as far as the similarities went.

But Ula offered her something to do, and there was part of her that loathed returning to her days of nothingness. It would be far worse to have time on her hands at Barras Castle because it would further alienate her. If she were a man, she would expect to find herself sleeping in the dungeon.

But that idea only gave rise to the thought that because she was a woman, she needed to worry about ending up in the laird's bed.

Who would detest it . . . ?

Her inner thoughts were becoming quite bothersome. Jemma ordered them to stay away from Gordon, but her mind was full of nothing but the man. He was well built, and she found his frame quite pleasing. She could not say just why, only that she noticed him more than other men. He was certainly different from the men who followed her brother. There was his kilt, for instance.

Her cheeks heated even more because she suddenly thought about what was beneath that pleated garment. Or, more precisely, how quickly the man might be able to *ride.* Scots had a reputation for tossing skirts, even lowland Scotsmen like Gordon.

She wasn't sure there was much difference. Gordon was far removed from the Englishmen she knew. His dress, his speech, and even his mannerisms made him Scottish to her.

Did he find me as foreign?

It was a fair question. In all her musing she had never considered how different she might be from the sort of woman he would have preferred for a bride.

Last night he had been certain that she didn't possess the necessary knowledge to be his wife. Well, sense was a better word. Her pride still stung, but there was the fact that he had returned and found her more to his liking the second time.

How would she fare tonight?

That was a dangerous thought, one that stirred up the embers of the fire he'd lit in her with his kiss. The sun was already high above her head and beginning to arch back toward the horizon. Emotions swirled through her, building in strength as the day progressed.

What captured her attention the most was the excitement brewing inside her. It stunned her and pricked her temper, but she could not deny that it was flickering in the pit of her belly, eagerly awaiting another encounter with Gordon Dwyre.

Jemma hissed at herself. The word "foolish" seemed to be firmly attached to her.

Barras Castle did have a fine bathhouse. Jemma sighed as she leaned forward and washed her feet. She was happy to discover that at least one rumor she had heard of Scotland was true, that the Celtic people liked to bathe often, unlike many of her English brethren.

She had never been among those who believed bathing too often led to a lack of immunity from disease. Amber Hill had a bathhouse behind the kitchen, and she used it every day.

Barras Castle put Amber Hill to shame. There were twice as many slipper tubs here. Quite a statement when one considered that each tub cost a large sum. There was also soap and linen for drying with. The bathhouse was built along the back of the huge hearths that were used to cook. The heat came through the wall, heating the room so much that the window shutters were wide open to prevent the room from becoming too hot. But the amount of heat made a cool bath soothing. A large water wheel gently lifted water from the river that ran alongside the castle. A portion of the bank had been dug out to form a pool that the water wheel might work from without risking damage to its wooden slats. The water poured into a long spillway that ran along the outside wall. Every few feet, a thick slab of wood was placed over a cut-out section of the spillway. With a tug it came free, and water spilled down into the tub below it. You only had to replace the slab to stop the flow of water.

There was a small hearth where iron kettles might be used to heat water, but the room was so warm that Jemma didn't bother. The cool water felt good against her skin, and she sat down in the water wearing her chemise so that the garment might gain a washing, too.

"Here now, there is no need for ye to worry about wearing soiled clothing."

Ula entered the bathhouse and placed a folded cream-colored garment on a nearby stool.

"This one should fit ye, but a dress will prove a bit harder to locate. Maybe on the morrow."

"I appreciate the chemise, Ula."

The housekeeper smiled. "Ye earned yer keep today. No one is forced to stink at Barras Castle. Perhaps the laird will bring a few of yer things back with him."

That would mean that she was staying at Barras Castle.

Jemma felt a prickle of a chill cross her nape. Ula moved to the fireplace and lifted one of the kettles. She tested it with her finger before bringing to to Jemma. There was a hint of something in her eyes that suggested she was preparing Jemma for her laird and that she was quite happy to do so.

"Let us give yer hair a good washing."

Jemma nibbled on her lower lip while she closed her eyes. The warm water soaked her head, running down over her chest to tease her nipples. The knowledge that the house-keeper was tending to her in order to please Gordon sent even more sensation across her skin until she felt like she was pulsing with anticipation.

Which was absurd, considering she was not interested in any further dealings with the man.

Liar . . .

"A clean head of hair always makes me feel better, more at ease."

Ula took up a dab of the softer soap that was kept in a pottery bowl and began to work it through Jemma's hair.

"You must have other, more important things to do." Jemma tried to take over washing her hair, but Ula flicked her hands aside.

"Nonsense, there be naught that is more important than seeing to someone me laird made welcome. Mind yer eyes."

Jemma closed her eyes, and Ula began rinsing her hair. The housekeeper even returned to the hearth to fetch another kettle of water to make sure there was no hint of soap remaining.

"Now let me have that chemise. Ye can nae get clean wearing that."

Jemma didn't bother to protest. Ula was already tugging the wet fabric up and over her head. It had been years since she had bathed with anyone near. Amber Hill had become quiet during her father's illness. As it did in late fall when even the animals were still and there were no more leaves to rustle in the wind.

A maid entered the room, and Ula lifted her face to look at the girl. "Good. Now find her boots and give them a cleaning."

"I'll look after my own things, Ula."

"Nae, ye will sit yerself in front of the hearth so that we can get yer hair dried."

Once again Ula insisted on her way. Jemma found herself sitting by the fire in the new chemise while the maid cleaned her boots and even polished them. Another girl entered bearing fresh stockings. Ula set the girl to shaking out Jemma's dress and making sure there was no dirt clinging to the hem.

A bell began to toll somewhere along the wall, the sound almost startling because of how quiet it had become in the bathhouse.

"The laird is returning."

Jemma could hear the joy in Ula's voice, but both maids turned to look at her and her throat went dry. They looked at her with assessing stares. From her feet to her head, they surveyed her, their eyes narrowing all the while.

"Come on with that dress. The laird will be wanting his supper, sure enough, having been out all day long."

There were suddenly three women all intent on dressing her. Jemma stood in shocked silence because it had been a long time since anyone had helped her. She had been the servant to her father, helping him and wearing only the simplest of dresses so that she might more easily lean over his bed. She didn't know the latest fashion, because none of it had mattered. There had only been her father and what he required.

Anything her brother might send from Amber Hill would be just as plain as the dress she now wore—a single cartridge-pleated pair of skirts that were sewn to one waistband. A modest hip roll helped to keep the weight of her skirts from pulling on her back, but the two-inch-padded roll that went around her hips also kept the garment away from her toes when she walked. Unless she was running, she wouldn't need to grab her skirt and lift it else risk stepping on it and falling on her face.

She had on a good set of stays. The corset fit her well, and over that she wore only a simple doublet that buttoned up the front. It had a French cut to it, coming down in a square neckline. She'd worn an over partlet that covered her chest and the swells of her breasts, but it was lost somewhere on the land between Barras Castle and Amber Hill where the rogue knights had attacked her.

Simple clothing. And boots just as practical. They laced up, and if set beside the ones the maids wore, there was no notable difference.

There had been a time when her mother was alive that she had dressed in pretty dresses with slipper shoes, but none of those garments fit her anymore. They were packed carefully away now in some quiet, sheet-draped room at Amber Hill.

Jemma reached for the tie that had held her hair in a thick braid.

"Ye should leave yer hair loose, being as ye are unwed, lass."

"Only brides wear their hair flowing." And that was on their wedding day.

"Here in Scotland, 'tis a bit different. Ye'll see the other girls letting their hair down once the day's work is finished."

Ula took only a small amount of her hair at the front and made thin braids of it that she looped around her head and tied at the back. The style kept her hair out of her eyes while the length of it still flowed down her back to her waist.

"Come on now."

Ula didn't give her a chance to protest being seen with her

hair loose. The housekeeper grasped her hand and pulled her out of the bathhouse. Jemma fought the urge to giggle because it had been a long time since she had played about with her hair flowing behind her. It brought back memories of spring festival and dancing on the green when her father had been ruby cheeked and jovial.

"Well now, lass, yer a right agreeable sight."

Jemma gasped and pulled her hand away from Ula. The housekeeper didn't resist the motion; in fact, Ula released her hand and stepped behind her in one motion. Ula dropped a quick curtsy to her laird before the woman disappeared in a flip of her wool skirts. A tingle crossed Jemma's nape again, but this time it was much more intense. Facing Gordon Dwyre instead of just her recollections of the man was to blame.

He was more imposing than her memory recounted. Too large for her comfort, because for some reason she was fixated by his broad shoulders and the fact that her head only reached his chin.

His dark-blue eyes moved to her hair, tracing the unbraided mass and flickering with something that looked like enjoyment.

"A right agreeable sight to greet a man indeed."

"I didn't dress for you." But she liked the look in his eyes. Liked it too much really, for it sent a flicker of excitement through her, and the sensation was unsettling.

He shrugged, and the ends of his shoulder-length hair left tiny wet spots on his shirt. She looked closer to notice that he must have just bathed, too, because his hair glistened with water and he wore only a shirt with his kilt. The cuffs of that shirt were rolled up past his elbows, displaying hands and forearms that were clean and without a streak of dust.

"Well, I'll be enjoying it all the same, lass. I've never been a man to pass up something I like because it was not intended for me."

"I wouldn't say that, exactly." The words were past her lips before she considered whether or not it was wise to confess her inner feelings to him.

"What would ye say then, lass?"

There was a hint of challenge in his voice that pricked her pride. Jemma raised her chin and returned his stare without flinching.

"I would say that your housekeeper took delight in preparing me for you as though I was some sort of . . . of—"

"Gift?" His lips curved up in a mocking grin.

Jemma pressed her lips together, refusing to rise to the bait he was dangling in front of her nose. He chuckled softly and moved closer to her, his gaze roaming over her hair once more. There was a flicker of something in his eyes that made her tremble. He reached out and touched a lock of her hair, his fingers making the briefest of contacts before she twisted away from him, hissing at herself for retreating but unable to conquer the urge to do so.

"I am not your gift."

"So do nae touch ye? Is that what ye are saying, Jemma?" He moved back and considered her. "Ye enjoyed being touched this morning."

"Why do you do that?"

"Do what, lass?"

"Bait me. Do you truly desire to bicker, or is it simply a way to outmaneuver me and gain what you wish without my true consent?" Jemma shot him a hard look. "Needle me until I slap at you, and then claim that touching me was my fault. Is that your game, Barras?"

He drew in a stiff breath and released it while he crossed his arms across his chest. The pose was intimidating, but Jemma refused to bend beneath his scrutiny.

"Many a lass has fallen to such tactics, but in truth I have placed a bit more polish on tonight."

He turned and extended his arm behind him, where candles illuminated a table with their yellow glow. The table was set with silver dishes that sparkled with the candlelight, and a salt cellar held expensive white salt.

"I thought we might dine together."

Her throat went dry once more as her suspicions with Ula proved true.

"Since I've made an offer to yer brother for ye, I believe it is proper enough for us to learn a wee bit more about one another."

Someone cleared their throat behind her, and Jemma turned to see a line of musicians entering. She wasn't even sure what chamber she was in, only that it was lovely with arches on the ceiling and windows that allowed a soft breeze to blow through the room. The musicians disappeared behind a wooden screen, and she could hear them sitting down. Music began to drift over the screen, soft melody constructed of mandolin strings and flutes, while the screen provided privacy.

It was a scene set for courting the most highborn lady. But in her deepest thoughts, she didn't care for it. Gordon did not belong in the courtly setting. Disappointment actually rose up inside her for the stately manner in which he was conforming to society and its rules.

"Or I could send them away if ye prefer to continue as we began yesterday."

He raised one hand, and the music stopped. Challenge flashed from his eyes, but it was the look of anticipation that forced her hand.

"It is lovely." Jemma forced her feet to move toward the table and felt her heart rate accelerating with every hesitant step. Gordon sat down across the table from her, but the small piece of furniture caused their knees to feel no more than a whisper from one another. His lack of doublet suddenly drew her attention, her gaze moving over the light fabric.

"We Scots are a bit more accustomed to the weather, lass. I don't need a doublet inside this time of year."

Her cheeks heated because he'd noticed where her eyes had settled. Well, in all truth she shouldn't be surprised, the man was facing her, but most men wouldn't have mentioned it out loud. She drew in a deep breath and reminded herself that Gordon was very far removed from the men she knew. Her brother was controlled and pensive, always weighing his thoughts before allowing anyone else to share them.

Gordon picked her up and carried her where he pleased if she refused.

"I believe that the idea is for us to have a conversation, lass."

She jumped. "Ah . . . well . . . I suppose so."

Maids were carrying in food now, but they didn't stay long. They left two large platters, removing the tops to reveal beautifully arranged plates. There were summer vegetables, roasted chicken, and even baked apples.

"Ye sound unsure? Does that mean we may dispense with the English tradition and go back to the Scottish ones?"

Jemma offered a roll of her eyes, but she couldn't help smiling at him. "You are a boy." She pointed her knife at his chest. "Right there inside you is a boy no more than ten."

He chuckled and speared a piece of chicken with the point of his eating knife. "Well now, that's just the playful side of me nature. Ye have one, too."

Jemma shook her head. "I have matured, sir."

His face turned pensive for a moment while he chewed.

"Nae, lass, ye just pushed yer own desires aside to take care of yer father. It's time for ye to allow them freedom from that chest ye have them locked inside of."

"I see, and does that mean you would have to wife a woman who was busy coddling her heart's desires?" Jemma shook her head. "Marriage is duty, and it is best met with maturity."

He frowned. "Now that is just plain pitiful. I swear I don't know if I need to put ye out of yer misery or"—his lips parted to show her his teeth—"chase ye around this table."

One of the musicians struck a wrong note, proving that they were listening intently to every word.

"Both would defeat your effort to court me gently." Jemma had to bite her lip to keep from smiling at the idea because it was so absurd. It was also quite exciting, because she had no doubt that he would capture her.

"Ah, but I think we might enjoy chasing more." He pressed his hand flat on the tabletop, rising partially from his chair. Jemma gasped and dropped her knife.

"You wouldn't dare." The words had barely left her mouth before she recalled his words from that morning.

"I'll show ye how much daring I have inside of me . . ."

He growled and his chair flew backward. The musicians stopped, but there were several smothered sounds that were anything but horrified. Jemma was grateful for her plain dress because it allowed her to slip out of her chair and make it around the table before Gordon gained the upper hand.

"This is absurd." But she was breathless and far from outraged.

"Aye, but 'tis fun." He lunged for her, and she danced away from his grasping hands.

"Stop it, Gordon, you are going to ruin all this fine table dressing."

"I employ good laundresses, and I know a competent silver-smith."

This time he thrust his hand over the table, using his large body to bend over the table and catch her skirt.

She let out a shriek, but no fear crossed her mind. It was sim-ply too ridiculous to become frightened over. Gordon growled with victory and pulled her into his embrace. He ended up be-hind her, crossing his arms over her body to cage her.

"My prize!"

"I believe the idea was to court me, not capture me, you brute."

" 'Tis the same thing in Scotland."

Jemma wiggled, but he held her firmly in place. It was an oddly comfortable position, one that didn't overwhelm her but allowed her to feel him against her without triggering the need to fight him off.

"Ask any Highlander and they will tell ye that stealing women is a time-honored tradition. In fact, I'm nae sure they get their wives any other way."

"I heard that one of your kings married his mistress."

"Ah . . ." He released her, keeping only one wrist clasped in his hand, and she turned to face him.

"Now that is seduction and I like that, too." He raised her hand to his lips, pressing a kiss against the tender skin of her inner wrist. Sensation raced down her arm, raising gooseflesh as it went. The excitement that burned in her belly began spreading through her, touching off a desire that made her breathless. He lifted his lips away and rubbed over the same spot with his thumb, clearly feeling the accelerated throb of her heart.

"I think ye may be liking it as well, Jemma Ramsden."

He folded her gently into his arms, moving slowly enough

for her to evade him if she chose. Jemma was too intrigued to do anything but comply. This was a side of him that threatened to undermine her resistance. His hand threaded through her hair, lifting the stands and drawing a handful up to his cheek. He rubbed against it for a moment.

"Silk. Rare and coveted and worth every bit of effort it takes to get yer hands on it."

She suddenly stiffened, recalling the musicians. Jemma turned to look across the room to where they had been. Gordon turned her face back to him with a hand on the back of her head.

"They're gone and not a moment too soon. I need to kiss ye."

Yes . . .

It was the only thought in her head. Her lips parted and her chin lifted, even without the hand on the back of her head guiding her. The first touch of his mouth against hers sent a shiver down her back. Just a brief touch, a mere whisper of a kiss that teased her more than it satisfied.

"I needed to kiss ye the moment ye entered this room with yer hair down."

His mouth returned to hers, this time lingering longer. He pressed a light kiss onto her lips, slipping his along hers and filling her with delight. A soft murmur escaped her mouth, and he pressed her lips farther apart to deepen the kiss. Now his mouth demanded, gentle at first and then increasing pressure. The hand cradling her head was tilting it so that their lips fit together even more. The tip of his tongue slipped along her lower lip before it thrust smoothly into her mouth, teasing her tongue in a long thrust. She shivered again, her entire body quivering in his arms.

"Aye, lass, now that is courting at its best."

She was suddenly free, Gordon stepping away from her. Frustration burned through her, but she clamped down the urge to demand that he return when she looked into his eyes.

Desire burned there. It was no mere flicker but a roaring blaze that she witnessed testing his control.

"I'll bid ye good night, lass."

"Yes, good night."

The church bell tolled at dawn, bringing an end to her dreams of Gordon. For everyone it was another day to struggle to finish all the tasks that needed doing before winter arrived. Jemma followed them to church and then into the hall for her morning meal.

But her temper turned her cheeks pink when she watched the same maid push the others aside so that she might serve Gordon.

How could she dream of the man?

How could she not?

Jemma rubbed her head before going to find Ula and something to take her mind away from the man occupying too much of her time.

"He is mine."

Jemma jerked her head up to find the girl she'd watched serving Gordon standing around the corner of where the hallways crossed. Jemma had to look around the stack of newly ironed sheets to see her. What she saw was a close-up view of the scowl that the girl had sent toward her fellow maids that morning.

"So keep yer English hands off him or I'll make ye sorry ye ever set eyes on him." There was venom edging each word and the girl inching closer with each one.

"What are you talking about?"

She laughed. "I'm Anyon and ye'd better dispense with yer innocent airs. The laird might believe such, but I know the truth."

"Which is what?" Jemma felt her temper rising. She was not going to suffer Anyon's wrath meekly.

Anyon propped her hand on her hip and sneered. "That ye are nothing but a doxy at heart. Ye dangle yer chastity in front of men, hoping to get them to bid against one another for the right to plow ye. But beneath it all, ye're selling yer flesh just like the rest of us."

"What do you suggest? That I refrain from polite behavior while you press your breasts into the man's face during his meal?"

Anyon snickered and actually rocked her bosom back and forth. "The laird likes me tits good and well. You wouldn't know the first thing about pleasing a man like him, nor would ye ever learn. He'd plow ye to keep yer dowry, and then come to my bed where he might gain true satisfaction."

"Well, I have no intention of wedding the man, so you may take comfort in that truth." What did a man like Gordon need to be satisfied? Her gaze swept the Scottish girl from head to toe, trying to judge what it was that she knew about pleasing men. Anyon smiled with glee.

"Ye know that I am right. I can read yer horse face very well. Don't be swayed by that display he put on for you last night. He is nae a gentleman, but a wild Scot who likes his women knowing how to please."

"Fine then. Be content." Jemma took a step away from the nasty creature. If that was what pleased Gordon, well, Anyon was welcome to him. She stiffened and refused to show the disappointment that surged through her. Instead she forced herself to look at the girl and see that she was not lying about knowing her way around Gordon's body.

It was very likely that he'd gone to her last night after leaving her standing there with her eyes wide and her body softly throbbing.

Anyon stepped into the hallway directly in front of her with both hands propped on her hips. "Ye are so stupid, English chit. Ye think I will swallow yer lies about not wanting the laird, but ye stay here, and that tells me that ye are a lying bitch. Ye're just trying to sway me with yer words, but ye remain here tonight just the same, tempting the laird as you try to snag him."

"I've heard enough of your spite. If you want that man, I suggest you go and find him. If I had the means to leave this place, I would, but I will not stand here and listen to you spit your venom at me for something that I cannot change."

And if the man spoke one further word about wanting to court her while his mistress lived beneath the same roof, she was likely to hit him.

Anyon scoffed at her. "Don't have a way? Another lie, not that I expect anything else from yer English lips."

"I do not have a way to leave, and if you know otherwise I would appreciate you sharing the information with me."

The Scottish girl smirked at her, obviously enjoying her moment of knowing that she possessed something that Jemma wanted to know.

"Well, speak up, I am listening." Jemma refused to put up with the girl's surly nature. Sometimes it was necessary to show that you were not meek if you did not wish to become the victim of those who enjoyed being nasty. "If all you are going to do is insult me, I was given a task to do by Ula."

"Proving what a good little wife ye will be? Is that yer game, English slut?"

"Enough! I am not a slut, and you have no right to call *me* something that your behavior says you are."

Anyon's face turned red. "I am the laird's mistress." The girl growled each word. "Ye'd better understand something about Scotland, English slut; here even the king has been known to wed his mistress. Scottish men like to know what they are getting before they marry."

"Well then, since I have no intention of showing your laird what he will get with me if we were to wed, you may go on your way, free of concern."

"Prettily spoken, but those words do not change the fact that you are still here, doing Ula's bidding while yer mare is standing idle in the stable."

"What?" Jemma felt her face heat. The Scottish girl smirked at her, but Jemma wasn't in the mood to be toyed with any further.

"Where is my mare?"

Anyon raised an eyebrow at her tone. "Listen to ye. Ye'd think ye were already the mistress of this castle, the way ye demand."

Jemma cast a quick look toward the window. The light was now coming in at an angle, telling her that sunset was approaching. She feared the coming night because it would bring Gordon back to his fortress for certain, and she doubted her ability to resist him.

"If you want me gone from here, tell me where my mare is and how to leave this place."

Anyon abandoned her taunting stance when she heard the determination in Jemma's voice.

"Yer mare is in the back stable, the one closest to the gate.

Saddle her if ye know how and no one will stop ye from taking what is yers and leaving."

So simple. Jemma swallowed and fought the urge to sputter with outrage. Gordon had never said that her mare wasn't in the stable. The man had cleverly avoided giving her that bit of information, and she had been too blinded by his presence to realize that she wasn't asking a direct enough question.

"Well, are ye going? Or just spinning more lies?"

Jemma thrust the stack of sheets at the Scottish girl and didn't wait to make sure Anyon took them. She relinquished her hold on them and turned her back on the woman. Urgency filled her, pushing her to quicken her pace. She resisted the warning that was trying to stop her. She had ridden every day for months; one bad encounter was not going to turn her into a quivering-kneed coward who hid behind the walls of a tower. Life was too full of wonderful things. Besides, she could feel Gordon. Actually feel the man tightening the circle he was walking around her. It wasn't the man she was running from.

It was her response to him.

Most men had a mistress, and she would have to accept that from any husband she wed, but there was something inside her that wanted to scream at him for having one. It made no sense, so leaving was the only logical thing to do unless she wanted to risk going insane. There was no controlling her responses to him, and that frightened her.

There was still plenty of activity in the main yard. Boys were training under the supervision of older men. They wielded wooden swords, and the sound of those blades striking against each other echoed off the curtain wall. Women were hurrying to bring in the last of the drying laundry near the south side of the yard where huge water wheels lifted water from the river to pour through slots in the curtain wall. Men were stationed up on that wall, but their attention was on the horizon. The scent of roasting meat drifted to her nose. The cook had a deer roasting in one of the huge hearths that served the kitchen. She had been carving strips off it all day long so that the meat underneath would roast. What she cut was diced and combined with vegetables to be cooked into pies for supper. The Barras clan ate well, which was yet another indication of their power. Lesser clans would not cross them for fear that they could not appeal to them in the dead of winter when their own stores ran low. Alliances were most often based on need. Her own sister-in-law had been handed over to Gordon because her cousin wanted to prove his loyalty to the laird of the Barras clan.

Jemma scanned the yard once more, seeking any hint that she was being watched. But she didn't find any. Everyone seemed intent on completing their tasks before the cook rang the supper bells. The older men training the boys were push-ing their young charges to teach them perseverance.

Just as she needed to persevere.

Entering the stable, she slowed down and waited for her eyes to adjust to the dim light. The smell of fresh hay and al-falfa filled her senses. The sunlight illuminated hundreds of dust particles floating in the warm air. Horses snorted and pawed at the floor. Jemma forced herself to move slowly among them. She reached out to rub a muzzle here and there, soothing the beasts before they alerted anyone to her pres-ence. Her eyes were becoming more keen, able to distinguish colors in spite of the low light. It was not dark, merely dim. She scanned the stalls and smiled when her mare appeared. Standing near the back exactly as Anyon had said.

For all the insults the woman had thrown at her, Jemma decided she would have to think kindly of her for giving her the means to leave.

Lament rose up from inside her, but she refused to let it stop her. She reached for her saddle, making sure it was well seated before placing the reins on the mare's head. She smoothed a hand over the soft neck and offered her a soft sound that made the mare's ears twitch with recognition.

"Yes, my beauty, we're off again."

"No, ye wildcat, ye are not."

Chapter Five

Jemma cursed. The words rolled out of her mouth instantly, and she meant every one of them. She turned to find Gordon standing in the aisle, his chin tucked low so that he could see her in the dim light. His body was tense and imposing, and she felt a ripple of apprehension cross her skin.

"Ye have a very bad habit of disregarding wise advice that is given to ye, lass."

Jemma choked before she sputtered with her outrage. "Advice? You purposely misled me when I asked you where my mare was."

The barbarian had the audacity to shrug in the face of her temper. "Well now, I did do that sure enough."

Jemma tossed her head and maintained her grip on the reins.

"So it is advice well ignored."

She held her chin steady and stared straight back at him. Their wills were clashing, and the friction produced enough heat to send a tingle racing down the back of her neck while Gordon considered her. Determination flickered in his eyes, but she refused to bend in the face of it. Her will refused to surrender while the feel of the leather was still against her palm. She was so close, and yet Gordon was such a large obstacle to overcome.

"Ye are nae going anywhere except back into me tower, lass. The only choice is how ye go there."

"You have no right to keep me here."

"I have yer brother's permission."

Her jaw dropped, disbelief flooding her. "That cannot be." Her voice was a mere whisper, but the emotion lacing it caused her mare to dance. Gordon reached forward to grab the reins, and Jemma dropped them in order to step out of his reach.

Why was it that she never seemed to judge just how close the man was until it was too late to avoid his reach? Frustration burned enough of her shock away, but an aching pain remained deep inside her.

She glared at Gordon. "You have spoken to my brother since I have been here? Curan gave you his blessing on keeping me?" It was two questions fired off together, but her mind was working too fast to slow down.

"It is true, lass, but I did nae seek out his permission to cause ye pain."

His voice was low, and she looked back at him to notice that he saw far too much of her true feelings for her comfort.

"I care not what your or my brother's reasons are."

She turned her back on him and left the stable. The pain followed her, digging into her heart like a dull knife. Curan was her brother. How could he grant such permission?

She felt like her throat was being squeezed past the point of endurance. As far as the law went, Curan had every right to decide whom she married. If it pleased her brother, she might warm the bed of some man old enough to be her grandfather, or someone like Gordon who would use her to breed his children while continuing to enjoy his riding with any woman who took his fancy.

But the memory of last night conflicted with her temper. There had been true effort applied to courting her, something that many a bride never received, especially in a time when two queens of England had lost their heads. Men followed their king's example, doing what they pleased no matter what misery their actions loaded onto a woman's shoulders.

Gordon hadn't treated her that way last night. The memory was precious, and she discovered desperation inside her to reach for it and pray that it was a glimmer of hope that would grow into a bright future.

The chamber where she had slept was the only place Jemma's wounded mind thought to take her. She really had no right to think that her brother would consult her on the matter of her marriage, or to believe that he would waste any more time deciding the matter. She would not be the first sister handed over without warning. Her agreement to meet with Barras had been more than enough discussion upon the topic.

"Does it truly displease ye so much to think of remaining with me, lass?"

Jemma jumped and stumbled when she turned. Her ankle complained as it twisted slightly, making her hop to relieve the odd angle she'd landed on. She growled and clenched her hands into fists because her frustration was so great.

"Why ask me? Neither Curan nor you seem to think my feelings on anything matter in the least."

Relief shone on his face, and she felt some of her temper cooling. She couldn't see what had troubled him so much, but something clearly had. Her heart leaped at the chance to think it might be her feelings. It had been a very long time since she had stopped to consider how she felt. Every hour had been about her father for so long, what he wanted, needed, and how she might give him enough of herself to heal him.

"Marriage is normally negotiated between men, lass, but I

was hoping to change yer mind last night and get ye to want to stay here so that we might court a bit."

Jemma felt suspicion ripple through her mind because Gordon's face was smooth and calm, telling her nothing about his mood.

"I appreciated the effort you placed into last night, but keeping me here is not courting."

His lips split to flash his teeth at her. "Well now, I disagree with ye there, lass. Name me another man that would have dealt with ye instead of yer brother."

He was correct and she hated it. Helplessness assaulted her, and she shook her head to deny it. "I suppose you think your grand experience in 'riding' has taught you how to court, but I must quibble with you, sir, for 'riding' often is not the same thing as courting."

"Oh, well I see yer thinking, lass. Ye're looking for pretty prose. Allow me to quote ye a few that I know . . . I once took a walk on a dock, Looking for to ease me cock—"

"That is the wrong sort of prose for courting." Heat returned to her cheeks because she instantly began thinking about his cock.

His lips were curled up in a mocking smile now, and it had spread to eyes sparkling with mischief. One of his dark eyebrows rose innocently.

"It is? Would that be the dock part or the—"

"Both," Jemma shouted, to drown out the word "cock." She didn't need to think about his cock. Knowing what his kiss was like was torment enough for her to try to resist. But his cock . . . The excitement that had swirled and flared so brightly in her leaped in response to that single word. She suddenly knew exactly what she craved. It wasn't her belly, but her passage, and it felt empty.

"Well now, lass, it does tend to cut the courting time down and get right to the point of the matter."

Jemma felt her cheeks burn bright with a blush. "You are the most audacious man. Go and find your mistress if you want to talk about your . . ."

"Me cock?"

"Exactly." Jemma slapped her hands on her skirts and turned her back on him. She knew it was a mistake almost before the fabric of her skirts stopped moving. Gordon was not a man who would respect her dismissal of him. His arms closed around her in the next moment before she had the chance to correct her misjudgment. He pulled her against his larger body, trapping her arms against her sides just as he had last night, only now she knew how much she enjoyed being held against him and her body rippled with delight.

"Now, sweet Jemma, where did ye get the notion that I'd tuck me tail and retreat just because ye turned yer back on me?"

He tilted his head, the warmth of his breath brushing the side of her face as his words filled her ears. His tone was low and dark, tempting her with all the things her body craved. The moment seemed perfect for it, and no one appeared to think she should do anything but surrender.

"It was a poor choice, I agree." She jerked against his hold, only to gain a chuckle from him. His arms were crossed over the front of her, and his hands began to rub along her arms. It was a delightful motion, one that sent enjoyment racing through her.

"I don't. 'Tis a fact that I like the result full well."

He pressed a kiss against the side of her neck and then a second one. A soft gasp escaped her lips, drawing a sound of male approval from him. She was pressed so close that she felt the sound vibrate inside his chest.

"I simply forgot that you do not respect me." Jemma forced her voice to sound prim when her thoughts were torrid.

He lifted his head away from her neck, and she felt frustration claw its way across her skin. Her body protested her desire to argue with him when submission felt so much better.

"Ye have that wrong, lass." He scooped her up and off her feet, cradling her against his chest for a moment while he crossed the distance to the bed. She stiffened when she realized that was his destination, but he tossed her onto it once more and stood over her while she bounced.

"If I held no respect for ye, I assure ye the kiss I claimed from ye last night would have gone much deeper. But I can see that ye are still distrusting of me."

"Of course I am, why do you expect different? I am not some meek little girl who will do as she is told with a lowering of my head. If that is what you crave, I am not it."

When she raised her head to glare at him, she felt a prickle of fear cross her mind. Her words were not annoying him. It looked as though he was hearing exactly what he craved. This was the man she had witnessed striding through the hall that morning. There was nothing teasing about his expression and no hint of any will except his own. His eyes were lit with anticipation.

"I do admire yer spirit, Jemma, and that is a compliment that I do nae give to many men, much less women. 'Tis a fact that I believe ye would have mounted that mare and set out without bending to the fact that danger lies beyond the walls of this castle. There is much to be said for that courage. 'Tis no often found in women and it is one of the reasons that I rode out and gained that permission from yer brother to keep ye."

"Your compliments are not gaining you any of my favor."

He chuckled, but it was not a warm sound. Instead it warned her that he was contemplating a new strategy for gaining what he wanted from her. There was a challenge shimmering in his eyes, and her insides tightened because she realized that he considered her something worthy of his time.

"I believe ye do like hearing that I admire the steel in yer spine, lass." His lips pressed into a line that reminded her of the hunger she'd witnessed on his face last night.

"I think there is a part of ye that enjoys it very much, because that part of ye is no interested in any man that ye can run off with a few barbed comments. Admit it, Jemma, ye are too proud to allow anyone to court ye who does not stand up to ye."

She quivered, his words striking her as true, but she pressed her lips together to seal any hint of that admission inside her.

Gordon blew out a short breath in response. It was a tiny sound, but one she had to hold steady to resist flinching from. All her senses were attuned to him. She noticed the way that his nostrils flared and the manner in which his fingers moved where they were lying on his thick biceps. Her heart increased its pace, and her hearing seemed to become keener. Everything about him, her mind drank in.

His gaze swept her from head to toe, studying her and missing not a single detail. "So something will have to be done to keep ye where I put ye during the day, because I've lands to see to and I'd prefer no to chase ye or to worry that ye are in the grip of danger again."

"You have already told me that my brother approves of me being here. That means I have nowhere to go." She couldn't conceal the emotion that edged her words, and that made her angry for she would not whine to him for comfort. She refused to whine to anyone. She would console herself; she'd been doing so for the past few years and now would be no different.

His eyes narrowed. "I never meant to hurt yer feelings, lass, and be sure that yer brother was nae an easy man to bring around to my way of thinking. I hear the hurt in yer voice, but I'll nae be trusting that to keep ye down past the morning. Ye have too much spirit."

His attention lowered to one foot that was sticking out past the hem of her dress. "I'll be having those boots."

"You will not."

His eyebrows arched as challenge lit his eyes again. "Well now, lass, are ye sure ye want to make another choice about gambling on whether or not I'll do what I please in spite of yer denial?"

Jemma pulled her leg back but felt every muscle tighten in her body. Her courage rose, refusing to allow her to submit.

"You shall simply have to deal with a little uncertainty, just as I seem to be forced to endure this agreement between you and my brother."

"It seems that the first thing ye will learn during our court-ing, lass, is that I never leave anything to chance. I'd be a dead man if I did."

The bed rocked, drawing a shriek from Jemma, but it wasn't a fearful one. The need to resist erupted in a flurry of motion that refused to be controlled. Gordon reached for her foot, his hands sliding beneath her skirts, and she launched herself at him, shoving his shoulders with every bit of strength she pos-sessed.

The man landed on his backside at the foot of the bed. He lifted a surprised look toward her that sent victory surging through her.

"I told you no!"

He rose up, looking larger and more muscular than she'd noticed before. Determination shone brightly from his eyes, and his hands planted themselves on the edge of the bed, each fingertip pushing the soft surface in.

"And I want yer boots, lassie, and what a Scot wants, he takes."

This time he pounced on her. His huge body sprung off the floor, cutting through the air before he pushed her down onto the surface of the bed. Jemma flung her arms up to resist, slapping at him, but he rolled her over onto her belly to trap her arms again.

"Ye are definitely a wildcat, Jemma Ramsden. Are ye sure yer mother did nae take ye in, because I'd swear ye had Scottish blood flowing through yer veins."

"I'm English, you troll! English! Do you hear me? Go and find yourself some Scots girl who likes this manner of rough wooing, for I detest it."

A hard hand landed on her bottom in response. The breath rushed out of her chest as outrage filled her. She shook with her rage, bucking against the hold he had on her.

"I heard ye sure enough, and most likely half the maids in the kitchen, too. Ye need taming." He slapped her bottom once again before flipping her skirt up to find her foot. He gripped one and began pulling the leather lace loose that held the buttons closed.

Gordon having both hands on one foot allowed her to roll over and kick at him with her other foot. She planted one kick solidly on the back of his head, breaking his grip on her foot.

"I do not need taming! You need to learn some manners. This is not courting." She tried to roll over the edge of the bed, but a hard arm hooked around her waist and lifted her up. Gordon dropped her back in the middle of the bed and pushed her thighs wide apart. He shoved his back against her spread body and leaned his weight down on top of her belly and chest.

"It's my form of courting, lass, so ye'd best do some better planning if ye intend to outfox me."

Her eyes widened as she stared at the canopy above the bed. Shock held her in its grip because she was indeed on her back and spread wide with a man between her thighs. He pressed his lower back against her mons and belly to keep her pinned. She'd never had anyone touch her in so private a place before, and even his back sent a pulse of awareness through her. Her face flamed but her pride refused to give up the battle. Gordon yanked the lace free and pulled one boot off her foot. He held it up for a moment like a prize.

"A bare foot will nae find the stable floor such an easy place to travel."

Jemma reached forward and grabbed his bonnet. One yank tore the thing off his head, gaining a snarl from him. "A bare head will not care for the cold weather, either."

"I should have spanked yer arse a few more times."

He flipped over and caught her hands. With ridiculous ease he pressed her arms down on either side of her head.

"But I find that I like this sight of ye beneath me too much to turn ye over."

She bucked, trying to dislodge his weight, but all the motion did was compress the pleats of his kilt against her spread sex. She gasped and froze, because sensation rushed up her passage and into her from the contact. Her skirts were raised, and there was nothing but the thin linen of her chemise shielding the opening to her body. It would be too simple for him to take her. But the worst part of it was how much her body seemed to enjoy the contact; her clitoris was throbbing, eager for him to move against her again.

"I won't wed with you, even if you rape me." She was frightened, more so than she cared to admit. It was a deeper emotion than the one that had filled her while facing down the English knights. She didn't want Gordon to value her so lowly that he would force himself on her, and she didn't want him to try for fear that she would yield.

But she had no reason to hope for such mercy.

"If that was my thinking, I'd have done it the first night ye were here so that I could face yer brother with the fact that yer virgin's blood had stained my sheets already. There would have been no reason to walk away from ye last night, either. I could have saved myself the torment of craving ye most of the night."

His hands released her wrists and pulled the linen cap off her head. He jerked the tie off the end of her braid and ran his fingers through the strands to free them. He didn't jerk his hands through her hair, but combed the remains of the braid out with careful stokes that didn't pull her scalp even once. His control over his strength astounded her, but it also touched her with a sense of tenderness.

"Why didn't you?"

Jemma could have bitten her tongue in half, but she could not take the words back. Gordon finished freeing her hair and lifted a hand full of it. He buried his face in it, inhaling the scent, which brought to mind how tender he had been with her last night. There were extremes inside the man, much like herself.

"Because I plan to court ye, just as I told ye." He raised his face away from her hair, and his expression lacked the mocking arrogance she had seen so often on it. Now his blue eyes were filled with something deeper, something that sparked hope in her that he wanted more than her fertile body for his seed.

"I've been watching ye race that mare across the edge of my land for months. Every damn person wearing me colors knows that I've turned me back on things that I should have been doing to go up there and catch a glimpse of ye. So when yer brother's bride made her way onto my land, it was too tempting to bring her here so that I might negotiate with yer brother for the chance to discover who ye are."

"But all we do is fight."

He growled softly and covered her lips with one of his hands. "Nay, lass, there is something else that we do very well, too. Kiss, and I'm wanting to discover just how far that passion runs in ye."

He lifted his hand away from her mouth and pressed his lips against hers. It was the kiss that she had been longing for since the last one they had shared. This time he didn't tease her but took her mouth with a hungry motion that pressed his lips against her with enough pressure to force the breath from her. Something about his strength drew her closer to him, and enjoyment blossomed inside her. She wanted to move with him, mimic his motions and learn the skill of kissing.

"That's right, lass, kiss me back." His voice was deep and hungry. His hands pushed into her freed hair to hold the sides of her face steady. The tip of his tongue swept along her lower lip before gently probing her open mouth for entry. She shivered, her body pulsing with needs that raced across her mind too quickly to be sorted into any manner of understanding. She could only experience them and bask in the delight trying to drown her. But she craved more, needing to touch him in return instead of waiting for him to decide where to stroke her. Hunger made her bold.

She sent her own hands up into his hair. It was soft and silky against her fingers, bringing another form of bliss to her senses. But she craved his hardness, her hands seeking out his shoulders and the hard muscles that covered them. His tongue speared down into her mouth, sliding along her own, and her passage suddenly became the point of focus for all the desire coursing through her. At the top of her sex, her clitoris began to throb with the same tempo as her racing heart. Her body was too full of needs to remain still. Her hips lifted, seeking out more pressure against that throbbing point.

"Exactly, lass. We seem to please each other when we stop talking."

He leaned down to press a soft kiss against the swell of one breast where it was uncovered above the top of her dress. She jerked, too overwhelmed by the amount of sensation to contain the response. His fingers followed, smoothing over the tender flesh before delving into the valley created between her breasts by her stays. The hooks that kept her bodice closed took him little time to open. He pushed the wool aside to leave her corset open to his gaze. He found the tie that held the front of her stays together and released the knot with a quick motion of his fingers.

"I want to know what ye look like, lass. The idea has haunted me."

She should tell him to stop. Her mind told her to forbid him to continue unlacing her bodice, but her body demanded that she remain silent.

"We bring out the extremes in one another."

His fingers froze for a moment and his eyes flashed with hunger. "Aye, lass, we do. Just think of how much better it might become."

He pulled the sides of her stays apart. She shivered when the air brushed across her breasts with naught but thin linen covering them.

"I wouldn't know." And she lost the battle to remain still, her hands coming up to cover her chest. She really couldn't stop him from doing what he pleased with her, but there was a part of her that trusted him not to force himself on her. She wasn't even sure where that idea had come from, only that she could not see the man who had taken the time to smell her hair as a savage who would take her innocence by force.

It was a fragile trust, but one that made it possible to fend off the fear that was trying to steal into her mind.

"Trust that I know that, lass."

"I'm trying to." Her voice became a whisper. There was no way to hide her uncertainty. But approval flickered in his eyes, giving her enough confidence to continue staring at him.

Trust him? She chewed on that thought.

He leaned down and kissed first her right hand where it cupped one breast. Beneath her palm her nipple was hard and aching for its turn to discover what a kiss felt like against its peak. But Gordon moved to her other hand to allow his lips to linger on it. He moved lower to where her chest rose and fell with her breathing. Another kiss landed on her belly, the warmth of his mouth easily making its way through the fabric of her chemise to her skin. Sensation ripped through her, drawing a sound of delight from her lips. But it also raced down to her passage where hunger renewed its grip on her.

Gordon nuzzled against her chest, kissing and moving upward until he gently dislodged her hands with his head. Once again her fingers were in his hair, and he turned to tease the side of one breast with his lips. She quivered, anticipation drawing her muscles tight. She had never been so aware of her nipples. The soft pink tips were alive with need so hot, her chemise felt heavy and suffocating. Gordon slid one hand up her body, crossing over her ribs, and then cupped the soft mound of her breast before his lips took command of her nipple.

She arched up off the bed, unable to remain still. There was too much heat, too much sensation to endure. A thin cry escaped her lips, and she heard an answering growl from him that made her fingers curl into fists in his hair. The fabric of her chemise became wet, sticking to the hard point of her nipple. Gordon licked over it, teasing the sensitive point through the fabric before reaching up to grab the neckline of the garment and pulling it down to expose her flesh completely.

"So sweet, lass. Like summer berries." He lifted his head and watched her face while his thumb glided over the wet tip of her nipple for the first time with nothing between their skin. "That's a favorite thing of mine, summer berries. Something that I enjoy feasting on."

His voice dipped down until it became husky. His eyes darkened, but she gained only a momentary glimpse of them before he returned to her exposed breast. She felt his breath passing over the wet skin of her nipple, rippling across skin a hundred times more sensitive than she could ever recall it being. His hand gently closed around the soft mound of her breast, pushing the hard tip upward in offering. Gordon took that tempting morsel between his lips, sucking the entire nipple into his mouth while Jemma gasped with shock.

It felt too good. Pleasure surged through her, wiping away any doubts that still lingered. Her hands slid down to his back where they might press him toward her. His tongue flicked over the tip of her nipple, back and forth while he continued to suck on it. She arched up, her back joining the effort to make sure he knew she wanted him to continue. She was suddenly too hot with the wool of her skirts and his kilt between them. Her fingers plucked at the fabric of his shirt but couldn't pull it down so that his warm skin might be hers to touch. He slid one arm beneath her waist and pulled her tightly against his body before rolling over onto his back. The bed shook, and Jemma ended up straddling him with her knees sinking down on either side of his hips. He gently pushed her up so that she sat upright, and that pressed her body weight down on her open sex and the little bead of her clitoris.

"Gordon—"

"I want to see ye, lass." He found the tie that held her waistband closed. He worked it through the eyelets quickly before sitting up and pulling her skirts right up her body and over her head. He tossed them over the edge of the bed and lay back down on his back with his hands working on the padded roll that helped support her cartridge pleated skirts. It followed her skirts onto the floor and he reached up to tug her open corset down her arms.

"Much better."

"Is it?" Her chemise was free to flow around her body now but the fabric was thin, allowing the light to illuminate her curves. The neckline had risen back up to cover her breast, but the wet fabric was translucent.

"Aye, lass, but not quite perfect yet."

She shivered, seeing the truth of what he craved in his eyes. She had never thought about whether or not her body was attractive. The knowledge that Gordon wanted to bare her and see what she looked like without anything to shield her sent a shiver down her body. He felt it, and his hands landed on top of her thighs, moving in soothing strokes along them. It was pleasing, the feeling of his hands on her legs, but at the same time startling. She nibbled on her lower lip with indecision.

"This is perfection." His hands slid all the way to her knees and beneath the edge of her chemise. He continued on up her thighs, his hands against her bare skin. It was too much, and she stiffened, pulling one knee over his body.

"Ye need to learn to trust me, Jemma."

His voice was deeply serious. He captured her waist and lifted her up once more to set her down on her back.

"You cannot expect me to simply do what you command. Not when we are talking about—"

"About being intimate?" He pinned her down with his weight but didn't move up her body so that their faces were even. Instead he remained lower on the bed, his hands returning to her thighs to stroke them with even motions.

"You are not my husband." She didn't say it unkindly. "I cannot shame my father. Understand that, please."

His eyes flashed with something that looked like a challenge. "Ye think I do nae comprehend honor? Marrying ye is the simple way to gain what I want, lass. This is no about that. 'Tis yer trust I want to earn at this moment."

He raised her chemise, pushing the fabric up to bare her thighs. His hands slipped back down along the length he'd uncovered until he cupped each knee, his fingers spreading over each one before gripping lightly.

"But making ye mindless with pleasure when ye don't have to lie in me bed and submit to me touch, now that's the challenge I'm taking up, too."

"That's sinful talk."

He pushed her thighs apart with the grip on her knees, spreading her once more and keeping her that way by placing his body between her open thighs. She gasped as the night air brushed against the folds of her sex. A small portion of her chemise still covered her mons, but it held very flimsy protection against the determination glittering in Gordon's eyes.

"It's honest, and isn't that more in keeping with God's law than everyone pretending that touching doe nae feel good?"

His hand moved over her belly, rubbing and kneading the place that was so full of excitement.

"Tell me ye don't like having me hand on ye, or better still, prove yerself the creature I believe ye to be and tell me the truth."

He rubbed her belly again, and pleasure rippled through her. It was deep and hot in a way she hadn't even imagined her body might feel.

But she liked it and craved more of it.

"I can see the enjoyment shining in yer eyes, Jemma, just as ye can see how much I like touching ye." His hand slid down to cover her mons. She gasped as pleasure spiked through her. It was hard and forced the breath out of her lungs. Her clitoris pulsed with sensation that was almost acute.

"I can smell how hot yer body is for mine."

His hand slipped over the edge of her chemise to gently stroke the folds of her sex. Just his fingertips touched her first, but she jerked with the contact because it was so strong. A bolt of need tore into her so strongly she whimpered. Her hands fisted in the bedding beneath her, and Gordon had to press his other hand down on top of her to keep her in place for his fingers.

"Tell me, Jemma, tell me to stoke yer sweet flesh some more. I promise ye, it gets even better."

"Better?" Her voice was harsh and breathless, but her clitoris begged for what he promised. Her question gained a flash of his even teeth as he smiled and made another pass of his fingertips across her slit. This time, he slid two fingers into the folds and swept them down to the opening of her body. He only touched her clitoris through the twin folds of her sex, but that sent a flame of pleasure up her passage.

"Aye, better, lass. Shall I show ye what pleasure it is that couples defy the Church to gain?"

"*Yes.*"

She felt as if she might die if she didn't know the answer. Her heart was pounding so hard, her hearing became nothing but a rushing of her own blood. Her back arched, trying to lift her hips up so that she could gain the pleasure he hinted at. She wanted it, craved it so greatly that nothing else mattered.

"I want it, Gordon."

"Then ye shall have it, lass, from my hand."

She craved attention on her clitoris. The little button throbbed at the top of her sex, making her mindless with need.

"God, ye're wet." Now his voice was raw with need. She heard it and knew exactly what it was. He pushed her chemise up to bare her and leaned forward to suck on her clitoris. His mouth was impossibly hot around the sensitive nub. But she didn't have time to care that she might be burned. He sucked on her clitoris and worked his finger in a small circle around the opening of her passage. The motion pushed her over the edge into a swirling pool of pleasure that was so intense she felt it tearing her apart. It was blinding and almost deafening, but she still heard her own cry echoing off the ceiling. Every muscle tightened, straining toward his mouth. The walls of her passage clamped down while the pleasure broke deep inside her.

She lay there, boneless, unable to move anything except to draw in breath. Her chest rose and fell in shallow motions because she lacked the strength to draw deeper breaths. Gordon sucked a few last times on her clitoris before raising his head to watch her. Smug satisfaction gleamed from his glittering eyes before he crawled up the bed to lie beside her. His arms gathered her close while she struggled to regain enough strength to think once again.

She didn't want to. All of the fight that had been coursing through her before was completely gone, and in its place was a contentment she couldn't recall feeling in far too long. She felt as if she was exactly where she should be.

Which made no sense at all.

But her body was glowing with delight, hands reaching out

to touch him because it felt so very right. His kilt brushed against the tender skin of her inner thigh, making her open her eyes to look at him.

"You didn't take any pleasure."

He was still fully clothed, and he moved the moment she spoke, sitting up and pulling her remaining boot off. That action recalled their quarrel to her thoughts. He stood up but turned and tucked the bedding around her in a tender action that confused her.

Extremes again. Tender and hard. She confessed to enjoying both.

"I don't understand you." *Or my own responses to you.*

He looked down at her, as if his gaze was memorizing the sight of her. Satisfaction glowed in his eyes when he was finished.

"Trust is nae something that can ever be demanded, lass. Too many men think that what they have from their brides is trust when it is actually fear. Frightened by their fathers and clergy, they lie on their backs and submit, all the while cringing. My first wife was that way and I swore that I'd never repeat the mistake of taking a woman that was a feared of being with a man to me bed again."

"You have a wife?" Jemma felt her skin turn icy in a flash of horror.

"Nae. I had a bride who could not enjoy being a wife, so I let her go to a convent when she begged me to. She says she is very happy there, and the Church dissolved our union in favor of her becoming a bride of Christ."

Jemma sat up, her eyes rounding with horror. She held the bedding tightly against her body to cover her nudity. The bed rocked, and a hard hand cupped her chin.

"Do nae look like that, Jemma. Ye have nae been whipped and broken with the notion that women are placed in this life to service men without any pleasure for themselves. Yer passion is natural, the way God designed ye, and I want ye just like that."

"So what was this? Some indecent test? To assure you that I would be passionate enough to please you?"

He chuckled, a harsh sound of male victory that was too arrogant for her pride to tolerate.

"Aye, it was. Part of courting is discovering what manner of woman ye are. I don't want to discover my bride hates the very idea of touching after the priest has blessed us." His expression turned dark. "I've already done that once. Nae again."

So he was not repentant one bit, even if she found it unsettling. "This is not part of courting."

His eyes flashed at her. "It is for me. I am not some beardless boy content with soft kisses, and ye would be dissatisfied if I trailed after ye begging for yer attention. Ye are too much of a wildcat for that, Jemma. Part of ye needs to be taken."

"Then why stop short of making sure that I am ruined for anyone else?" Maybe she shouldn't have asked that question, but it was one that burned for an answer, eating away at her until she could not resist the need to know.

He released her chin and caught her hand in his. With a controlled pull, he drew her hand beneath his kilt and pressed her fingers against his cock. His flesh was hot and rigid beneath her fingertips, and she couldn't suppress the shiver that went through her.

"Feel me, Jemma." Sharp and commanding, his words were edged with unsatisfied desire. "Open yer hand and feel just how hard my cock still is."

"That is indecent."

"It's natural. Admit that ye wanted to touch me as freely as I was touching ye. With nothing between us, only skin and pleasure. Lying there and being touched is not enough for ye is it . . . wildcat?"

It wasn't. She had yearned to feel him . . . so much so that the craving had almost consumed her.

Her fingers opened and closed around his member, the hot flesh too tempting to ignore. Need ate at her, blurring the line between right and wrong until there was only hunger and what she wanted to satisfy it.

"That's it, close yer hand around me staff and watch how much it pleases me."

His nostrils flared and his eyes filled with delight. His length was hot and smooth against her hand, but it was also hard, the length rigid and swollen. She slid her hand up to the top of it and felt a thick ridge that crowned it.

"That is what yer passage was wet and eager for. My finger was but a tiny offering compared to what ye really hungered for."

He stood up, pulling his cock from her grasp. A ripple of satisfaction moved through her, reminding her that he had fed her hunger while keeping his.

"But why did you not take me?"

"Because I intend to wed ye, and I want ye kneeling beside me because ye know that I am yer match, not because ye believe I ruined ye. I want yer trust and yer surrender, and nothing else will do to satisfy me."

He picked up her other boot and walked toward the door, but he turned to look back at her.

"If ye still want to fight with me over the issue, Jemma, be very sure that I will meet ye on the field as many times as ye insist before ye consent to wed me, but I will nae give ye what ye truly crave until ye are my wife."

He opened the door and shut it with a solid sound behind

him. She sat poised on her knees once more in the center of the bed, completely stripped of everything that she had believed important in life. Everything she had been back at Amber Hill meant nothing here.

But did she want to return to being that girl?

Jemma sat down to contemplate that question because it was a very good one, considering that she did indeed like being pleasured like a woman. She looked around the bed and saw not a place to rest, but a place to feed the throbbing in her passage. It was lonely now that Gordon was gone; she felt the chill that had nothing to do with the open windows and everything to do with her choices.

Surrender?

Her pride bristled, but she couldn't quite reject the idea altogether because he had been correct in one thing. There was a part of her that enjoyed being challenged when she tried to cast his advances aside. Deep down in that place where she enjoyed his strength was something that wanted to shout with joy because he had not taken her, and kissed her in spite of it.

But more important than all that was the spreading glow of contentment that came from the fact that she was still a virgin. She ached for his possession and could not have reproached him for taking her when she asked him for it. The warm feeling wrapping around her came from the fact that he did indeed have honor, an unbending sort that kept him from taking her just because passion had been licking her unmercifully.

Trust? Well, that was growing, and she feared that there was nothing she might do to hinder it.

Anyon was waiting on him again.

The sight of her did nothing to soften his mood; in fact it sent him to growling. His mistress smiled. Somehow, he'd failed to notice that the woman was very crafty. She knew him better than he believed and had used that knowledge to secure herself a position in his bed. Now that he was thinking about it, he had never asked her to be his mistress, but he knew that everyone thought she was. After all, he had done nothing to prevent it being said.

"Anyon, I do nae want to be unkind to ye, but I will seek ye out no more."

She fluttered her eyelashes, but the motion only struck him as another ploy to bend him to her will.

"I'll be marrying Jemma Ramsden."

Anyon offered a disgusted look. "Why would ye wed a woman who just tried to run away from ye?" She walked toward him, her body wiggling in all the places that normally pleased him. Tonight even the extreme amount of cleavage she had on display failed to snare his attention. His mind was full of the soft rose-colored nipples he'd left behind the chamber door. Thinking of those buds sent a fresh bolt of need through his cock.

Anyon pressed her hands flat on top of his chest and rubbed her breasts against him. "Ye deserve a woman who values ye. I would nae shame ye."

"Enough. I told ye, I'll not seek ye out again." He clasped her wrists and set her away from him. Anger flashed in her eyes, but she lowered her lashes to conceal it.

"I will nae set ye out, Anyon, and I'll see ye settled with enough coin to get yerself a husband who pleases ye."

"The only one who pleases me is you, Gordon."

He didn't care for the sound of his name on her lips. How had he never noticed that she used his name to secure her own position? There was no hint of wounded feeling in her eyes, only taunted ambition.

"And ye'll mind how ye address me from hence forward. Ye

were nae pure when ye came to me, Anyon, and ye are the one who came to me."

"Something ye seemed plenty happy about at the time." Anyon failed to keep her temper under control, and it flashed at him.

"As were ye, but it is past. I'll have a bride very soon, and she shall be yer mistress."

Anyon laughed. "You may call her what ye will, but that weak-kneed creature will never be my mistress. She'll hide in her chambers or run away from ye, mark my words on it. Then ye'll be back looking for a woman who does nae whimper because yer grip is too tight."

"Anyon—"

She blew out a hard sound, interrupting him and not caring if it was a slight to his authority as her laird. "I am a woman, Gordon, and that is what the beast inside ye needs. That girl will never satisfy ye. Never."

Chapter Six

"Tell me about the girl Gordon was wed to."

Ula jerked her head about, looking more startled than Jemma had ever seen her.

"Who told ye about Imogen?"

It was clear that the housekeeper wouldn't tell her a thing unless she answered the question in a way that she deemed acceptable. The warning in her eyes spoke of loyalty to her laird. "Gordon did. He said he was wed and that the girl is now a nun. I believe this is a matter that I need to know about if he is considering marrying me."

"The laird should have told ye, but I agree that 'tis something ye have the right to understand." Ula drew in a deep breath and looked about to make sure they were alone. "The girl was no good at being a wife, did nae care for it at all. She cried until her eyes were puffy every time he told her he intended to enter her chamber. She claimed that bed sport was sinful, and the awful truth was that she believed it."

"Many think that. Why do you say it is awful?"

Ula stopped looking tired for the first time. The housekeeper placed her hands flat on the top of the stack of ironing she had been working to fold.

"That poor girl had her thoughts twisted beyond what normal parents do with their daughters. I'm no talking about instilling a healthy respect for remaining pure, that is right, but Imogen took to lashing herself every morning after the laird left her." Ula lifted her face and shot Jemma a hard look. "'Twas a horrible sight what that girl did to herself because someone twisted up her thinking. She could nae tolerate knowing that she enjoyed being a wife. Her back was a bloody mess when we discovered what she was about."

Ula stopped and drew in a deep breath. "The laird was a kind man when he let her go. I know men who would have set a guard on that girl to keep the dowry she came with. Her own father knew she wanted to be a nun but forced her to wed because of the alliance it would gain him with the Barras clan."

It was a sad tale but not an uncommon one. Marriage was a business first. It was strange the way the world worked. A poor girl was granted the right to marry where her heart led her, but she longed for the better life that came with being born to a higher position. Those born to better, to titles, often discovered themselves envious of the chance to decide whom they would have affection for.

"I'm glad to see that ye are nothing like Imogen. The laird has refused to open any of the offers sent to him from other clans. He claims that he cannot stomach the sight of ink on parchment when it comes to marriage. Ye're different, lass. He's taken with ye because he set his eyes on ye. 'Tis a good thing for the laird, and ye being kin to our neighbor makes it a good match for the Barras."

So simple, unless someone, anyone recalled that she had not lent her agreement to the match. Of course it was not needed; she might be wed by the clergy with only her brother's word on the matter. Her dowry would be handed over, and Gordon would have the right to keep her on his land any way that he deemed appropriate.

I'm not being fair . . .

She truly wasn't, but knowing that didn't bring her any peace. It should have, for Gordon had treated her more than kindly.

"Yer thoughts are too troubled." Ula handed a stack of linens to her with a quick flick of her hand to indicate a large cabinet that stood open for them. It would be locked when Ula was finished ironing what had been washed the day before. There were enough linens to change them out with fresh ones from this storage cabinet, but it was kept locked because fabric was expensive.

"Ye need some work to keep ye from turning matters over in yer head the way ye do." Ula considered her for a long moment. "Go and fetch up the laird's shirts that should be drying along the back of the west tower, and tell me if those laundresses are working or lying on the slope sunning their noses."

It was only midmorning, so it would be best if the laundresses were working. Jemma decided that she wouldn't care to have Ula cross with her. Such was a good thing in a housekeeper. If she failed to keep a tight fist around everyone drawing pay from the laird's coffers, there would be dark times ahead for the castle. More than one great noble family had found themselves bled dry of silver by servants who spent more time resting than working while still expecting their pay. Ula didn't seem to be the sort to allow laziness to flourish under her watchful eye.

Jemma made her way from the north tower where she had been working with Ula. The west tower was used for washing because the sun would shine on it last, allowing time for washing in the mornings. Laundry was left hanging all night if the weather was fair, and she heard dry cloth snapping in the breeze when she came around the side of the tower.

"I warned ye, ye English whore!"

Anyon was in a rage, the girl shoving at Jemma before she realized that an attack was imminent. The force of it sent her tumbling down the slope with its harsh stones that scraped and cut into her hands and face.

"I warned ye that the laird was mine!"

Anyon came down the slope after her, aiming a vicious kick at her head before Jemma regained enough of her senses to move. Pain shot through her neck and back, but she snarled and rolled out of the way of the next kick the girl sent at her.

"Enough, Anyon! I am not going to fight with you."

"That's because ye think yerself so much better than me, but ye aren't! Ye're a slut, and I will nae let ye take Gordon from me."

The edge of the river was mere inches from her nose and the ground muddy beneath her hands when Jemma tried to push herself off the ground. She staggered to her feet, wondering why Anyon seemed to be waiting for her to stand. Her ignorance ended when the girl lifted her skirt and stuck her foot directly in the center of her belly, shoving Jemma into the water.

Jemma fell into the river, and the water rose up around her, burning her eyes and nose as she struggled to push her head back above the water's surface. Her muddled senses caused her to flail about in the water, trying to decide which way was up.

A hard hand hit her between her shoulder blades. The blow was harsh and sent her remaining breath out in a whoosh that filled the water in front of her eyes with white bubbles. Anyon didn't stop there. The girl held her down, pushing with all her weight to keep Jemma beneath the water.

She should have been frightened, but her temper rose in a burning rage. The water cleared, allowing her to see Anyon's ankles. Reaching out, she grabbed one and used all the fury that was burning in her to yank it out from beneath the girl. Anyon fell back into the river with a huge splash and a startled screech.

Jemma stood up, gasping for breath. Her lungs burned and her vision was blurry from the soap left in the water from the washing. Strong lye soap that made her eyes tear.

"Stupid whore!"

Anyon came up out of the water with her fingers curled like talons. She launched herself at Jemma like an animal attacking.

"You still want to fight? Well, I won't stand and let you drown me, that's for sure." Jemma balled up her fist and sent it straight toward Anyon's face.

Pain exploded in her hand, but Jemma carried through with the blow. Anyon howled with outrage, but her neck twisted and she fell into the water with a snarl. The water suddenly splashed all around her as men plunged into the river between them.

"That's enough out of ye, Anyon." One of Gordon's captains hauled his clanswoman out of the water with a disgusted frown while she kicked and fought them. Someone gripped her arm, and Jemma shrugged it off.

"I don't need restraining. It wasn't my idea to fight, but I'll surely not stand idle while someone is attacking me."

Jemma turned and discovered that the laundresses that Ula had set to working along the riverbank were lined up watching her. More men came around the tower at a dead run with a couple of women trailing them, telling her how they had known about Anyon's attack.

But there were far more standing and watching.

That was the blow that hurt most of all. Jemma wiped the

water from her eyes and took a second look. These were Anyon's friends and blood. The fact that Anyon had tried to drown her didn't seem to distress any of them too greatly. None of them had tried to stop her.

Of course not, she was English. No doubt most of them had lost kin to her countrymen.

"What manner of devil play is this?" Gordon's voice made all the women flinch. Their eyes widened as they turned to face their laird. He came around the corner and swept the scene, his keen gaze stopping when his attention landed on her still standing knee deep in the river.

He snarled something in Gaelic and turned a furious look on Anyon.

"Put her in the stocks. She's to be lashed."

The laundresses gasped, gaining them their laird's attention. "And the lot of ye will join her for standing about while this savageness was being done."

"I don't need you to rescue me, Laird Barras."

Gordon turned an incredulous look on her, and the laundresses gasped in unison once more.

"Oh, enough of that gasping. The lot of you seemed to be sturdy enough to watch one of your own try and drown me; I hardly see why you are so shocked by a few disagreeing words now."

Jemma trudged out of the water. Her legs felt weak as though they might crumble beneath her at any moment. She drew a deep breath to fend that off.

"No one disrespects my orders, Jemma."

Gordon was furious, but she refused to bow her head. "Of course, but I need to make it clear to your clanswomen that I do not need anyone coming to my aid simply because I am English. I took care of Anyon well enough, and I will defend myself if any of them find it necessary to attack me, even if I do find it horrible to harbor such hatred for complete strangers based only on where they were born."

Several sputters arose from the laundresses, and Jemma turned her head to glare at them. "Do you deny it? There is nothing that you object to in me but the fact that I was born ten miles from here on land that is considered English. It is naught but something you learned from your—"

She lost focus of what point she was attempting to make, her mind simply going blank. Shutting her mouth, she stared back at the laundresses until she forgot why she was looking at them. Turning her head, she discovered Gordon standing only a foot from her.

"Well, as you see, I handled everything myself. I meant no disrespect of course."

"Aye, of course."

"Yes, that's right." Her thoughts began to turn hazy. "I believe so . . . hmm . . . what did I say again?"

His blue eyes suddenly fascinated her. He caught her arms and she sighed, because it was the most perfect moment. His gaze settled on the top of her head, and he reached up to touch her, triggering a startling pain that spread through her head.

"Yer head needs stitching, Jemma."

She offered only a soft mutter before everything became a blur of morning sunlight. Bright and perfect with each point of light shattering into a brilliant display of colors that she smiled at.

"So why is she still sleeping?"

Jemma winced and opened her eyes to see Gordon pacing. He didn't pace like any other worried person she'd ever seen walk the floor. Gordon stalked. His feet taking huge steps that covered the length of the bed she lay on in three short strides. He froze when he noticed her looking at him.

"There, ye see? Exactly as I said. The girl is fine. She was lucky to sleep through the stitching."

Gordon grunted. Ula stood near the bed along with another woman who had white hair. She seemed unimpressed with her laird's disgruntlement.

"Leave yer head be, girl. I had to stitch ye up, but it's in yer hair so the scar won't bother ye any once it's healed."

"Stitched me up?" Jemma didn't stop, but reached for the throbbing spot on the top of her head. She fingered it gently, wincing at the pain that bled out from the light contact.

The woman grunted. "Ye don't mind very well. Maybe the laird is right to be suspicious. Could be her mind is wounded."

"My mind is not wounded."

Gordon snorted, but there was relief in his eyes. "She sounds quite normal to me. Ye have my gratitude for yer service, Vanora."

"Seeing the lass well is enough for me. Do ye want me to get on with inspecting her so that ye can marry?"

"I didn't promise to marry him."

Vanora turned a curious stare toward her. "Well now, girl, if that's so, I wonder where ye get the idea to argue so publicly with the laird. I thought surely ye were his bride, and even then, I still wonder how ye thought to escape being chastised for such. But if ye are nae his bride-to-be, well, I believe that Anyon will have a bit of company in the stocks."

"Give us a moment alone."

Ula and Vanora both inclined their heads before leaving the chamber.

"I shouldn't have argued with you in public, I know that, but I'm not saying it to avoid the stocks, either."

"Then why are ye saying it, lass?" Gordon crossed his arms over his chest, looking far too forbidding. It was another glimpse at that part of him accustomed to being in command.

"Because it is true. This world needs its rules. Without authority there would be nothing but lawlessness."

His expression softened, but that only drew her mind back to what had happened the last time he was alone with her in the chamber.

"That doesn't mean I agree that Anyon should be lashed on my account."

He growled at her, low and deep, leaving no doubt that he was growing frustrated with her.

"Since ye just agreed that rules are needed to maintain order, ye can nae disagree with me having her lashed. She tried to drown ye."

Jemma sat up and felt her muscles ache with the effort. She tried to conceal the pain, but Gordon read it off her face and his eyes narrowed dangerously.

"She'll be getting those lashes, and those who stood there watching will be paying for it, too. I won't stand for having the women of this castle acting like a pack of wild dogs."

"To what end? Punishment will only make your people detest me more. Besides, I gave her what she deserved and I hope she has a bruise marking her face." Jemma crawled to the edge of the bed, determined to make her point to the stubborn man. "So you can save your pampering, Gordon Dwyre. I have no need of it."

"Well now, Jemma, that would leave me only tenderness and passion to give ye." His eyes flashed with hunger as his hands cupped the sides of her face. "I suppose I could yield to yer desire if ye agree to become my wife."

"But why would you want to wed me? Your people detest me." She shook her head but stopped abruptly when pain shoot through her skull. "All you and I do is fight when we are alone."

And end up kissing . . .

Her cheeks burned with her thoughts.

"That is nae the reason ye hesitate to agree, Jemma. I would know yer reason to resist our union."

His eyes filled with challenge, but she shook off his hands to stand up.

"You want to know my reason? Well, sir, I don't believe I know it myself. You brought me here only a few days past and set me here to deal with your mistress while taking away my boots to keep me from leaving. The hallway is rather chilly in the morning on bare feet, I can tell you. However much you might say you are outraged, I notice that you said nothing of sending her away. Did you soothe your desire last night with her once you left me? That would account for her temper this morning."

Gordon crossed his arms over his chest. "She would have been content and smiling if I'd taken my hard cock to her yesterday. We had words last night that I should have realized might enrage her."

Jemma felt her eyes widen. "You admit that you went to her last night after leaving me?"

Gordon shrugged, his body looking far too relaxed for the topic. Jemma felt as if her emotions were going to burst through her exterior and send her lunging toward him just like Anyon had attacked her. She was jealous and had no idea how to deal with it.

"I'll tell ye straight that she was waiting on me when I left ye last evening, and offered herself to me." He lifted a hand and pointed a thick finger at her. "But I didna use her, which accounts for her rage this morning. She'll receive her lashes, and that will make an example to anyone else who might think to argue against who I bring here as my bride. Ye'll be mistress here."

"You mean I will be your wife."

His forehead creased with confusion. "My wife will be the mistress of this castle. They are one and the same."

"I don't believe so. Those that you enjoy your riding with will always be considered more powerful than the English-woman you bring home for her dowry."

He shook his head, but there was anger burning in his eyes. "Didna I prove anything to ye yesterday, Jemma? 'Twas yer trust I was hoping to secure by leaving ye a virgin." He snorted. "I can see that has nae happened yet, but I swear that I will have ye one way or another."

"Is that a threat?" She tossed her head and squared her shoulders. "Well, I am not frightened of you Gordon Dwyre."

Only the way you make me feel.

He closed the distance between them, one hand cupping her chin in a firm hold.

"Which is why I promise ye that I will be sharing yer bed tonight. Ye aren't afraid of me because ye feel the same attrac-tion that I do, 'tis a powerful thing and neither of us will be happy until we stop denying it. I wanted to give ye time to be-come accustomed to it, but I will nae have yer place here questioned again."

"Don't you dare try to protect me."

"And why not?" he snarled through his clenched teeth at her, obviously frustrated. "Not only am I laird here, but I brought ye here, Jemma, so protecting ye is a point of honor."

"Would you allow me to step between you and any man that threatened you?"

He drew in a sharp breath. "I would not."

"It is the same thing when you insist on stepping between me and your clanswomen. I'll deal with the women who try their hand at intimidating me, and I want you to stay out of it. There will be no lashings unless I order them."

"That would only be yer place if ye are my wife, Jemma."

"Our courtship is not a classical one, grant me my will, Barras, even if you don't agree it is my place to insist on it. I don't want you sheltering me."

He stiffened but held his next words back. Jemma watched him fight back the urge to order her to accept his will. She was asking too much for the world that they lived in. A woman's place was beneath the authority of a man. She might also end up in the stocks with her back lashed for saying that she did not want to follow that natural order. It was considered unnatural and obviously something that needed to be cured.

Gordon suddenly chuckled. It wasn't a nice sound but one of contemplation.

"I'll grant the women mercy because I see that the only way I'll earn yer trust is to recognize that ye need some of the same things that I do. Ye need to know that ye aren't helpless, 'tis something I can see the value of. That is the reason we're so drawn to each other, Jemma, we're very much alike."

"I disagree."

He snorted with male amusement. "Exactly my point. Ye disagree because ye do nae care for me telling ye what to think. I like to keep me own counsel, too. Ye can speak yer mind freely behind closed doors, lass, but when it comes to the others ye will recall what ye said about this order coming from there being rules."

"So I will remember my place? Is that your warning?"

"Nay, lass, my promise to ye is this. Ye may have the Church's blessing or not, but be very sure that I will be back to make sure ye have no doubt who eases my cock tonight."

He hooked his arm around her waist, pulling her against his body while his mouth claimed hers in a hard kiss. There was nothing tender or teasing about it. His mouth demanded submission, and hers opened to allow his tongue to thrust deeply inside. Her passage ached for the same treatment. She wanted to be filled and all of her ignorance destroyed forever.

"You have no right."

He snorted before releasing her. "What I am is honest, Jemma. Ye are a good match, but the thing that has me saying to make yer peace with wedding me today is the fact that even though I can nae see yer breasts, I know yer pink nipples are hard. Ye long for me as much as I do for ye, and I have the experience to tell ye that it will nay be easing. We're drawn to each other, and nature has her way of being stubborn. I'll be at the church at dusk." His eyebrow rose. "And in yer bed by dark. I swear it to ye, Jemma, ye will be mine tonight."

The door slammed shut behind Gordon, making Jemma flinch.

Excitement burned along her limbs and pooled in her belly. Her clitoris throbbed with longing so intense it stopped only a tiny bit short of being painful.

In yer bed . . .

She shivered as she recalled his words. The rest of the day's events paled and fell aside as she became absorbed with recalling the deep timber of his voice. He was correct, her nipples were hard. The woman in her wasn't interested in the reasons why she didn't want to wed Gordon, and worse still her mind offered up the fact that he was far more accepting of her nature than any man she might hope her brother contracted.

But would Gordon remain that way? It wasn't the way men expected their world to be. It might just be that the burly Scot was once again employing a clever strategy to gain what he wanted before he closed his hand into an iron fist and lowered it upon her.

But even that fear wasn't a good reason to not marry him.

There was always the chance that Gordon was exactly as he appeared and that would be a far better husband than she might have dared to hope for. The reason was simple, she did desire him. So much so that she had to admit that she doubted her ability to send him away tonight if she refused to marry him. His kisses were intoxicating, and she knew that he would kiss her.

Someone knocked on the door, and it opened almost immediately. Ula pulled both sides of the doors open, and two boys carried a bathing tub in.

"I can bathe in the kitchen."

Ula snapped her fingers at the boys who had stopped with the tub only halfway into the chamber. They jumped and hurried to finish their task.

"That wouldn't be fitting for the mistress of this castle."

A line of maids entered, and every one of them lowered themselves before hurrying to lay out things to please even the most noble lady. One added wood to the fireplace, poking at the thick layer of ash to get at the coals. Soon there was a crackle and pop of wood catching fire. Lengths of linen were laid out carefully before the growing flames so that they would be warm and cozy when she finished bathing.

"I've fetched up a few dresses that belonged to the laird's mother. Silk does endure well, it seems. The styling is a bit older, but yer dress is showing a little too much wear for a wedding."

"I still don't mind going below to bathe. It is a great deal of effort to haul water."

Ula snorted. "I only wish I could set some of these over-prideful maids to carrying water. I believe it would do them well for it seems there is too much unkindness to suit me. A bit of hard work will fix that."

The maids kept their heads down, but that didn't stop them from cutting quick looks at one another.

"But this tower has a water line, 'tis a fine comfort." Ula pointed toward the window with pride ringing in her tone.

One of the lads opened up a set of shutters that did not reveal a glass window. This one was open to the afternoon air, but the opening was dipped in the center and one of the lads placed a copper trough into that spot, forming a deep "v." It was long enough to reach the tub, and he reached out the window to pull on a rope that ran very close to the wall. A small wooden pitcher appeared on that rope, and when he kept pulling, it went over the top of the pulley wheel to spill its contents into a wide pan that extended past the window. The water rushed down to the low point in the window opening, into the trough, and then into the tub. Another pitcher was fashioned to the rope and then another. The boy worked the rope, and the chamber was filled with the sound of running water.

"How clever."

"Aye, it is. One of the lads thought it up to save his hands from wear."

The tub was filling rapidly, and one of the maids came through the door with an iron basket full of glowing red coals. She angled it carefully through the chamber, making sure to avoid touching anything. The basket had feet on it, and she slid it beneath the tub. A second basket was carried in to join the first one, and Ula went over to the tub to begin stirring the water about. The iron baskets almost touched the bottom of the tub. Since the tub was made of copper, the heat from the coals began to warm the water quickly. The lad finished filling the tub and tugged on the corner of his knitted bonnet before he and his partner left the chamber. The maids took their chance to scurry out behind them.

"Good for naught." Ula sent a shake of her head toward the door. "A few lashes would have done them good. Ye are kinder than I, but even if ye are my mistress, I'll tell ye straight that I think ye should put Anyon out. That girl is trouble, and she is no done upsetting this house, mark my words."

"It's not entirely her fault."

Ula grunted and walked over to help Jemma begin taking her dress off. The tub looked very inviting. Her skin felt as if it had sand clinging to it, and that was entirely possible.

"Being unhappy does nae give her the right to attack ye. That is her fault."

"I know." Being mistress would mean making hard decisions. Ones that made her no friends. Yet that was the cost of making sure that a castle was run well. A noblewoman wasn't anything if her holding didn't run smoothly. If laziness was tolerated during the summer, there would be empty bellies in the dead of winter when the food stores ran dry. Gordon was charged with seeing to the protection of the castle, but she would be expected to make sure the kitchens ran smoothly and that her husband was not cheated by servants who failed to earn their pay.

That was the reason most men contracted a bride years before they intended to wed them. They wanted a woman who was raised to know the skills necessary for running a castle. Many a noble mother had dangled the account books of her own estate beneath the nose of a daughter's prospective groom, proving that her daughter came with expert knowledge on how to run an estate.

She realized she was looking forward to having the workload again. She had run Amber Hill for years until her brother brought his new bride home. It had been right to turn over the books and the authority to her, but that had left Jemma with even less to keep her from riding.

Another rap came from the door. Jemma hugged her arms around her bare chest and looked over her shoulder to see Vanora making her way into the chamber once more. A prickle of anxiety crossed her skin, raising it into gooseflesh. It was normal enough to have a midwife such as Vanora look at her before she went to her groom. An age-old practice that protected women from accusations of greedy men who wanted to collect dowries by claiming there was something wrong with their wives once the marriage was consummated. It could take years for divorces, and all of that time the dowry might be kept.

"Well, I can't look at ye with yer hands up like that." Vanora made a motion with her hand. "Let me see ye, girl. Ye're not the first bride I've taken a look at. The sooner started, the sooner finished."

It was a practical idea but one that Jemma found little comfort in. Vanora made a slow circle around her, her keen gaze sweeping her from head to toe.

"A good bath and ye should please the laird," Vanora announced with an approving grin.

Ula pulled the baskets of coals out so that the bottom of the tub would not burn her. Jemma went into the water gratefully. At least it felt as if something was covering her, even if it was transparent.

Different pieces of soap were laid out on a small table near the tub. The aroma of flowers drifted up to her nose, and she reached out to pick one up. It was scented with rosemary. Jemma reached for another and discovered the smell of heather mixed in with the soap. The third one was spicy cloves from gillyflowers. She kept it and began to run it along her arm. Ula watched her with a keen eye, noticing every detail.

Another knock on the door and two maids entered. They didn't consider their presence during her bath anything to worry about. No one would think such a thing. Privacy was something only traitors and plotters craved to cover up their sins.

But she had become accustomed to being alone. Jemma bit her lower lip and sat still while Ula directed the maids to begin washing her hair. They worked carefully around the new stitches in her scalp while still more maids entered with the dresses Ula had spoken of. She closed her eyes but could hear the footsteps all around her. Nervousness and excitement brewed inside her until she was flooded with a combination of the two emotions. The sun seemed to be arching toward the west remarkably quickly today. Maids flowed in and out of the chamber. They brought her trays of food that she left untouched, and warmed cider that she only sipped. The dresses were tried on, and then more women appeared with their sewing boxes in hand to begin stitching quickly on the one that was selected.

A hush remained, and Jemma realized that she was the cause of it. The staff was waiting to see what sort of woman she was. No one wanted to be the one who chattered too much and gained the displeasure of the new mistress. Everything felt as if it was rushing too quickly toward the moment when she would be expected to make her choice.

You've already made it and you know it, she told herself.

Knowing that didn't ease the tension. It tightened and filled her with anxiety while Ula brushed her hair until it shone. The dress was a soft blue silk with velvet edging. The neckline was square and the sleeve had thick cuffs that turned back to lay against her forearms. Ula looked at the hat that came with it but shook her head. It was a style once favored by Catherine of Aragon, built high to represent the desire to achieve heaven's favor.

"I don't understand the court fashions at times, but ye do nae need a hat since it is yer wedding day. It's a pity there is no ivy left, everything has turned to color now."

"I don't need decorations."

Ula nodded approvingly, and the housekeeper raised her voice just a bit when she answered so that every maid in the chamber was sure to hear.

"A wise thing that is, knowing that decorations are naught but a waste of resources."

The last thing set out for her was a pair of silk slippers. Jemma stared at them for they appeared too fragile to be anything but a figment of her imagination. But she stopped before stepping into them.

"Gordon took my shoes away." Saying the words awoke her temper—she was still quite displeased with the manner in which the man had tried to keep her inside his fortress. But her cheeks also heated with a blush as she recalled just what had happened when he took her boots off.

"I wouldn't be calling these shoes, they are more slippers, and pretty as they might be, they are quite useless for much more than supping and dancing."

Of course, court ladies would have slid their slipper-clad feet into over-shoes that kept the delicate silk creations from being soiled on the way to their banquets. Costly Persian carpets would have been rolled out to cover the hallways so that they might step out of their over-shoes and onto carpet that would not mar their pretty slippers.

She wasn't going to wear them.

Turning around, she walked toward the table and picked up a hand mirror that lay there.

Was she pretty? She really had never contemplated the question. Her father had told her she was fair beyond all others, but he was her father.

"Ye will please the laird." Ula spoke in a soft tone.

"Hmmm . . . perhaps." Jemma placed the mirror carefully back on the table. "But will he please me?"

There was a collective gasp from everyone in the room except for Ula. The housekeeper held her silence for one long moment before erupting with laughter. She slapped the top of her skirts and continued to shake with amusement.

"I do believe the laird may have met his match. 'Tis a grand day indeed."

Gordon couldn't recall when he'd been so nervous in the past. His shoulders tingled with the strain, every muscle tight with anticipation. Would she come? He debated the alternatives if she didn't appear.

But the truth was, he wanted Jemma to walk down to their wedding of her own free will. Part of him needed it more than he wanted to admit. Trying to tell himself she was a logical choice for a bride didn't change the fact that he yearned to see her submitting by choice.

That was something too many men didn't understand the value of. It was something that they failed to see in their own mistresses. Part of what drew them away from their marriage beds was the freely given affection a mistress offered. She embraced a man because she wanted to, not because of some contract. Many would tell him he was insane to want that from a wife, and there was a possibility that they were correct, but that wouldn't keep him from hoping. He looked toward the door and sighed when it remained empty.

He ground his teeth against each other and moved down the aisle. He wasn't abandoning his ideas, but he would have her tonight.

Even if that was outside the bonds of matrimony.

Jemma took a deep breath and tried not to turn and look at all the women watching her. She could feel their eyes on the back on her head, but she kept her pace slow and steady as she crossed the courtyard.

Gordon suddenly appeared at the doorway of the church, his face a mask of disgruntlement. She stopped, staring at that expression and trying to decide what to do next. Her firm decisions didn't hold up well against that dark expression. She stood in place, trying to recall what her reasons were for joining him.

But his eyes suddenly lit with joy. There was no other way to describe it. The emotion erupted clearly in those blue centers before his lips parted and his teeth flashed at her in welcome. He held out a hand with his palm up in invitation. Jemma took a step forward and frowned when she lowered her foot onto a sharp stone. His smile faded but not completely as he closed the distance between them.

"Are ye losing yer courage now when ye are so close? Where's the spirit that got ye this far, Jemma?"

"It is annoyed by being barefoot." She kept her voice low so that her words did not drift to those watching. The men along the curtain wall had turned to witness the moment, and the priests filled in the doorway to the church while the nuns peeked through the stained glass windows.

Gordon's eyes filled with wicked merriment, something that she was beginning to understand was a major facet of his nature.

"Brides used to wed in their shifts to demonstrate their submission to their groom."

His hand was still out, and she placed hers in it before digging her fingernails into his skin. He choked on his amusement.

"Well, I suppose that if you see naught wrong with every man seeing my body through the thin fabric of my chemise . . . I believe the light is just right to shine through and show every curve I have."

"Barefoot is submissive enough."

"Too much for me."

His hand closed around her, and his expression became pensive. "Then why did ye come, Jemma? Somehow, I doubt it was my promise to return to yer bed even if I believe that ye know I mean to do exactly as I said."

She raised her face and stared at the joy that was still glittering in his eyes. Her heart absorbed that single emotion and cradled it close.

"You are correct that I am not here because you promised to take my innocence tonight. Maybe I am here because you left me a virgin last night." She offered him a guarded look. "It is possible that I do trust you even if I detest the idea of wedding you barefoot."

"I rather like the notion." He leaned down to whisper in her ear. "It means I'll be able to undress ye so much faster."

She dug her fingernails into his skin once again, but the priest narrowed his eyes at them both.

"Are ye ready, lass?"

"As ready as I am ever going to be, I believe."

Gordon took the first step, leading her by their joined hands toward the church and the priest waiting to bless their union. She forbade herself to think, trapping her emotions down beneath all the reasons why taking her vows was the correct thing to do.

And in an impossibly short amount of time, she was wed.

Chapter Seven

The Barras clan was waiting for them when they made their way out of the church. Jemma was astounded at the number of people crowded into the yard. They were straining to see her and Gordon, fathers lifting their sons up to sit on their shoulders while rows of children stood on the few wagons dotting the area. A cheer rose when they followed the priest out of the sanctuary. There had not been one inch of pew space left inside, either. The small procession that preceded them included the altar boys; one held up a crucifix and one held a small painting of the Virgin Mary. The priest followed while swinging the incense burner to spread the fragrant herbs over those who came to see their laird wed.

They were led all the way to the great hall and then inside. The priest remained until she and Gordon sat at the high table. The man gave a final blessing, and the hall erupted into cheers. Jemma couldn't contain her smile because there was just too much merriment surrounding her. The cheering died down and the music became louder, and her toe began tapping beneath the silk skirt of her dress.

"Ah, something that pleases ye." Gordon reached out to capture her hand beneath the table. He gave it a soft squeeze. "I'll have to be remembering that."

Large platters were brought toward them from the long tables in front of the hearths. The cook was turning back linens draped over the food to decide the order it was to be served in.

It was far more effort than she had anticipated. While she had been bathing, there must have been a flurry of activity in the kitchen.

Gordon squeezed her hand once again, and she turned to discover him watching her.

"Did ye think I'd just take ye upstairs straightaway without celebrating?"

Her cheeks heated because she had been completely focused on the next important part of marrying.

The consummation. Her mind offered up the fact that tonight she would do far more than feel his cock. She could expect her groom to remove his clothing. That idea deepened her blush, and the warm fingers clasping hers gently stroked her fingers.

"As much as I'm eager for that, lass, 'twould be a blackguard that did nae offer ye a wedding feast."

"But there was so little time."

He leaned in so that his words remained between them. "Aye, there was indeed, but look, Jemma, it seems that everyone is very eager to lend their effort to making tonight special for us."

"I did not expect such, but thank you."

One of his eyebrows arched arrogantly. "Have I given ye the impression that I do nae know how to celebrate, Jemma? Well, that is something that is going to have to change."

His tone suggested that he was more serious than teasing. Her eyelids fluttered because it was another hint of tenderness she had no idea how to accept. He released her hand and a moment later cupped her chin to raise her face. His eyes simmered with happiness.

"I can see that it is definitely something I am going to have to work on proving to ye, for I care not for the fact that ye doubt me."

"There has been little happiness between us."

He tilted his head to the side. "Aye, well, it was a wee bit of an intense moment that I found ye in, Jemma."

Another cheer went up, and Jemma turned to see that men were pushing the tables back to clear a large section of the floor. The moment they completed their task, couples flooded the area and began dancing. Several men and even some women were gathered together with their instruments to provide music for the dancers. There were handheld drums, flutes, violins, and Scottish bagpipes. They blended together in a lively offering of music that kept her toe tapping.

"Do ye play any instruments?"

"Yes . . ." Jemma stumbled over her response because she realized that Gordon was making an attempt to know her. It surprised her because she suddenly realized that she had never taken any time to attempt to talk to him, either.

"I play the mandolin. My father enjoyed the soothing sound very much."

"Would ye play for me?"

Her lips tugged up at the corners, and she had to fight the urge to lower her lashes again.

Sweet virgin . . . she is simpering, he thought.

"If you like. Is it possible to have my things brought from Amber Hill?"

Gordon looked slightly uncomfortable for the first time. "Aye, 'tis something I should have seen to before, but I confess that I was distracted by ye too much to consider that ye had not even a clean chemise."

"Ula brought me what I needed."

He grimaced. "Aye, and slipped a few barbed words into me ear when she made mention of the fact."

Jemma couldn't resist laughing. Just a low sound of amusement that gained her a scoffing sound from Gordon.

"Do nae start laughing at me. That woman knows how to strip the flesh off a man without muttering a single word that ye might be able to take offense at."

"I have noticed that, but that is her experience rising above our own."

"It is that, lass, I hope ye'll be considering that valuable."

Jemma suffered another jolt of shock hitting her. He hoped? So the man was not going to usurp her authority when it came to the running of the house, even if he disagreed with her choices?

"I have never disrespected ye, Jemma."

She snorted and lowered her voice. "You spanked me and took my shoes."

He offered her a cocky smile, one that flashed his teeth at her.

"Now that was just playing, lass. I admit that placing my hand on yer bottom was quite enjoyable."

"Playing?"

Jemma kicked him beneath the table, but her bare foot took more pain from the blow than his shin did with his knee-high boots to help protect him. He chuckled.

"Ye see? There is evidence as to what I am saying . . ." He leaned toward her and she was too curious not to do the same. There was something about the man that was far too hypnotic. "Ye like to play, too, which is why I indulge ye so often."

Jemma pressed her lips together and narrowed her eyes. "You toy with me too often, sir."

His expression turned sensuous, and his eyes filled with dark promise. "I've only just started, lass, but it would be a poor groom I am to take ye above stairs the moment the priest finished the blessing. Ye might think I only think of two things in life, fighting and *riding*."

Jemma smiled sweetly at him. "Do you mean to say that you do think of other things?" She kept her tone innocent and honey coated, exactly as her nurse had once instructed her.

He snorted and then laughed out loud. He tipped his head back and let his amusement bounce off the ceiling. Heads turned to glance at them, and Gordon picked up his tankard and raised it toward the assembled company.

They cheered and grabbed their own mugs, everyone tipping them back to drink long and deep. Gordon slammed his mug down and pushed his chair back.

"Come, wife! I want to dance with ye so that ye are too tired to lead me on a chase around our bed tonight."

His words gained hearty approval from those who heard him, and they were happy to repeat what they heard to those who weren't close enough. Jemma blushed as the men all cheered on their laird and the women offered her tiny smirks.

"You are incorrigible."

"Aye, lass, I am."

But he still knew how to play, and that was something she realized she had missed. Amber Hill had been too structured, a necessity while her father was ill, but she couldn't recall the last time she had danced anything but slow pavans.

Gordon pulled her into the middle of the dance floor, and the music picked up its tempo. The dancing was Gaelic with some of the younger girls rising all the way up onto their toes. They pulled their skirts up to show off the quick motions of their feet, and the men roared with approval while clapping in time with the musicians. Everyone joined in, from the young to the old. Even Ula passed by, her skirts held in her hands while she wove in and out of the men. There was flirting and boldness such as Jemma had never seen in her dancing instructions. The dances were not the orderly Italian steps she had been taught in case she went to court. They were more like the ones danced at festivals outside the walls of Amber Hill.

Gordon pulled her along, but she took to the beat of the music well, reaching down to grasp her skirts and pulling them up as the young women had done. The stone floor was smooth and cool against her bare feet.

Ula danced by and caught her hand to pull her along. The housekeeper wove and dipped through the men while women joined them, forming a long line of linked hands. The musicians played faster, and Ula pulled Jemma toward the doorways. A snarl and growl rumbled from behind her, and she turned to see Gordon being held back by his clansmen.

But it was done with a great deal of jesting. Gordon would frown, but he couldn't maintain the harsh expression for more than a couple of seconds before his lips returned to smiling.

"Here now . . . I think he needs a bath, lads!" Kerry shouted over the noise the other men were making.

"A cold one!" someone else added.

Ula pulled her down the hallway before she heard any more. The noise coming from the hall became a blur of male excitement. But it was drowned out by the laughter of the women escorting her. They giggled and crowded around her, all the time sweeping her toward the stairs, but not the set that led to her chamber. They kept going until they entered the west tower. There they took her up the stairs, passing three floors before they pulled her into a chamber.

Without doubt, it was the laird's chamber.

A huge space, it took up the entire area between the walls of the tower. They were on the top floor, and the ceiling was covered with arches that made for a breathtaking view. Candles cast their flickering orange and scarlet light over the rugs covering the floor. Persian ones and also thick fur ones. The chamber itself was round, with glass windows set in all the way around it with only two-foot sections of stone to interfere. Thick curtains, which undoubtedly cost a huge amount of money, hung on either side of those windows.

She didn't get the chance to look at the room anymore. The older women clustered about her, gently unlacing her dress. They lifted her unbound hair up carefully while the silk and velvet garment was removed. The scent of rosemary touched her nose and the sweet fragrance of flowers. She could see the younger, unmarried girls pulling the heavy bed covering back to expose the sheets. They folded everything down to the foot of the bed, leaving only the creamy expanse of the bottom sheet. Vanora peered at it, reaching out to run her hand over the smooth surface before grunting with approval.

Jemma blushed and felt her limbs quiver. Nervousness assaulted her in a flurry, threatening to buckle her knees.

Vanora would be back at sunrise to look at that sheet. It was an ancient custom and one she had seen played out many times at the village that clustered around Amber Hill. When the merchant's daughters married, the next morning there would be a stained sheet hanging from the window of the house or there would be deep disgrace for the bride and her kin.

She didn't fear disgrace. No, the anxiety that flooded her came from the knowledge that there would be a stain on that sheet come the morning. For all the playfulness Gordon had displayed in the past couple of hours, it was passion that had led them to this night. He would have her, and his cock was no doubt hard with hunger right that very moment.

She sat down while someone brought a basin forward to wash her feet. Hushed bits of conversation drifted to her ears, but she was far too absorbed with contemplating her groom.

Cool water splashed over her toes, drawing her attention to the women eagerly preparing her for her wedding night. She'd missed out on helping brides in the past few years, and she discovered that her memories were those of a little girl, because as soon as her feet were rinsed and dried she was pulled to her feet and her chemise plucked right off her.

A soft sound of shock passed her lips. That drew more attention to her.

"Make a path for Vanora."

The women tending her parted, and the old midwife crossed the floor toward her. Jemma tried to remain poised, but it felt impossible to remain still. She wanted to cover her breasts with her arms, but forced them to remain at her sides. She mustn't act as though she had anything to hide. Gossip was a vicious thing, and brides suffered from it more than others. If she refused to have the midwife inspect the entire chamber to her satisfaction, there might be talk that Jemma had hidden chicken's blood somewhere to stain the sheets.

The midwife stopped in front of her, and the chamber went silent. The women behind her lifted her hair to show there was nothing hidden. Jemma forced her hands to open wide, her fingers spreading for Vanora's gaze. It took every bit of nerve she had to remain still, but every wife in the room had tolerated the same on their wedding night, so she stood steady. She would not cringe like the pampered Englishwoman many of them called her behind her back. She would show them courage.

Vanora took a linen square from a nearby table and ran it up the inside of her thigh, across her sex and down the opposite side before pulling it back to look at and confirm that she was not having her monthly flow. Several woman stood on their toes to see the surface of that fabric. One of them was Ula. Jemma felt her cheeks sting because her blush was so hot, but she waited for the midwife to send her to bed.

Vanora nodded. "I am well satisfied. There will be no talk or ye shall answer to me in front of a priest." The midwife turned to point a finger toward some of the laundresses who were standing in the back of the chamber. They were not helping at all, but there to watch with suspicious eyes. "Mind me well, for I am not so convinced that mercy is the way to instruct ye on decent behavior. Now be gone if ye have no help to offer. The mistress has tolerated far too much from ye already, but she has done so with courage. Wag yer tongues about something true for a change."

There was a hushed silence, but a good number of the women surrounding her turned to glare at the ones standing near the walls. The laundresses did not hold up well. They hurried out, pushing on one another to escape.

That did not leave her alone. The chamber was still full of nearly thirty women, but the mood changed. They smiled and led her toward the bed.

"Come now, before the men show up with the laird."

Someone had strewn late autumn herbs across the sheets. There were no flowers, but the sweet scent of heather and peppermint filled the air. Ula pulled up the covers to protect her modesty, and not any too soon. They heard the men escorting her groom from several floors below. They were trying to sing a bawdy tune but kept losing the rhythm because they were laughing too hard.

No one truly knocked on the doors, they ran into them, making a racket while trying to sing out the next line of their lusty song. Two of the women pulled the chamber doors wide open to admit the pile of chanting, kilt-clad males. They snickered before thrusting their laird forward.

"Be gone!"

They didn't mind him very well. The group rolled back into song, several of them swinging their mugs back and forth to help keep time. It worked rather well, and they belted out the final few lines of the song. The women didn't care much for their tune. They began to beat the group back toward the door, and the men grabbed them to take along with them out of the chamber. Ula was the last to leave, closing the door firmly behind her.

"Bloody lot of trouble."

Jemma got a good look at her groom and laughed. She couldn't hold it, Gordon Dwyre was soaking wet from his bonnet to his boots. Water dripped from the pleats of his kilt making a ring around him. He frowned at her.

"Ye're nae helping matters, woman. The water was cold, and I bathed this afternoon."

"Somehow, I don't believe their goal was to clean you, Gordon. More, I think, to slow you down."

She pushed the bedding back and stood up. His mouth shut with a click of his teeth. His expression became tight as though he was in pain, but in his eyes she could see hunger flickering. Those flames reinforced her courage. She strode slowly toward him, actually enjoying the way his eyes followed her every motion. The sonnets that she had read in a book of love suddenly made sense. This was what they meant when they spoke of not being able to look away. Gordon was devoted to her, and it was more than lust. Something else in his eyes shimmered brightly.

Approval, yes, but there was also relief. A relief born from the experience of his first marriage that had seen him entering his chamber to discover a woman cringing beneath his bed sheets.

"Yer more beautiful than words can express, Jemma. Thank ye for wedding me."

She reached up to open the first button on his wet doublet. The fabric was stiff and resisted.

"We are well suited." The button opened, and she began to work on the next one.

He cupped her chin and raised her face so that their eyes met. "I wed ye for more than the facts that might have been written on a parchment, Jemma."

The words were tender. So tender and unexpected. Her heart eagerly soaked them up, refusing to allow any doubt to wipe them aside. He leaned down and kissed her. The fingers that had been opening his doublet turned into a fist that pulled him closer. She was no longer concerned about her lack of clothing; it seemed perfectly suited for the moment. What bothered her was the stiff fabric held in her closed hand. But his kiss was too delightful to postpone. She mimicked his motions, opening her mouth and tilting her head so that their lips fit more snuggly against each other. She even teased his lower lip with the tip of her tongue as he'd done to her in the past, taking a gentle pass along his lower lip. She felt him jolt, and then he pulled away from their kiss, confusing her.

Gordon snorted. "It is not that ye displeased me, Jemma. Quite the opposite." He stepped away from her completely, and the action allowed doubt to invade her thoughts. Her arms rose up to cover her breasts.

"I suppose I can nae expect ye to understand what I mean." He was busy unbuttoning his doublet with hands that moved far faster than hers had been.

"Then try explaining it to me." Her voice was whisper soft, and she didn't care for how vulnerable it sounded.

He surged out of his doublet and tossed it onto a chair. When he looked at her she gasped, because what she had thought bright about his eyes before was nothing. His eyes glowed now like the harvest moon. Hunger was a living force in them.

"Yer boldness makes me want to meet it measure for measure, lass, and I swear I hate these clothes right now for they keep me from holding yer lovely body against mine."

"But isn't it a wife's duty to tend her husband?" Jemma wasn't sure where her boldness came from, only that it restored her balance, allowing her to uncross her arms. One of Gordon's eyebrows arched in question.

"Are ye toying with me, lass?"

"Maybe. If I am, it is something I have learned from you, I believe."

He pulled his belt open, and the soggy wool of his kilt slumped to the floor in a wet heap. "Good, I like to think that we shall be fine playmates."

Jemma barely heard what he said. His shirt was the only thing shielding his body from her gaze. Since it was wet, it molded to him like a second skin. The fabric was translucent, allowing her to see the darker hair that grew on his chest. The man seemed to be composed mostly of muscle. It ran down from his broad shoulders to a lean waist and on to powerful legs.

But his cock held her attention. It pushed the fabric of his shirt out. Ridged and swollen, the shaft was thick and long.

"Have ye changed yer mind?"

The hint of tenderness in his tone struck her as pity. Jemma didn't care for that because if she took even one morsel of it, she feared she would be reduced to shivering with dread. She had wanted him before, so much so that she had been angry when he left. That was the fact that she held fast to, and she forced her hesitating feet forward to lift one of his wrists up so that she might untie the cuff.

"Yer courage is astounding, Jemma."

She lifted her eyes to see appreciation filling his. He reached out and combed one hand through her hair, beginning at her scalp and drawing his finger down to the ends of the recently brushed strands. For such a simple touch, it sent a spark of anticipation down her body.

"Close yer eyes."

She hesitated, and he slid his hand back into her hair near her head. He closed his grip on the delicate strands gently, but it was enough to dispatch another ripple of enjoyment through her.

"Close yer eyes and feel for a moment, without yer sight to interfere."

"Oh . . . I see." But in truth she didn't. Her eyelids fluttered shut, and he pulled on her hair just a tiny bit more. Without the distraction of what he looked like, the sensation felt as if it were doubled. It raced down her spine and into her belly where it awakened the passion that had been sleeping since the last time he lay with her. Everything happened much faster this time, her body recalling in detail the intense pleasure that he had produced with his finger and mouth. She was eager for more, her clitoris beginning to awaken.

"That's the way, lass, trust me."

Though she wasn't cold, when his hand left her hair she felt the loss of its heat.

His heat.

All across her body, her skin was demanding to be touched. She wanted to feel his hands on her breasts and her belly, and even over the curves of her hips. The idea of it was intoxicating. Her senses became heightened, and she clearly heard the slump of the wet shirt as it dropped to the floor. Excitement rippled across her skin, and she opened her eyes, unable to remain still.

He caught her up against him before she got a clear look at his body, his mouth seeking hers out to press a demanding kiss against it. Passion burned brightly inside him, which his kiss reflected. He captured the back of her head in one large grip, holding her captive while his mouth pillaged hers. His tongue thrust deeply inside, stroking along hers, and her passage begged for the same attention. She felt empty again, and this time the need did not build slowly. It burst into flames that tormented her as much as they pleased her. Jemma reached for his shoulders, her hands seeking out the warm skin she had longed to feel against her own.

He swept her off her feet and carried her toward his bed, the laird's bed, and that sent a shiver of dark possessiveness through her.

"Did you bring Anyon here?"

He laid her down on the heather-scented sheet, one hand lifting her hair up and out of the way so that it would not become trapped by her back.

"Nae."

His voice was gruff, and it was darker in the bed with only a teasing flicker of candlelight making its way to them. That only heightened her senses once more. She heard tiny sounds, such as her own heartbeat. She lifted one hand to press it against his chest. Beneath her fingers she felt the steady beating of his heart, and her lips rose into a smile.

"Exactly, lass, we are nae so different when all of the trappings of this world are taken off us. Here, our bodies fit together very nicely."

"We've yet to see about how well you will fit."

"Ye're the boldest virgin I've ever heard of."

She settled against the sheet and felt him rising above her. He remained on his side, lying next to her, but she felt small and petite compared to his harder and larger form.

"Or did I build a desire in ye for more of the pleasure that I gave ye the last time we were in a bed together?"

His voice was husky but playful. "I believe the word you used was trust."

He reached out and trailed his fingers over the mound of one breast. She shivered as pleasure spread out from that touch.

"It is something I value greatly, lass." He gently cupped her breast, forming his hand around the tender globe. Her nipple drew tight until the top was a hard pebble that eagerly anticipated his kiss. "Something that I plan to put to good use tonight."

"I suppose that I am hoping that is so."

He tilted his head, raising his attention up to her face. "Ye question that? Why? I know that ye were pleasured the last time I touched ye."

His pride was slightly wounded; she heard it in his voice.

"You did, but I believe you have something else planned for this evening that I have never experienced, so the only thing I may say is that I hope it is so. But I seem to recall that doing *this* pleased you." Reaching for his cock, she closed her hand around it. The flesh was silken soft, but the staff itself hard. He drew in a stiff breath, his expression becoming strained.

Jemma moved her hand to the top of his shaft to where a thick crown circled the head. She touched it gently, feeling it and listening to the sounds of his breathing.

"Ye have a wickedly clever hand, lass."

"Ah, does that mean that my actions meet with your approval . . . my lord and husband?" She offered up her last few words as a test. There were plenty of men who liked to hear such from their wives; some who demanded it.

Gordon opened his eyes. "Leave that bit of expected speech for when there are others about to hear ye, lass. That has never been my way with ye when we're in private, but I can understand ye wondering about it."

"I see. Aren't you afeared that I will become bold if you do not keep me in my place?"

He flashed her a wide smile that was full of mischief. "I believe I'm dreading the fact that ye might be meek, madam. There is something that I fear. Truly I do."

"We could not suffer such, not fear from the Laird Barras himself." She moved her hand back down to the base of his cock, watching his face to see what he did in response.

He made a soft sound beneath his breath, his eyes narrowing to mere slits. "I'm suffering, lass, but 'tis a pleasant sort of suffering."

She moved her hand up and down his shaft, gaining a sort of rhythm. He growled softly, rolling slightly more onto his back to offer her access to his length. Apparently his cock was as sensitive as her clitoris. Her gaze moved to it. The head was swollen and crowned with a small slit that held a drop of fluid. Bringing her hand back up to the top, she ran her thumb over that slit, her skin slipping easily across it. Another moan rumbled up from his chest, but it was not nearly as hungry or passionate as he had driven her to.

Of course, he had been using his mouth on her, too . . .

Before she considered the idea any further, Jemma leaned down and opened her mouth and licked the head of his cock.

"Sweet virgin's tits!" His huge body jerked, bouncing on the bed and pulling his cock from her grasp.

"Gordon . . . such words will see you in the stocks."

He snarled while glaring at her. Jemma rolled up until she was poised on her knees in the middle of the bed. "Didn't you like that? I enjoyed it when you used . . ."

"When I sucked on yer clitoris, aye, I recall it well."

His cock looked more swollen now, the head ruby red. "Men don't enjoy the same?"

He laughed, low and deep. "They do, lass, but I don't trust my control to last if ye took to Frenching me. I'd likely spill my seed."

There was a tone in his voice that told her he found the idea very appealing. Her pride latched on to it, craving an opportunity to be the one commanding his pleasure.

"I've heard that men can spill more than one portion of seed in a night."

He stiffened, his eyes filling with bright hunger. "Aye, that's a truth."

"Then I do not see any reason for you to argue against my *Frenching* you, unless you were not sincere in your claim that you have no care for a submissive bride behind closed doors."

"That word is nearly enough to unman me, coming from yer lips, lass."

But not enough? She grabbed the challenge and stretched out toward him on all fours, walking her hands across the surface of the bed until she lowered herself onto her stomach. The candles turned his skin crimson, and she used both her hands to cup the sac hanging below his member.

"Since we are newlywed, I believe I should confess that I have never been satisfied with being nearly good enough at anything, Gordon." She stroked her fingers up the soft skin encasing his cock, lightly teasing it as he had done with her sex.

"I've always admired those who seek excellence, lass."

His breath was becoming rough. Closing her hand around his thickness, she leaned forward and trailed her tongue over the top of it again. She felt him shiver. The little response fanned the flames of her determination. She licked his cock again, this time with more than just the very tip of her tongue. She leaned in closer and allowed her mouth to open wider so that more of her tongue connected with his cock. Fluid had returned to the slit, and it tasted slightly salty when she ran her tongue over it. She could hear him breathing roughly, but it wasn't anywhere near the same mindless condition he had reduced her to.

Lifting her head, she looked up at his face. "Tell me how to French you." He snorted at her request. "Why not tell me? I don't know because bed sport was something I expected to learn from my husband, not from the local light skirts."

His hand grasped the back of her head, and his lips thinned into an expression that was almost harsh until she recalled how tight her own emotions had been stretched when he was sucking her.

Is he on that edge?

"Open yer mouth and suck some of my length inside."

She swallowed hard and shivered. Excitement brewed once again in her belly. It was strange how hearing the words made her quiver with anticipation. Her hands stroked his member, drawing another snort from him.

"And do that with yer hands."

She looked back down at his cock and opened her mouth. She had already tasted him so there was no hesitation in her. Relaxing her jaw, she took the head between her lips while her hands played up and down the portion that was still outside her mouth. His hand tightened on her hair, and she heard his breathing become small pants. His hips thrust toward her mouth, driving his cock deeper and then withdrawing in shallow thrusts.

He groaned. Low and deep, it was a sound that confirmed he was as flooded with pleasure as she had been. That knowledge sent a flicker of heat through her clitoris. But she wasn't ready to allow him to reverse their roles yet. She allowed more of his cock to penetrate her mouth while her hands closed around his cock in an imitation of her passage clasping the entire length. He snarled something beneath his breath, his hips quickening their pace before the fingers in her hair tightened and his hips drove his cock into her mouth in a hard motion. She felt the warm spurt of his seed bathe her tongue and flood her mouth. His body shook while he let out a savage-sounding moan.

He pulled her head away from his cock, but she continued to stroke it with delicate touches while he drew in rough, rapid breaths. His face was drawn into a hard expression, but he opened his eyes and she witnessed the pleasure shimmering in them. His lips suddenly parted to display a smile at her. The expression, full of promise, sent another ripple of intense excitement through her being.

"One good Frenching deserves another, woman."

He hooked an arm beneath her waist and flipped her onto her back in one powerful motion. The amount of strength the man had was frightening, but he controlled it expertly. The bed shook beneath her back, and Gordon lunged right over her to come up between her legs. He slid his hands up the insides of her thighs, sending pleasure through her, and then pressed her legs wide. He did it with just enough strength to allow her to feel like he was indeed reversing their roles. His hands held her thighs wide to expose her sex while he raised his head up to look at her stunned face.

"I'm going to enjoy tonguing yer pearl, lass."

"My what?" Her voice was a croak because she'd never imagined that husbands and wives talked so much about bed sport.

His hand moved to her spread sex, gliding up the center of her folds to the top where her clitoris was unprotected now. He pressed his thumb down on top of it, gently moving the finger in a tiny circle.

"This little pearl, sweet wife. The only one that I truly care to see on ye. I'm going to enjoy giving it a great deal of attention."

The man was not boasting idle promises. He leaned forward and captured her clitoris between his lips. She cried out because it was even more sensitive than she had thought. Arousal had seeped into her while she pleasured him, and now it was like dry tinder and his mouth the spark.

Her hands became claws, pulling at the bedding. His lips sucked, and the tip of his tongue flicked back and forth across her clitoris. She couldn't seem to pull enough breath into her lungs, her chest heaving to try to keep pace with her accelerating heart. Her hips lifted to his mouth, seeking out enough pressure to fling her into that same pleasure pool as before. This time she knew her destination, and her body was even more eager for the culmination.

"That's it, lass, raise yer hips and demand yer pleasure."

He trailed one fingertip down the center of her spread fold to gently circle the opening to her passage.

"Take yer pleasure from me, Jemma."

His voice was strained, as though his control was being tested. She lifted her eyelids to look at him and discovered hunger glittering in his eyes. She watched his fingers take over working her clitoris, pressing and rubbing it. She lost the ability to keep her eyes open, the pleasure becoming too much to ignore in favor of anything else. She closed her eyes and felt her body tighten, each rub from his fingers intensifying the pleasure. He leaned forward and replaced his fingers with his mouth, muttering something against her clitoris that vibrated against the sensitive point.

Pleasure ripped through her, pulling her into a moment filled with nothing but blinding delight. It raced out to the farthest points of her body and then back to her belly where it bathed the hunger gnawing at her in satisfaction. Her cries echoed off the arched ceiling and the canopy stretched over the bed. He trailed his fingers back down to the opening of her passage to gently tease it. She felt empty and as though she wasn't yet truly satisfied. He allowed one finger to penetrate her, just a small amount, but the walls of her passage instantly registered it and how good it felt. The motion recalled her to the task in front of her. That thing that had been so much talked about.

Taking his member inside me.

For certain she had heard more coarse words for it, but she could see the hunger in his eyes and feel it still glowing in the deepest part of her. She was still needy, still yearning for something more.

"Are ye ready, Jemma? Ready to become me wife?"

His voice was rough and coated with need as great as her own. She lifted her arms in invitation.

"Come to me, Gordon. Be my husband."

He growled and pulled his fingers from her passage. Rising up, she caught a glimpse of his rigid cock and shivered. But he crawled up to cover her, and his warm skin connected with hers to send a flood of contentment through her, as though it was something she had always yearned for but never realized she needed. Her hands rose to clasp his shoulders, and she felt the first touch of his cock against the opening of her body. It slipped easily against the wet skin, nudging its way . . .

Gordon suddenly froze, his head tilting sideways. The windows all vibrated with the ringing of bells. They increased in volume as more of them joined. He let out a vicious curse, and a second later she lay alone on the bed.

"What is it?"

"Trouble."

He cast one look back at her and snarled something else that would have gotten him locked in the stocks for cursing. He grabbed the heavy coverlet and tossed it up the bed to cover her. Someone pounded on the chamber doors a moment later.

"Enter!"

Two of his captains burst into the room. "Fire in the village."

"Assemble the men."

His captains didn't waste any time delivering their laird's orders. They quit the room in a flash while Gordon stalked toward the far side of the chamber. She hadn't realized the maid had set out his clothing in case he might have to dress quickly in the middle of the night.

It was his duty to protect his people. Such was a dangerous task that was so often bathed in blood. He pulled a shirt on and stepped into a pair of boots. Bending one knee, he laced one quickly and then the other. A kilt was already pleated along a table built at an angle. The length of tartan evenly placed and a belt running beneath it. He placed his back in the center and tugged the ends of the belt around his middle.

"Stay right there, exactly as ye are." He leaned into the bed and pressed a hard kiss against her mouth before turning and grabbing his sword on the way out of the chamber.

Jemma heard the doors close, and her eyes filled with tears. She failed to keep them from falling, the salt drops falling down her cheeks to wet the sheets. She wept for the chill that crept over the chamber and for the moment that they had been denied, but most of all she cried because of the fear that dug its claws into her.

The fear that she might become a widow before she sampled the joys of being a wife.

Gordon smelled the smoke the moment he set foot outside the tower. He took the stairs two at a time and gained the top quickly. Kerry was looking through a spy glass at the bright orange glare below them. It wasn't in the village but one of the farmers on the outskirts.

"I suspect that would be the work of those bloody English."

"The ones I granted mercy to." Gordon took a quick look through the glass before passing it back to one of the men standing nearby. "I warned them that there would be no second chance of that happening again. Mount up!"

Every lad over the age of five was already helping to saddle horses. They came running in their night shirts to lend assistance to their clan. Gordon's foot touched the ground, and his stallion was tugged toward him. He offered the animal a firm pat along its neck before swinging up onto its powerful back.

"Open the gate!"

There was a groan as the chains were wound up and the iron gate began to rise. The Barras retainers didn't wait for it to finish; they ducked their heads across the necks of their horses the moment the iron gate was high enough for them to ride beneath. The sound of the horses' hooves combined with the night. They streamed out of the castle, uncaring of the darkness. Nothing was more fearsome than they.

Chapter Eight

J emma rubbed her eyes at dawn. Sleep had proven elusive, and she was already out of bed when Ula arrived. The housekeeper was without her customary smile this morning, her lips slightly pinched instead. But she was also not alone, for several women followed her.

"Don't bother, Ula, there is no stain on the sheet. We hadn't . . . um . . . the bells interrupted . . . us . . ."

Jemma stumbled over her words, never having imagined that she would have to explain the lack of blood on her wedding sheets. She would have laughed indeed at anyone who told her such a tale, but there was naught amusing about knowing that her bed was as clean as it had been the night before. Being English in a Scottish castle was not the place for any bride to try to explain pristine sheets on her first morning as a wife. At the very least, her marriage was unconsummated. Anne of Cleaves had found herself divorced for the same circumstance.

"I see. 'Tis nothing to fret over, Mistress. The laird will return."

"I shall pray that he does."

Jemma shivered, feeling the icy dread that had been her constant companion since her father died. Ula was worried; she read it off the housekeeper's face. Gordon should have returned before sunrise. Other maids came into the chamber and set to work dressing her. Jemma stood still out of shock and the dread that felt like it might stop her heart with its grasp. He would return, she had to believe that.

Why?

Was she so foolish as to have allowed affection for him into her heart?

Jemma scoffed at herself. There had been nothing allowed. That was the difficulty with tender emotions; they slipped past every defense like poison in a goblet. You never knew that an assassin had gotten close enough to snatch your life away until you felt the evil concoction eating away at your insides.

But evil was a harsh word. Jemma hugged herself and crossed the chamber to look out the windows. The maids had opened some of the glass panes just like shutters, allowing fresh air to sweep through the room. It carried the scent of fall and blew out all the traces of smoke left from the candles that had burned last night. She had never imagined sleeping in such a grand room; it was something from a tale of a palace somewhere far away. Not something she might actually step into. It was easy to see far into the distance.

The view did not ease her mind because there was no sign of the Barras retainers nor their laird.

Her heart longed to see them, and that only made her more unhappy. Dread unleashed its tension on her. Like any storm there was no way to block out the chill completely, because even standing in front of a fire you felt its icy touch on the back of your neck.

She followed the other women to church where the priest sent out prayers for the retainers and laird. But her thoughts were centered on the man she worried so much about.

"Come along, Mistress, best to keep busy; that will pass the time better."

Ula was correct, but her voice betrayed that the house-keeper was no happier about waiting than Jemma was. They began to work, racing the end of the season to make sure the castle was prepared for the ice and snow. Every work room was piled high with dried fruits, oats, and grains. Men worked on the hen houses where the birds would roost during the winter while providing eggs. The birds were still being al-lowed to graze on the drying hillsides, and the young girls were sent out to find their eggs with large baskets to carry them back to the cook.

The afternoon turned dark long before sunset, black clouds dominating the sky. They huddled together while the wind ripped at her skirts. Jemma climbed up onto the hillsides to call the last of the girls back. They struggled to bring their heavy baskets with them, and she reached for two that were full of fresh eggs. With abundant food, the hens were laying twice a day.

"Go on now, it's going to storm."

The girls needed no further urging. They grabbed the front of their skirts and ran toward the side gate that led into the yard behind the curtain wall. Jemma followed but at a steady walk to ensure that she did not crack any eggs. She stopped outside the gate, hearing Ula's voice raised on the other side of the stone wall.

"Are ye mad? Allowing the mistress out without an escort? The laird will nae be pleased, mark my words."

"The way I hear, my laird will be plenty grateful to be rid of her. The sheets were white this morning. She's a slut. An Eng-lish slut that we have no need of."

Jemma gasped. Thinking that it might be said was different from hearing it. Her face heated with a blush, and tears stung her eyes. She drew in a stiff breath and raised her chin, refus-ing to allow those tears to fall. She blinked them away and stepped boldly through the gate. The man arguing with Ula jerked his head around when he noticed her and his eyes narrowed in distaste. Thunder boomed in the hills above them, loud enough to make conversation impossible.

It was better that way. Kindness seemed to have abandoned her. Ula reached for one of the baskets, and they carried them both into the kitchens. The long rooms that served as kitchens were bustling with women coming in to avoid the rain. The cook snapped at them when they began to chatter, making the room an impossible place to concentrate.

Anyon stood near one of the hearths with other laundresses, all trying to dry their skirts. The girl smirked at her as she carried the basket toward a long table where the cook was laying out her ingredients.

"Better be careful that ye didna break any. The cook likes to hand out slaps." The laundresses snickered.

Jemma raised her chin and shot a firm glance toward Anyon. "Well, I suppose that would be better than being ambushed for no reason beyond spite."

Anyon propped her hands on her hips, and the action pushed her breasts out. "Ye see, there's the problem with the English, they never did know how to fight."

"Enough, Anyon, I have no time for pettiness." Jemma turned her back, but the girl raised her voice.

"Oh, yes, I forgot. Ye have to be off to think of ways to get the laird to share yer bed since he could nae stomach the sight of ye last night long enough to plow ye."

Jemma turned to face the girl once more. If she wanted to be mistress of Barras castle, she could not hide.

"But he was in my bed when the bells rang, not seeking out yours."

Anyon stiffened but closed her mouth when the majority of the women working at the long tables refused to cross the laird's new bride, even if the sheets had been clean this morning. They looked down at their work, abandoning Anyon to her temper.

Jemma raised her chin, casting a glance around to make it clear that she expected her words to be obeyed by all. "I was raised in England and therefore under the Protestant church. Since this is a Catholic nation, I expect that Christian values shall be used in this castle. My wedding-night celebration was interrupted. Any who claim any other reason for the lack of a stained sheet this morning will have the privilege of telling your laird that charge against me when he returns."

Eyes widened, and several gasps made it past the hands attempting to smother them. Tension drew the muscles along her back tight, but Jemma remained firmly in place. She swept the room, aiming a hard look at anyone who did not lower their eyes when she met them. Only the cook stood up to her, the older woman staring back at her for a few moments. The woman wiped her hands on her apron before speaking.

"Aye, Mistress."

Jemma turned around and felt everyone staring at her back. But she maintained her dignity, leaving the room with her chin level. Many a noble bride had failed to take her house in hand when she arrived. Failing to do so would earn her nothing but a staff set against her.

Jemma scoffed at herself. Her words might have ensured that the Barras staff was indeed set against her, for Anyon was one of their own. But a sharp slap came from the silent kitchens, a solid flesh-upon-flesh sound that Jemma could not mistake. The cook was clearly a woman of her word, and it would seem that Anyon was learning that the hard way. A flurry of work sounds followed, chopping and dishes connecting with the hard wood tabletop. The cook resumed issuing orders, but there was not one word in response.

"I'm glad ye put that girl in her place." Ula nodded with approval. "I'm ashamed to claim her as kin."

The thunder cracked above their heads so loud it felt as if it shook the very air. Jemma shivered, something raising the hair on the back of her neck. It was more than the wind, something other than the storm raining its fury down on the towers. She could feel the hate being directed toward her. It was thick and choking, frightening her with its darkness.

"I hope it brings peace. That is all I seek, Ula."

The border land . . .

"Damn miserable rain." Curan Ramsden offered his opinion in the place of a greeting. He pushed the visor up to expose his face. "Makes a man want to seek out his home and *family*."

There was no mistaking the barely concealed threat in his tone. Gordon turned his hand over to feel the rain pelting them and shrugged. "Ye have spent too much time in France if ye find this weather disagreeable, my brother by marriage."

Curan held his emotions behind a tightly controlled expression. It was admirable because not every man learned to hide what he was thinking so well. The only hint was the way the man's stallion jerked its head, clearly feeling the man tightening his thighs around the saddle.

"Is that so, Barras?"

"Yer sister did me the honor of becoming my wife yesterday."

There was a flash of something dangerous in Curan's eyes. It was something Gordon knew about the man, that he was a noble who took action rather than talking. Curan was a knight who backed up every word he spoke.

"Yesterday? And you failed to invite me to the ceremony."

"I had yer permission." Gordon returned the baron's stare,

refusing to back down. Jemma belonged to him. "That was always my goal, and I told ye plainly."

"But did my sister agree?" Rage edged each word.

Gordon leaned forward. "She did."

Curan glared at him, holding his next thought while lightning flashed around them. The thunder came next, and Curan's expression looked just as fierce as the rumble sounded. "But you have no way of proving that, Barras, seeing as how you moved forwards without sending someone to inform me of your impending wedding so that I could ask Jemma that before the vows were taken."

"I do nae send any men out without a full escort with yer English knights roaming these hills looking for me queen. They nearly ended yer sister's life, and fired one of me farms last night, dragging us both out here to enjoy the weather."

"Your point is well founded."

Gordon nodded, accepting the slight easing of tension between them. "Ye are welcome at Barras Castle to ask Jemma yerself."

"That will not resolve my question now that the deed is done." His eyes narrowed with judgment. "Nothing can."

"Well now, lad, that's where ye're wrong." Gordon watched his neighbor's face register surprise. Unlike most men, Curan waited for him to continue instead of blurting out another comment that would delay him gaining the answer he sought.

"I married yer sister and took her to bed, but the attack on my people took me away before I consummated the union." Gordon felt his frustration peak once again, but he offered Curan a smirk. "Ye might recall that little challenge from yer own attempts to celebrate yer wedding with pretty Bridget."

"And you have no issue with sending my sister to me outside your walls to tell me she is pleased to be your wife?"

"If that is what is needed."

"Possibly." Curan's reply lost some of its edge when his eyes lit with satisfaction. "I am pleasantly surprised, Barras. I didn't believe there was a way for you to prove the matter to me; I stand corrected."

Gordon nodded, feeling the tension release between his shoulder blades. He valued his neighbor's goodwill even if there was little the man might do to reclaim his sister. It was a harsh fact but one he realized he'd have resorted to if it was the only way to keep Jemma.

"Then I'll leave ye now, Ryppon, for I have a bride to seek. Ye might recall the feeling."

"I do, Barras."

"And as much as I like ye, I'd appreciate some time alone with me bride before ye come to visit."

"Something else I understand." Curan considered his next words. "A few days."

He'd never enjoyed hearing three words so much. But Gordon couldn't let her go now. Not after last night. She had come to him, cementing something inside him that refused to bend. Like mortar it was solid now, unmovable deep inside his chest. He didn't know what it was, only that the idea of not seeing her waiting for him was unendurable. It was more than the desire to bed her. He wanted to smell her hair again and taste her soft kiss when she leaned forward to press her lips against his of her own free will. That was the gift that filled him with tenderness when he'd always considered such emotions merely the stuff of sonnets, the babbling of insane men.

Maybe he had just gone soft, Gordon didn't care. He tightened his hand around the reins, and his stallion pawed at the ground, eager to begin covering the miles between them and home.

Home, aye, that was what he craved, and was what Jemma made Barras Castle feel like now.

* * *

The bells rang again well after sunset. Jemma sat in her chamber unable to stomach returning to Gordon's. She pulled a brush through her hair, lifting it gently so that the heat from the fire could help it dry. She felt on edge while she waited.

Would he want her tonight? Or would he decide to rest before taking up the challenge of consummating their union? Both were valid questions. In truth she knew very little about Gordon, his likes and dislikes or his expectations of their marriage.

She knew full well that the man desired her body.

Was that lust? For certain it was, but was there more between them, some deeper emotion tugging them together? She felt like there was.

Many would brand her foolish for thinking such.

But her brother loved his wife Bridget. There was no way to deny it, because she had witnessed it. The Church would tell her love was insanity, a sickness that needed healing, but she had seen how her brother and his wife looked at each other. If that was suffering, she would give herself into its keeping willingly.

She felt Gordon before she heard him. A tingle brushed over her nape and down her back. It rippled over her skin, and her nipples contracted until they were hard points behind the dressing robe she wore. It was her only garment because she couldn't seem to bring herself to dress any further when she was so newly a bride.

But not yet a wife . . .

She drew the brush along her hair again and felt his attention shift to the motion. There was not much light in the chamber, only the fire casting deep scarlet shadows onto the floor near the hearth. Gordon stepped out of the darkness, looking for all the world like some highlander from legend.

His hair was curling slightly and held back from his face by a thin braid. His knees peeked out from beneath the pleats of his kilt, and his doublet was missing. The sleeves of his shirt were rolled up and tied at the shoulders, exposing his forearms. There was such a raw appearance to the man, as though he could survive anything the rugged Scottish hills gave him.

"I approve of yer attire if not the place that ye choose to wait, lass." He reached up and pulled something from his bonnet. "But I brought ye a token of my affections to soften yer heart toward me."

It was a small stalk of heather, the flowers delicate and the scent teasing her nose with sunshine and afternoon breezes. The fragile stem didn't fit with his powerful body, but that was what sent her lips upward in a smile. The fact that he had taken the time to bring her something that most men thought silly woman foolishness. Girls wove flower wreaths, but men preferred the beauty of a good sword. The stock was cool against her fingers, and she trembled for it was such a tender gesture. One she had never imagined.

"Ah, does that smile mean I shall not have to carry ye to my bed?"

"Only if you wish to."

He chuckled and reached out to grasp a handful of her hair. He dropped to one knee and held it against his face while he inhaled its fragrance.

"I didn't put any perfume in it. Some ladies do."

"Do nae become one of them. I daydreamed today about the way ye smell, and I enjoyed every moment of it, but the reality is far better, I assure ye."

He stood up. "Come and greet me with a sweet kiss of welcome, wife."

She placed the brush aside and rose to her feet. "A sweet kiss?"

"Aye."

Jemma felt her belly quiver and her knees threaten to collapse, but she mustered her determination and closed the distance between them. She noticed how much larger he was than her; somehow that fact impacted her more deeply now than it had before. Laying her hands on his chest, she smoothed them up and over his collarbones until she gently clasped the top of his shoulders. Rising up onto her toes, she placed her mouth in contact with his, pressing her lips until they sealed against his.

"Welcome, my lord."

He chuckled, the sound warm and promising. "How very innocent that was."

"I am innocent."

She moved away from him, but he followed her with slow steps that were a chase of sorts.

"Nae that innocent, lass."

Her cheeks burned, but her lips remained curved, only this time her smile was a wicked one and he wore one that was its reflection. She wove her steps in an uneven line, unsure why she was moving away from him. Her body certainly wanted to be closer, not farther away. But she kept walking, looking back over her shoulder to watch the way he followed. His keen eyes roamed over her, watching the sway of her hips and the way her unbound hair flowed. She moved deeper into the shadows, and her highlander pursued her.

"Are ye ready to be caught?"

Her throat felt tight, anticipation making her breathless. She nodded, and he quickened his stride. His arms slid around her, bringing her into contact with his body. One hand cupped the back of her head, and he lowered his face to press a kiss against her mouth. This one was sweet but full of budding passion. It built in a steady increase of heat, the tip of his tongue teasing her lower lip before he demanded she open her mouth for a deeper taste. His tongue thrust down to stroke across her own only once before he broke away from the kiss and offered her a cocksure grin.

He bent and lifted her off her feet. "I could say something sweet, but I confess that the truth is, I plan to take ye to me bed and have my way with ye."

"Oh, wait."

His arms tightened around her and his expression told her he had no liking for her words. Jemma placed a hand on his frown, smoothing it with her fingers. He shivered, a barely noticeable response but it shook her to her heart.

"I mustn't leave my gift behind."

He lowered her feet to the floor, and she went back toward the fireplace where the sprig of heather lay near her brush. She closed her hand around it gently for it was a treasure, brought to her by a hand that should have crushed it. Instead he had controlled his strength to bring something of little value but great importance.

It was a token of his affection.

"Now I am ready."

"What is that?" Jemma wasn't sure how she might have missed such a thing. It was huge.

"A bathing tub." Her husband encircled her waist with one of his thickly muscled arms, pulling her back against his body. Her head brushed beneath his chin, feeling as though she had been molded perfectly to fit next to him. The tub in front of her was like three tubs all placed side by side. Only it was a single tub and someone had already filled it with water. The window near it was open, displaying glimpses of the moon that the clouds allowed through. Coal baskets placed beneath the tub brought gently steaming water.

"It's far too large."

"Well now, lass, I've heard that before, but I do assure ye that ye'll find the size to yer liking." He was teasing her, and her cheeks turned red when she realized he was insinuating something else entirely. She jabbed one of her elbows back into his ribs.

"I wasn't talking about that, sir."

"Ah but ye were thinking about me cock."

"I was not."

He nuzzled against her neck, placing a kiss against the tender skin. Pleasure rippled down her skin, making her smile just because he was near. The warmth of his body was so pleasing she would have been content to remain standing so long as he was there.

"Considering how we parted, my mind has been returning to the very moment I heard those cursed bells ringing. Can I not hope ye were thinking about it, too? Dare I admit that the idea of hearing ye confess that would bring me much happiness?"

"I was thinking about you." The words rushed right out of her mouth with no consideration at all. What was there to think about? He made her happy, why should she deny him the same?

His arm tightened, and he pressed a harder kiss against her throat and then several more. "Sweet English wildcat, come share a bath with me."

"Share?"

He released her and pulled his shirt over his head, baring his body. There was an arrogant look on his face, one that spoke of experience she discovered she was jealous of.

Jemma crossed her arms over her chest. "Not if you invited Anyon into that tub."

He laughed, and she felt her temper simmer. "I mean what I say, Gordon. I'll not be the next in line for your riding."

He closed his lips to contain his amusement, but his eyes were still filled with mischief. "Ye're jealous, Jemma."

"You may be certain that I am, sir. Why is it I am forced to stand bare while every inch of my body is inspected and the bed, too, all for the sake of proving that I am innocent, yet my groom is allowed to *ride often?*"

His eyes darkened. " 'Tis unfair, I agree, but I suppose it is a matter that men kill over jealousy, lass, and I swear that I feel like I'd gladly choke the life out of any man who touched ye."

"Barbarian." She sniffed at him. "Take your bath alone."

He placed his hand over his heart. "I swear to ye, Jemma, I never had another woman in this tub."

"On your honor?"

His voice had turned somber. "Aye, lass. Now take yer dressing robe off. I want to see if me memory is playing tricks on me or if ye are more beautiful than any woman I've ever met."

His gaze was fashioned on her, unwavering and completely devoted. Excitement flowed through her, waking from where she had thrust it down when fate had taken him from her. Reaching down, she pulled the single tie that held the dressing robe closed. Rolling her shoulders sent the heavy garment slipping down her arms, past the curve of her hips, and down her legs.

Gordon watched her intently, his keen eyes following the fabric as it bared each new part of her.

"Ye are stunning, Jemma, and ye are mine." His raised his attention back to her face. "And I enjoy that fact, lass, more than I can tell ye."

He swept her off her feet, cradling her against his chest, and carried her to the tub. He lowered her gently to make sure the water wasn't too hot. A soft sigh escaped her lips, and he chuckled.

"Aye, it's a fine thing, isn't it?"

He knelt down to move one of the coal baskets out from beneath the tub.

"Where did you find such a thing?"

He lifted one leg over the edge and then the other, sinking down into the water next to her. The water level rose as he displaced a large portion of it. The tub wasn't just wide, it was deeper than any other she had ever seen, but she realized why when Gordon leaned against the back of it. The side of the tub rose high enough to support his back. He sighed and offered her a satisfied look.

" 'Twas made here by one of my own blacksmiths. I read about one in a book brought back from the holy land." He wiggled his eyebrows. "It told a tale of a sultan who had one of these for traveling. It seems the man liked his concubines to attend him at all moments."

"Right in his bath?" Her voice had turned husky and low, but she couldn't help but be captivated by the forbidden topic. Gordon reached down and grasped his cock.

"Aye, lass. Those Moors teach their concubines that men can nae experience pleasure unless the female rides him to it."

"You are toying with me . . ." But the idea was exciting her. Her passage was alive with need and her clitoris begging for the chance to try what he was suggesting.

"Ye're sitting in the tub, are ye not, lass?" He reached out and captured one of her feet. "That book had many suggestions, Frenching a woman among them."

He began to rub her foot, working over her arch with small kneading motions.

"And it also mentioned pressure points that build passion in a woman."

"On her foot?"

"Aye." His fingers worked some more. "Here I believe."

He pressed and rubbed and sensation shot up her legs. It tingled and awakened feelings that twisted through her.

"Such a book must be forbidden by the Church."

"Ye can be sure of that." He reached for her other foot and treated it to the same massage. Her body was growing warmer, the water suddenly becoming too hot for her taste.

"But ye want to know what else was in it, don't ye?"

"Yes," Jemma answered quickly, drawing a cocky smile from him.

"Ah well, the book mentioned a few things about nipples."

He pulled her forward and right up onto his lap. She squealed because the hard length of his cock pressed against her slit, the folds of her flesh opening to lie on either side of his thick member.

"Now put yer hands behind ye so that yer sweet breasts are thrust forward to please me like a good concubine."

"That would be brazen."

"Aye, and ye sound breathless with the idea, wife."

She was. Hunger was flooding her, and her own thoughts were helping to drive it. He grasped her arms and gently folded them behind her back. Her breasts did thrust out toward him.

"Ah, the perfect picture of submission. Ye know those Moors insist on their concubines being slaves to their every desire. Will ye stay there, waiting for my touch with yer little pearl pressed against my cock?"

His hands cupped her breasts, the water making it a delightful sensation. His fingers smoothed over her skin, and he lifted his fingers to drip water on the top of her breasts where the skin was still dry. She made a low sound of approval, and he offered her a male one in return.

"Sweet, sweet wife. I am looking forward to the winter."

She laughed. A single sound but her cheeks brightened once more. She felt pretty. It wasn't due to flowery words or thoughtful gifts, but the feeling stemmed from the look in his eyes and the way his attention was focused on her breasts. He was still happily toying with her breasts, thumbing her hard nipples and spreading his fingers out around the tender mounds. Soft arousal continued to build inside her, making her more and more aware of the hard flesh pressing against her clitoris. It became an effort to remain still, her hips wanted to twitch and move. She bit her lower lip but lost the battle to remain still.

"Aye, I could nae agree with ye more, lass. A bit of action is called for."

He moved his hands down to her hips, cupping her curves with his hands and pressing her down onto him harder. He thrust his hips up in soft, tiny motions that moved his cock against her slit.

"Gordon . . ." She was truly breathless now, the motions of his hips rubbing against her clitoris. The pressure from his hold on her hips kept his member against his body and away from the opening to her passage. By thrusting up and holding her steady, his hard flesh worked against her slit, rubbing back and forth. Pleasure spiked up into her. The water splashed against her breasts and nipples while he continued to thrust. She couldn't maintain her position and reached for him as need began to force a moan past her lips.

"Gordon . . . stop . . . before—"

"Take yer pleasure, Jemma, I want to see ye cry with it."

There really was no choice. She was powerless to hold it back. Her thighs grasped his hips, making sure that their bodies were even tighter against one another. He thrust faster, and she felt her fingers clawing into his shoulders. The cry he desired broke from her lips as pleasure tore through her. It raced into her, where it became a glowing knot of tension that held for one blinding moment and then broke apart into tongues of white-hot flame touching every part of her. She gasped, and her head lowered onto his shoulder. Her heart was beating too fast, and the hands holding her hips were almost too tight, but they held her steady while she drew in rapid breaths and felt her sanity return.

He cupped her chin and raised it to meet his eyes. They were full of bright need that made the water feel cold.

"I enjoy pleasuring ye, but the next time ye cry out, I am going to be deep inside ye, Jemma." He leaned forward to press a hard kiss against her mouth, his hands raising her up so that his cock sprang up to position itself for entry into her body.

"Not yet."

She reached forward and clasped his cock while scooting down to sit on his thighs. The water made it easy to work her hand up and down the thick staff. His face tightened as she moved her hand faster. His cock grew harder, and his hands gripped the sides of the tub until the knuckles turned white.

He suddenly caught her hand, forcing her to stop. "Enough, Jemma. I want to be inside ye."

His eyes were bright with need, the same hunger that was coiled up inside her belly.

"Not here. We need to go back to the bed."

She stood up and stepped out of the tub before he realized her intention.

"Come back here, wife. I've waited too long to claim ye." His voice was strained, and there was a dangerous glint in his eyes.

"No. In the bed." The frustration on his face drew a soft laugh from her.

"It's not comical, wife. The moment is now."

Jemma tried to compose herself, but failed. His demands reminded her too much of how need made her feel. She enjoyed knowing that he was just as susceptible to passion for her; in truth she was proud of her ability to push him to that edge. It fortified her confidence and made her bold enough to stand completely nude in front of him. He liked her in such a way, and she enjoyed seeing his enjoyment.

Her husband growled.

"Admit it, Gordon." She plucked up a length of toweling and wrapped it around her nude body to prod him into following her. Her action drew a fresh round of snarls from her companion.

"With all your boasting of how much riding you do, it is amusing to consider how difficult it has proven for you to . . . gain the saddle . . . in this instant . . ."

She laughed again but backed up when he rose from the tub. His body was magnificent. His chest was thick with muscle that continued down to a lean belly and thighs that were defined with ridges. He reached down and grasped his own cock, his fingers stroking it and drawing her gaze to the swollen flesh.

"Now, lass, it is not only the stallion that wants to cover a mare. The mare leads him on a merry chase to fire up his appetite before allowing him to mount her." He climbed over the side of the tub and didn't bother to use the toweling set out for his pleasure. The water streamed down his legs, the candlelight making him glisten.

"Ah . . . the chase . . . well then . . ." She unwrapped the toweling and tossed it aside. Gordon's face split with a smile. He spread his arms out wide and bent slightly at the knees. The man was ready to lunge at her. The knowledge sent a crazy twist of excitement through her that was rooted deep inside her feminine nature. She turned and ran.

She heard his wet feet slapping against the floor, but they dried too quickly, leaving her no way to gauge how close he was. The hair on the back of her neck stood up, and she couldn't control the need to look back over her shoulder.

Gordon's face was a mask of savage pleasure. He offered her a growl moments before he scooped her up and tossed her over his shoulder. She squealed, but he laughed heartily and spread one large hand over her bare bottom. He turned and covered the space to the bed with quick strides. She bounced in a tangle of limbs when he tossed her onto the sheets. His body rising up over hers looked impossibly hard and demanding. Her teeth bit into her lower lip as nervousness invaded her. He placed a knee on the bed, crawling up to join her.

"Do nae lose yer trust in me now, lass. That would wound me more surely than an arrow."

He placed one solid knee between her thighs, and she flinched in spite of every bit of confidence he had built in her. His expression tightened, his eyes filling with concern.

"I do have faith in you, Gordon." Jemma lifted her hands, reaching for him. He lowered his weight, spreading her thighs with gentle motions of his hands before allowing his body to settle on top of hers. A soft murmur of enjoyment crossed her lips. There was something intensely satisfying about having his weight on top of her, something that she had never expected.

" 'Tis something I treasure, lass."

He framed her face in his hands and pressed a kiss against her lips. It began as a slow motion of his mouth against hers, but his passion burned too hot to maintain the slow pace. His kiss became harder, more demanding, and she opened her mouth to allow his tongue to penetrate. Her body ached for the same thing, and her thighs rose up to clasp his hips in invitation.

She felt the head of his cock nudging at the opening to her passage again. Her hands tightened on his shoulders as he began to move forward. It was slow but steady, his hard flesh tunneling into her softer core. Her head arched back as pain began to burn along her passage, hundreds of pinpoints of pain where the skin was refusing to stretch.

"Easy, lass, ye can take me. 'Tis the way ye were made, to take my length."

His words were soothing, but her body still hurt. His hips pulled back and thrust into her once again. This time his cock split her, burrowing into her in spite of the resistance her body offered him. His flesh was harder and it pressed onward, opening her passage with a slow thrust that sent the breath rushing out of her lungs. He withdrew again, offering her relief from the worst of the pain, and she dragged a deep breath in but it went rushing back out when he thrust smoothly into her again. This time his cock traveled deep, the hard flesh lodging itself all the way inside her. The bed beneath her back kept her in place, making it impossible to move away. She was forced to endure the burning pain while her passage adjusted to being penetrated.

Yet the pain subsided fast. Jemma opened her eyes when she realized that there was naught but a dull ache remaining.

"Aye, lass, that's the worst of it." He pulled his length free and then thrust forward again. This time, without the burning pain, she was free to feel his hard member stroking along her clitoris. It produced a spark of delight that traveled to where her passage echoed it when his flesh was once more deep inside her.

"And now, I'll introduce ye to the best of it."

He began to thrust in slow motions, but there was still a hard edge to each stroke. Jemma heard herself moan, and she couldn't have controlled the sound if she had tried. Her body was completely focused on the hard flesh tunneling into it, her passage eagerly taking him now while her hips lifted to ensure that he penetrated deeply each time. There was no reason to think or even keep her eyes open. She wanted to sink back into the pool of sensations produced by the action of their bodies moving together.

"That's it, lass, work with me, show me the pace ye like."

"I will . . ."

His breathing was turning rough, and his hands twisted in her hair. His thrusts came faster and harder, shaking the bed beneath them. But she enjoyed the pace, her body eagerly meeting it. Pleasure tightened inside her with each deep penetration from his member, the sliding motion of his withdrawing building a growing desperation to have him impale her again. She lifted her hips up, almost frantically seeking out his next plunge. Her heart raced and she could feel his pounding when he pushed his length deep inside her and their bodies were pressed tightly together for a moment.

The pleasure he'd given her with his mouth paled to the delight boiling inside her now. This was deeper and more intense. Her hips bucked off the bed to take his next thrust quicker, and when he pressed completely inside her it burst, forcing a cry from her lips. She arched, and her thighs grasped his hips while the sensation tore through her, wringing her body and bathing it in satisfaction. Gordon plunged a few final times into her with rough thrusts before he let out a harsh sound and she felt his body pulling taut. Deep inside she felt his seed spurting out to soak into her womb. The hot stream of fluid triggered another soft contraction of pleasure from her body. This time her passage tried to milk his member, tightening around it to pull his seed forward.

The pleasure reduced her to a quivering mass of muscles. She lay on the bed, uncaring if her hands were flung out like a broken doll. She lacked even enough strength to pull them closer to her body. She only had the will to breathe, her chest rising and falling in deep breaths while her heart beat with hard motions beneath her breasts.

A soft kiss was pressed against her lips before Gordon rolled off her. He slid an arm beneath her waist and pulled her against his side. Her head was pushed down onto his chest, and she heard his heart rate matching her own.

"I swear it is going to be the warmest winter ever in this chamber."

Jemma smiled, but she wasn't sure if it was due to his words or the soothing strokes his hands were making over her, long passes of his hands over her back and along the curve of her hip. Gentle strokes that were tender, so tender she felt tears stinging her eyes because he certainly didn't have to be so caring; he was her husband not her lover.

Maybe he could be both . . .

Jemma tried to hush her inner voice. It was a dangerous idea, one that promised her heartache if it did not blossom. But she failed because there was already too much tenderness between them. She could not shut the doors to her feelings; they felt as if they were blocked open.

"Why did ye insist on the bed?"

Gordon sounded sleepy, but his hand froze on her shoulder. "I did nae think to ask ye before. Ye had a reason, yea?"

Jemma buried her face against his chest, hoping the man would think her exhausted. She didn't want the tensions of the day to shatter the moment.

"Tell me, Jemma. I will nae have ye keeping things secret from me that are important to ye."

"And I do not plan to be a wife who whines to you of every trifle."

He drew in a stiff breath because it didn't take him long to deduce what her reason was now that passion wasn't distracting him. "Who questioned yer virtue?" His tone was hard now, and he sat up, taking her along with him to sit her next to him. He cupped her chin and raised it before giving her the chance to do it herself. His pride was wounded, and it shone in his eyes.

"That is it, isna it, lass? Who spoke against ye?"

She shook off his hold. "Don't treat me like a child, Gordon."

"Then answer me like a woman who is nae trying to hide the answer."

She shrugged. "It does not matter who spoke, what is important is how many listened."

He frowned. " 'Twas Anyon. No one else would dare or worry about yer place here so much."

Jemma scoffed at him and tried to move off the bed, but she froze when she caught sight of the sheet. Bright red blood marred its surface, drawing a shiver from her in spite of her desire to see exactly this.

"I am going to put her out."

"You will not, Gordon Dwyre." Jemma didn't care if her tone was something no wife should use with her husband. The Church would chastise her for it, her brother would disapprove, but none of that seemed to matter. Her dealings with Gordon had always been poised on the border of uncivilized behavior, and it was a truth that she enjoyed it.

"There are rules beyond the confines of this chamber,

Jemma, that you know must be observed. She was my mistress, if ye may even call a few tumbles by such a title. She is to be turned out."

He stood up and stalked across the chamber to swipe something off the floor.

"Those rules are exactly why I am telling you that she shall not be turned out by you." Jemma followed him, determined to gain her wish.

"Ye are nae making any sense, woman."

"Exactly." He snorted at her triumphant tone. "You do not understand because running the house is a woman's duty. I would not comprehend many of the things that you order your retainers to do because I am not a man and was not raised to understand the duties that are yours. So I tell you again, Gordon, leave Anyon be. I set her down and will do whatever else is needed."

He drew in a stiff breath, his expression remaining inflexible. "Except that Anyon is nae causing trouble over her duties, she's questioning my devotion to the vows I took with ye."

He shook her dressing robe out with a snap that betrayed how much his temper was still burning. He held it open for her, and she lifted one arm with confusion turning her mood dreary.

Was he going to send her back to her old chamber now that he'd had her?

She couldn't help but think it. Too many couples that wed for the same reasons they had slept apart.

Well, she would not whimper. She was a woman now, not some child wed too early because of her fortune and her groom's taste for a girl in his bed who would be simple to dominate because she was too young to know her own thoughts. She would also speak her mind even if it displeased her groom. Her heart ached, the tenderness that had been hers but a few moments ago now wilting.

"I am your wife, Gordon, and I shall do whatever is necessary to run this house. Your doubt insults me. Do you want a wife or a pampered princess who is useless besides her ability to take your seed?"

He cursed. Jemma held her chin steady while she knotted the tie to keep her dressing robe closed.

" 'Tis something I understand, lass, the need to know yer word is respected." He picked up his kilt and wrapped the fabric around his waist a few times before tossing the rest of the fabric up and over his shoulder. It lacked the normal pleats and wasn't as accommodating to his stride, but he seemed to care little about that. He yanked the door to the chamber open and grabbed a rope that hung next to the threshold. He yanked it several times before turning around and sending the door shut with a hard motion that slammed it.

"I'll grant ye that, lass, the need to nae be thought too weak to command those under yer authority."

"Thank you."

He laughed, and it was not a kind sound. Gordon covered the distance between them, and she was able to see his expression once again. It sent a shiver down her spine because this was not a man to cross, not in his current frame of mind. Something dangerous glittered in his eyes.

He lifted one finger and pointed it at her as the sound of booted feet began to pound on the stairs leading up to their chamber.

"But be very sure that I will be setting the matter clear as far as me men go."

Whoever was on their way up the stairs didn't stop to knock on the chamber door. They pushed right inside, and Jemma found herself stepping back into the shadows the edges of the chamber offered because her confidence in being so scantily covered did not extend to anyone except Gordon. Two of Gordon's captains tugged on the corners of their bonnets and kept their gazes on their laird while they waited for him to tell them why they had been summoned.

Gordon pointed toward the bed. "There seems to be some discussion about my bride's purity. Ye will witness the fact that she came to me a virgin and that there was no blood on the sheets this morning as I did nae jump on her last night the moment the doors were sealed like some beardless boy that does nae know how to stroke his bride's passion. We were interrupted last night before I got to deflowering her and I am nae happy to hear there has been talk to the contrary."

Several women entered the open door in time to hear their laird's words. One was the cook that pressed her lips into a hard line. The woman slept in the kitchen and had clearly come straight from her bed, for her long hair was hanging down her back in a single thick braid.

She joined the captains near the bed and lifted a candle lantern high to illuminate the sheets. Jemma stepped back farther into the shadows, tears prickling her eyes. It was ridiculous to cry over such an expected thing. Being English only meant she dare not overlook any detail. Brides suffered such exhibitions all over the world; it was very unwise to allow it to upset her so.

"Now begone and make sure it is known that I will nae have the matter questioned."

"Aye, Laird."

The captains offered Gordon a tug on their bonnets before quitting the room. The cook snapped her fingers at the other maids who had arrived behind her, and she herself pulled the soiled sheet from the bed while they brought forward a clean one.

"Leave the sheet on the table since it is raining."

"Aye, Laird." The cook did as instructed before snapping her fingers at the maids once more and shoving them toward the door. It closed behind them in a hard sound that drove a spike through the last of her heart.

She shouldn't expect anything different. It was the way things were and the world was an imperfect place. Mustering her strength, she walked toward the door, intent on playing her part, but she couldn't quite bring herself to stop and lower herself before leaving. It was too submissive, and Gordon would know it was false.

Well . . . the doors were shut so she would be herself while behind them.

For the moment all she truly craved was an end to her duties as bride.

Chapter Nine

"Where are ye thinking to go, Jemma?"

That dangerous note was still in Gordon's voice. Her fingertips had not yet even touched the door.

She turned to discover him moving toward her. "Clearly we are finished consummating our union. I wish to sleep."

He stopped a single stride from her and aimed a hard look at her.

"Ye sleep here."

"But—"

He didn't care for her hesitation and he acted upon that displeasure just as quickly as he had always done, scooping her up and carrying her to where he wanted her. He reached into the bed and yanked the tie open before reaching behind her to pull the dressing gown up and over her head with one powerful motion of his arms. She was dropped back onto her knees with nothing except her hair to cover her.

"Here, Jemma. Ye want me to respect yer authority over the house, then ye shall accept my will when it comes to how to manage me men." He tore his plaid off and crawled into bed with her. His cock was hard once more, and she shivered because no matter how much her feelings ached, she desired him.

"Ye sleep here, in the place that I never brought Anyon or any other who was not my wife."

He pulled her up against him, binding her to his larger body with solid arms.

"That will send the message to my men that there is no doubt who is mistress here."

He pressed a hard kiss against her mouth, demanding compliance with one hand cradling the back of her head to hold her still for the ravishment. Sweetness flowed from the kiss, soothing the raw emotions that had sliced at her. His cock was hard against her, but Gordon finished their kiss and lay down behind her. He bound her to his length with strong arms, tucking her head beneath his chin and pulling the bed covers up to cover her. One of his feet tucked over hers, but he did nothing to try to relieve the swollen cock that was hard against her bottom.

He sighed, nuzzling against her head and inhaling the scent of her hair.

"Do not think me harsh, Jemma. Men are different from women."

Confusion settled over her, but the trust that she had felt so strongly overwhelmed it. The corners of her mouth tugged up into a satisfied grin. His body was so warm against her, his arms so tender, and the night the perfect shield against the harsh reality that sunrise would bring.

"You never brought anyone here, to this bed? Not even your first wife?" Her voice was soft, and she heard him sigh behind her.

"I changed chambers after I gave Imogen her wish to join a convent. I could nae stomach sleeping in the bed she detested so much."

"You wouldn't call Anyon your mistress?"

He snorted. "A mistress is a woman a man has affection for, Jemma. All I did with Anyon was take what she flaunted beneath me nose. I see that she was scheming now, but I did nae at the time."

A hint of weariness reflected in his voice. As laird there were many times that women had tried to secure what they wanted from him by offering him tumbles.

"I shall have to make sure I flaunt myself before you often so to keep you from noticing any others."

She heard him draw in a stiff breath. Jemma nibbled on her lower lip while she waited to see what his response might be. Many a bride had also been forced to face the fact that her husband would wander where he pleased, with whom he pleased, and she would be expected to remain silent upon the matter of his indiscretions.

" 'Tis something I will look forward to, lass; indeed, I will mostly likely dream of it tonight." He groaned. "Now go to sleep, Jemma, else I lose the restraint to keep out of ye while ye are yet so tender."

He stroked her hip and she allowed her eyelids to shut. There was comfort and tenderness in his embrace, and she allowed it to carry her off into slumber.

"Mistress?"

It was Ula who woke her. Jemma rubbed her burning eyes and tried to focus her thoughts. Her mind was a foggy mess that defied her demands to clear.

"Ye have missed service, but the laird bid me allow ye to sleep. It is growing late now."

Jemma opened her eyes and saw the sunlight shining in the open windows to make large bright rectangles that stretched across the floor. She sat up and gasped when the bed covers fell down to her waist, allowing her breasts to be seen.

"I'm so sorry for sleeping so late. I can't imagine why I did."

Ula was more composed than Jemma. The housekeeper held up a chemise that she eased over Jemma's head and arms to cover her before she stepped out of the bed.

"It has been an eventful week for ye, Mistress. I imagine ye are in need of a few hours of rest now that things are more settled."

Ula raised her voice so that the maids working in the chamber were certain to hear her.

"Ah yes, things are far more settled now, Ula."

There was a splash of water and then the sounds of flowing water. Jemma turned to see one side of the huge bathing tub hoisted into the air by a pulley that she had not seen hanging from the ceiling last night. There was a thick hook holding one end of the tub, and one of the maids pulled on the rope to lift the tub. On the opposite side of the tub was a lower point in its rim. A gutter was fitted against it while a smaller opening in the wall was revealed at the floor level. One maid pulled on the rope raising the far end of the tub while the other held the gutter in place and all the water rushed out to flow down the side of the tower.

So clever.

"Ye may have bathe every day, Mistress, no matter what weather."

Ula was making a point of addressing her as Mistress.

"The laird has gone on to help rebuild the home that was burned two nights ago. He'll return tonight."

"Of course. It is good to hear that he is seeing to his people."

So she would see to her duties as well. Jemma took one last look at the bed, smiling when she considered how much she longed for the shorter days of winter because it promised longer nights with Gordon.

She was a wanton. There was no doubt but she was happy. In fact it felt like a bubble of contentment encased her. There was nothing she found distasteful, not even the flapping of the soiled sheet in the wind from outside the chamber window.

She hurried off to the church, and the priest frowned at her for missing service, but he welcomed her into the sanctuary and began a quick service for her. Only the nuns and younger priests were in attendance, but as she was Mistress of the castle, they stopped their duties to stand and observe the service. Jemma took the Mass, sipping from the golden chalice and taking the small piece of bread he offered. She refused to quibble over the fact that such a service was illegal in England. She was married to a Scot, and women often had to be more practical than men when it came to adjusting their thinking. A princess such as Mary or Elizabeth Tudor might be allowed to place their foot firmly on the floor and refuse to bend to the whim of their royal father, but the rest of the country had to live in peace with the favored church.

The great hall was nearly empty, but the maids there lowered themselves when she passed them. The cook began snapping her fingers, and the little popping sounds echoed in the mostly empty hall. Maids brought forth a fine meal of cereal and fruit along with warmed cider that had been mulled with cinnamon. Jemma took a moment to inhale the scent of the costly spice before sipping at the drink. She would have to tell the cook not to use such expensive things on common days. But since the cider was served, she savored every drop and chewed on the small brown piece of cinnamon.

Another snap popped from the long worktables, and Jemma turned to see Anyon gaining the cook's attention once again. This morning Anyon wore her linen cap correctly. It was tied securely beneath her chin like the other maids' and her hair was tucked up into its gathered back. Although Anyon's chemise was tugged up to cover her breasts more properly, the cook was still riding the girl unmercifully. With another snap from the cook's fingers, Anyon carried a small copper pitcher toward the high table where Jemma was seated.

The girl's lips were white from being pressed so tightly together, but she lowered herself before carefully refilling the cider mug. Jemma felt her stomach sour, but she clamped down on her own pity. Anyon had spent too many days acting as a better to everyone, and now she would have to face those she had spit in the face of.

But the unease in Jemma's belly persisted, so she rose from the table and went to find the estate books. It was time to begin the duties of a wife.

Gordon wiped the sweat from his brow and smiled. The afternoon sun was bright with no sign of the rain that had blanketed the countryside yesterday.

"Whoa there, laddie, who's that dreaming the day away?"

It was Kerry who teased him. His captain tossed up another bundle of thatch before climbing up to help him secure it to the roof supports.

"Ye're jealous, Kerry, and I'll tell ye straight, ye have every right to be."

"Och now, that's unkind. Just unkind in the worst way."

Gordon bent over and felt his back give a twinge of discomfort for the number of hours he'd been working on the roof. They were nearing the top of the house now, and soon he'd have the right to ride home to the woman he'd been thinking about since he left. The sound of children drew his attention. He straightened back up to see the family's four youngest playing in the yard. They wore bright smiles while they watched their new home being built.

"It will be a blessing to have a few of those following ye

around." Kerry shot him a smirk. "Hopefully all girls, because if they're boys, the poor sods will look like ye, and that would make them ugly creatures for sure."

"Kerry, I have a fine memory, and ye are going to marry someday."

"I could never choose between all the lasses that adore me, Laird. 'Tis a fact that I can't bear to give up any of them in favor of the other."

Gordon bent back over. "Ye just wait, Kerry, the Church is going to lock ye in the stocks yet and nae release ye 'til ye repent and wed."

"Not if I keep slipping the priest the wine he likes so well."

Several men snickered in response because their priest was a plump man in spite of his vows of poverty. His robes were fuller than most of their kilts, but the man was fair, taking what was offered and only taxing those who could afford it. There had been worse clergy on Barras land before.

A sharp whistle drew Gordon's attention back to the ground.

"Rider coming up fast, Laird!"

Every man stopped to watch the youth riding his horse like the son of Satan himself was chasing him. Dust rose up behind the horse in a dull-colored trail.

"That's young Travis."

"Aye." Gordon climbed down from the roof, his neck muscles tightening. Travis was only twelve and not yet old enough to ride out with the retainers. But the lad could sit a horse and stay in the saddle better than some of his men. If someone had sent the lad out, time was essential.

"Laird, yer bride is ailing!" Travis began yelling before he even stopped his horse. The animal walked in a circle, trying to cool off. The youth pulled hard on the reins to turn the animal so that he was facing his laird again and might be heard.

"The cook suspects poison."

* * *

Jemma opened her eyes and stared at the blurry haze in front of her. Voices surrounded her, but she couldn't seem to force her brain to make sense of the sounds. It was almost as if she had suddenly been taken off to a land where no one spoke English. Everything moved too slowly, swirling around her in nightmarish motion. She wanted water, but her hand shook when she stretched it out, her strength failing her before her arm reached out far enough to gain any attention. Instead her body felt like it was falling through the air. Down, down, and still farther down. She waited for the pain that would be hers once she hit the bottom of the abyss but it never came, because she never stopped falling.

Gordon threw someone out of the way and didn't know who it was. He didn't care, either. His room was full of people once more, only today they lacked the sense of joy that had been present on his wedding night. No one was doing much but watching and waiting. His attention shifted to the priest, and Gordon felt his mouth go dry.

The priest was already there. His vestments on and his lips muttering the final words of last rites. He finished, and the assembled people all raised their hands to cross themselves. Two of the church nuns knelt near the bedside, their fingers moving on their wooden rosary beads while they concentrated on saying prayers for the woman lying there.

"I'm very sorry, my son." The priest passed him by with two younger priests in training following him.

Several of the maids began wailing, the sound driving a stake through Gordon's heart. He staggered, lacking the strength to cover the remaining distance to the bed.

How could she be gone?

"What are ye crying for?" The cook burst through the door,

her hands full with a steaming pot. "Get out of my way, ye useless lack wits!"

"But the priest gave the mistress her last rites."

The cook scoffed and kept moving toward the bed. "Well, that's well and good, but no one's dead yet so stop yer whining. I don't abandon hope so quickly, else I might have sent half of ye back to yer mothers on the second day ye served in this house."

The cook suddenly noticed him. "Good, a pair of hands that are strong enough to help me."

"Help?"

"Aye." The cook reached into the bed and whisked the covers away from Jemma. Her lips pressed into a hard line. "She's too hot beneath all of this. Poor lass has enough to deal with without being smothered."

The lack of bed coverings allowed him to set eyes on Jemma. He stared at her and watched her chest rise and fall. It was a shallow motion, barely noticeable, but it filled him with strength.

"Get out! Anyone who isn't helping, get ye gone from this chamber!"

There was a flurry of motion toward the door. Several shrieks came from those trampled in the frantic crush of bodies trying to obey the laird's commands. Gordon dismissed them from his mind. He ripped the bed clothing even farther away from his wife, throwing it toward the nuns.

"Gordon?"

He gasped, sitting heavily on the side of the bed. Jemma's eyes were open just the tiniest amount. He reached out to grasp her hand.

"Aye, lass, I'm here."

She nodded and opened her mouth, but nothing came out

except a dry rattle of breath. Her face was the same color as her chemise and her lips bloodless.

"Sit her up now, Laird, as gentle as ye would a babe."

Gordon realized that he was afraid to touch her. His hands shook, and he discovered he was grinding his teeth while he reached for Jemma. Her eyes remained on him, giving him the strength to slip his arms beneath her shoulders and raise her up.

"Now support her head. I forgot that ye have most likely never held a babe."

"I hope to." He shifted one hand so that it clasped Jemma's neck. She felt too delicate, too small now. The woman who had wrestled with him had somehow vanished, and left in her place was this mere whisper of life. But it was the most precious thing he had ever felt. Gordon gathered her up, placing one of his bent legs behind her and sitting behind her to make sure she was steady.

"What do ye plan?"

The cook was stirring something into her pot. Steam rose from it and a bitter scent. He suddenly frowned. "And why don't I know yer Christian name? Everyone calls ye Cook."

"Because I detest me given name, but to say so would be to disrespect me father, so call me Cook. 'Tis a better name than the one I was baptized with, for sure."

The cook pulled a small ladle from the waist tie of her apron and used it to measure out some of her brew into a pitcher. It was the smallest pitcher in the house, a pewter one used for serving cream.

"We need to help her drink, or she'll be a ghost by tomorrow for sure."

The cook gently placed the dimpled part of that pitcher against Jemma's mouth and tipped just one spoonful of the fluid against her tongue. Gordon's wife jerked and lifted her chin.

"Forgive me, Mistress, for I know 'tis a bitter concoction."

The cook placed another measure of it in Jemma's mouth, and this time she swallowed it. Gordon felt sweat trickle down the side of his face. Every muscle felt as though it was tight enough to snap. The cook kept placing spoonfuls of her brew inside his wife's mouth until Jemma sighed.

"Better . . ." Jemma turned her head to rub against him before her eyes slid closed and her breathing became shallow. So shallow it sent fear through him once again.

"That will have to do for the moment."

The cook stood up and blew out a long breath. Her eyes swept Jemma from head to toe, and her face became clouded with serious thought.

"That was an antidote?"

"It's something I learned when I was a young woman, but I don't know if it will be doing the job needed."

Gordon gently laid his wife down and pulled up just enough sheet to cover her.

The cook continued. "Ye see, we don't know what was used to poison her, so I don't know if what I mixed up was what she needed or if it came too late. The mistress was working on the books, and no one knows how long she was ill before Ula discovered her. It's possible that the evil person behind this has already done the wicked deed by stealing her away from us."

Gordon felt a shiver go down his spine. Anger flashed through him like a spark through black powder. Rage exploded inside him, and the helplessness in his wife's pale face only made that anger burn hotter.

"Anyon." He snarled the word.

The cook's eyes went wide, and horror clouded her face.

"Tell me, woman, why do you look like that?"

The cook wrung her apron with nervous hands. "I sent the girl to serve the mistress cider this morning. I thought it would impress upon her the place she needed to learn was hers. I never thought Anyon had evil in her heart."

"That bitch tried to drown my wife earlier this week."

"Lads fight and then they drink together when their tempers have cooled, Laird. I thought Anyon just needed a firm hand to teach her to be content with what God had given her. I never thought she'd turn to murder. It still baffles me; I've knelt in church beside her. How could that be—how could so much evil be right there and none of us see it?"

Gordon ground his teeth together. "I don't know." He forced himself to think, to make his mind work despite the rage burning in his gut.

"I don't know, but I do know this. Someone did this foul deed and I am going to see them hanged for it."

Chapter Ten

"The Baron Ryppon is on the road with his men."

Gordon turned and followed Kerry up to the top of the wall. He looked through the spy glass and inspected the flags being carried by the men preceding the baron. Those flags danced wildly because Curan was riding hard. The horses were lathered, and his men were stripped down to only breastplate armor and helmet to lighten them.

"Allow them through!"

There was a hustle along the walls, his men filling the positions in spite of his order to allow the English force to enter. He couldn't blame them for that, inviting an English party of knights inside the curtain wall would have most of his Scottish neighbors questioning his sanity.

He felt on the verge of losing his mind. He could feel the rage melting his principles until he was nothing but a savage willing to strike out at anything that might have been responsible.

That was not the way to trap the guilty. He knew it and was trying desperately to maintain his wits. Descending the stairs, he went to meet his friend. Desperate times called for equally desperate measures. There was no one in the castle he might trust. Whoever had poisoned Jemma was one of his own. It infuriated him, it sickened him, but it was the truth.

Curan was out of the saddle and moving quickly to meet him.

"She still lives."

"I want to see her, now."

Gordon grunted and turned with an English baron following him. His father was sure to rise from his grave tonight for the fact that he was making an English army welcome in his home, but that was a torment Gordon would gladly suffer if he gained what he desired.

Jemma.

That was it. He needed his wife and didn't want to think about the very real fact that she might not live to see the next day.

Gordon held up a hand and pushed the chamber doors open slowly to keep them from making noise. Whispers came from inside where the nuns were still on their knees praying. They took shifts with their other sisters, an hourglass set on the bed to mark their allotted time.

"Send them out, Barras. We need to talk."

"Aye." Gordon crossed the room and stood near the bed. One of the sisters lifted her face. He pointed at her, and she looked at the hourglass.

"Go, Sister. My wife's brother would be in private with his sister."

The nun hastily crossed herself and grabbed the hourglass. "The English are heretics. You should keep them from her and save her soul."

"That sounds as though you are judging me, Sister." Curan stepped up closer to the bed and eyed the nun. She grabbed her fellow sister's arm and pulled her off her knees.

"God will judge us all."

"Yes, He shall." Curan leaned forward with his response, and the nuns slipped on the floor because they tried to run so quickly. The chamber door burst open as they hit it hard. Curan shrugged.

"I seem to have forgotten how to deal with nuns."

"I hear being raised in England has that effect."

Curan knelt down, and his armor shifted and filled the chamber with the soft sounds of metal moving against metal. He sat his helmet aside and reached for his sister's hand.

"Open the bed drapes, I need light."

Gordon slid the drapes back to allow the afternoon light to illuminate the bed. Jemma's breath was the only sound in the room, and it was far too faint. Her brother lifted her hand, tilting it so that the light fell on it.

"What are you looking for?"

"A blue tinge on the fingernails. It's a sign of eastern poisons." Curan continued to inspect his sister's hand but finally gave a grunt of satisfaction. "There is none, and for that we should be grateful. The Moors brew poison that is deadly."

The chamber door opened, and several people slipped inside. They walked carefully, mindful of their steps. Curan turned to speak to one.

"Her nails are white but not blue."

The man was thin and lanky, obviously young. Gordon glared at Curan. "How can someone that young know anything of value when it comes to poisons?"

The knight behind the youth reached forward and lifted the helmet off the youth's head. It proved an easy task because the youth only measured up to the knight's shoulder. The helmet had hidden a face that was clearly female. She was quite a beauty, even lacking feminine clothing.

"This is the Lady Justina." And the woman was dressed every inch like a boy. A pair of baggy britches hid the curves of her hips, and a solid armor breastplate covered up her other feminine curves.

Gordon crossed his arms in front of his chest. "The same lady who betrayed ye by betraying the location of the side gate that yer bride used to escape through?"

"Aye." Curan nodded. "She has been my guest since that time for I cannot in good conscience send her back to a guardian who charges her with such tasks."

"You take too much upon yourself." Lady Justina sent a hard look toward Curan.

"I disagree, Lady. If the one who sent you wants you back, he can ask me and admit that he sent you."

Lady Justina shook her head but Gordon had no patience for their quarrel. He only had time for Jemma.

"Why is she here? I have enough people I distrust around me. I don't need one of yers to watch me back for."

"She is here because she has spent her entire life at court and knows far more about poison than any of us, because that is the place where such evil is used often."

Gordon narrowed his eyes, but the lady didn't crumple beneath his displeasure. She offered him a serene look, but if one took a moment to peer deeper into her eyes, they could see the strength hidden there. She looked delicate, but she was solid like stone. It was something he was more accustomed to seeing in knights. That look which a man gained from witnessing death.

"Reject me if you wish, Lord Barras, but I will tell you plainly that I am your best hope of catching this assassin, and that you need to reconsider sending me away."

Gordon felt one of his eyebrows rise. "Ye've caught so many of them, I suppose?"

"A few."

"Which is more than I have." Curan cast a look back at his sister. "If Jemma survives, she will only face waiting for the next attack or returning home with me."

Gordon stiffened. He clamped down on the denial he wanted to issue to Curan because he had to. Never once had he been defeated when fighting against men he could see coming at him, but this manner of attack was one that he knew no way to challenge.

"What is yer plan, Lady?"

Justina held up a hand and turned in a full circle, inspecting every bit of the room. She began to walk, looking at the floor and pushing at any boards that appeared uneven. It was the sort of inspection that placed confidence in him when he had been so sure mistrust was the only thing he might have for the Lady. Justina finished and came back to drop to her knees and crawl beneath the bed that Jemma slept in. They heard her tapping on the boards with her hands before she emerged from the other side.

"First we shall move Jemma, but it must be done in secret and I must inspect the chamber before she is taken there."

Justina stood up and wet one fingertip before reaching out to run it along the sheet that Jemma lay on. She tasted her finger gingerly.

"Ye think there is poison in the sheet?"

Justina licked another finger and ran it along the chemise his wife wore. "It would not be the first time, and do not doubt that assassins are very clever. I have seen gloves and saddles poisoned, food and fabric, too. There is no decency in these assassins; they will poison bedding and not care that a husband or wife dies along with their intended victim. Poison the wet nurse to get at the child she suckles."

"I didna take ill and I slept in that bed."

"Except that your staff most likely changed the sheet this morning before she was found, and if someone truly wishes her dead, they would be wise to use more than one dose."

Justina pressed her fingers against Jemma's face, peering intently at her skin. "It looks like common toxins such as hemlock or toad stools."

Curan gave a soft grunt. "You see why I brought her."

"It is becoming clearer, if not more disturbing, to see such knowledge in one so delicate."

Justina frowned, the harshest expression that had crossed her lips. "Delicate does not survive long at court. My husband died of poison."

"My condolences."

The lady lifted her fair face to stare straight at him. "My only regret is that it took him too gently to hell and that I was not the one who fed it to him. He was a very cruel man and killed too many innocents before his ways came back to haunt him." The lady suddenly looked older than her years. "And my father knew it well when he wed me to him. That is court; nothing matters but ambition. Not even murder."

Justina look into Jemma face. "But perhaps some good might come of it now."

Lady Justina searched his towers. Gordon paced the floor in front of his wife's bed while he waited. The lady had not enlightened him on the rest of her plan, saying only that she needed to keep the information from as many ears as possible.

"Gordon?"

He turned in a swirl of kilts to discover Jemma watching him.

"Good evening to ye, lass."

Jemma tried to smile but her lips were dry and the skin cracked. Pain went through them, but it was mild compared to the burning that was in her belly. It was even more than her belly because the fire licked over her back and down into her legs.

But the sight of Gordon soothed her. He moved toward her, and the bed shifted when he sat on its edge. Just that small motion sent pain spiking through her. It must have been plain on her face for Gordon frowned.

"Do not."

He picked up one of her hands and held it gently between his two hands. "Do nae what, lass?"

"Do not treat me so." Two tears eased from the corners of her eyes, bringing relief from the dryness she hadn't realized tormented her, but the salt stung. "You have never been anything but bold with me. I like that."

"Well then, lass, ye'll have to be getting well so that we can get back to that."

He wanted her to, she could see the need shimmering in his eyes. The pain increased, burning hot now that she was fully awake. Poisons were horrible things; some of them took a long time to kill, eating away at their victims before finally snuffing out their lives. She had always known that she would die someday, but it had never been something that she feared. Living had been the challenge when her father died. Now she had a reason to want to cling to life. Her hands tightened around Gordon's, and the feel of his warm flesh against her own was soothing.

"I love you."

He flinched, a muscle twitching along the side of his jaw. He leaned closer, laying her hand on her stomach before stroking his fingertips along her cheeks.

"Do nae do that, lass."

The hard edge to his voice drew a soft smile from her in spite of the pain it sent along her lips.

"But I do and—"

"And ye will nae say good-bye to me now, Jemma. Ye will survive this and ye will be my wife."

If the force of his will could force fate to heed him, then Jemma would live. She stared at the determination in his eyes, trying to absorb some of it, but her body hurt too badly.

Gordon turned and lifted something off a table that had been placed beside the bed. It was a small pewter cup, such as a child might use.

"Some water will make ye feel better." He lifted her head and supported her neck with a firm hand while sliding behind her to brace her with his body. "I may take to feeding ye, lass, because it gives me the chance to hold ye."

"Hmmm . . . I find it strangely attractive myself, except for the part where I recall that I am helpless."

"Drink, lass, and yer strength will return."

"Do not drink that."

Gordon jerked the water spilling onto the bed. With one fluid motion he pulled his sword from where it was leaning against the bedside. There was an answering slide of steel against steel as the knight trailing the boy unsheathed his sword. Jemma felt surprise flash through her, for the knight was Synclair and it seemed as if it had been a long time since she had seen him.

"You must not give her anything that has come through your kitchens."

Gordon slid out from behind her and lowered her onto the pillow with one arm, but he kept his attention on the boy who was telling him what to do. Jemma stared at the youth, trying to decide what it was about him that she found odd.

"What ye must nae do is surprise me, Lady Justina, else there will be dire results. I am nae in the mood to ask too many questions."

Gordon replaced his sword, but he kept an eye on Synclair until the man followed suit.

"Lady?" Jemma turned her head and recognized Lady Justina. Synclair nodded at her in response. Gordon turned to sweep her with a keen look, ensuring that she was settled well before turning back to look at Lady Justina.

"Why are you dressed like a boy, Justina?" It was a dangerous thing to do because the Church spoke against women dressing in men's clothing. Punishment was harsh, but even worse were the superstitions that attached themselves to those females who donned britches.

They would be sterile or too small to take a man's member or become diseased, and the list continued. There were even those who claimed witches were girls who had worn britches, and the clothing had turned them against the natural order of the world.

"Fine, nothing from the kitchens." Gordon walked over to the window the water was drawn through. He pulled on the cable and turned over more than a dozen buckets before he filled the small cup with water and carried it back to the bed.

Justina walked to the open shutter and looked down. Synclair was right behind her, and he even reached out to pull on the rope and watch the buckets rise from the river below.

"That should keep them busy for a moment." Gordon lifted the mug to her mouth, and Jemma sighed as the cool liquid soothed her dry lips.

"I have decided on which chamber she shall go to."

Gordon released the back of her head and settled her against the pillows before turning to look at Justina.

"And how do ye plan to feed her if nothing may come from the kitchens?"

"My maidservant Claire will do all that is needed and use

only those things that were brought from Amber Hill. I will re-side here and sample what is sent up from the kitchens."

Jemma didn't think she might feel worse, but hearing Justina make her suggestion filled her with dread.

"Justina, no, you must not risk yourself."

The lady moved across the floor with a smile on her lips. "Do not worry, Jemma, I will not eat much, only enough to catch the guilty one if they attempt to finish what they have begun. We must make them think you are here, so a woman must take your place. Believe me, I am glad of the chance to do something for your brother."

That brought another feeling of discomfort to her for she hadn't really thought of the woman her brother had at Amber Hill. Lady Justina had betrayed his trust by aiding his bride in escaping the castle. Curan wasn't being vindictive in keeping the lady within his walls; someone powerful at court had sent her there to betray her brother's trust. Curan was keeping Justina away from that man, but the fact remained that Justina had been living there, without a place, and that was some-thing Jemma had tasted recently. It was bitter indeed.

"Synclair will show you the chamber I selected. There is only one window, and that will hopefully keep you from being seen. It is imperative that everyone down to the smallest kitchen girl believes you are still in this chamber and recover-ing well. If it is believed that you are regaining your health, an-other attempt might be made."

"Justina—"

Justina looked at Gordon. "Take her now, she has not the strength for arguing against what is needed to end this threat for good. Rest is what she must have to recover. Do not be foolish enough to think because she is awake, all is well."

"Gordon, don't listen to her—"

"I have no better idea, lass, and keeping ye from harm is something I will do anything to achieve."

Her husband scooped her up, and she couldn't help but curl toward his heat. Her body was too cold, and the heat from his body helped soothe the ache that was threatening to send tears into her eyes. In truth, she felt her small amount of strength beginning to fail. She did feel those tears run down her cheeks because she was grateful to Justina for telling Gordon to take her away.

Her husband carried her through the hallways with Synclair walking ahead of them to make sure no one watched their journey. They left the tower that held the laird's chamber and headed to the oldest one. This tower was round, and the stairs were steep and narrow. Gordon carried her up to the second floor and through a single door.

Her husband stopped and surveyed the room. It was humble but clean. The bed was made with fresh sheets, and thick pillows were piled up so that they would support her. He settled her on them and brushed a hand over the tears that had wet her cheeks.

"I didna mean to hurt ye, lass."

"You didn't. I detest being helpless, and I am too weak to not cry over such an unchangeable thing."

He leaned toward her and kissed one cheek. It was a soft pressing of his lips, but she shivered with the contact. His hand was still cradling her nape, the fingers moving in soft, soothing motions.

"Yer tears wound me, lass. I swear I feel each one more deeply than any cut I have ever received."

"Stay with me."

She was weak and couldn't hold back the words.

"I can nae and make the staff believe that ye are in our

chamber, but I will come often, and be very sure that I will feel the separation keenly, lass."

The door opened, and he jerked his head up.

"I am Claire."

She had her arms full, and Gordon rose to help her. There were small bags and more sheets and towels; even a cooking pot was dangling from the woman's arm. The room had a small fireplace set into the wall and a single window. The window did not have glass but wooden shutters that could be used to close it when the weather was too cold.

"You should go now. I will look after her needs."

Claire was soft spoken, but there was no missing the sound of experience in her tone. It sent a shiver down Jemma's spine, and it drew a cringe from her husband.

"Aye."

He leaned down and kissed her once more. Jemma reached for him and had to force herself not to cling. She was afraid, but so was he. She caught a glimpse of it in his eyes, and her heart clutched that bit of knowledge close.

If he was frightened for her, he might learn to love her. It was an odd hope when she considered the fact that she should be more worried about opening her eyes again. Instead all she had swirling around in her mind was longing for affection from the man who had touched her heart. She took him into her dreams, and that brought her more comfort than any of the prayers that had been muttered at her bedside.

Time became indefinable. Jemma awoke at odd hours; sometimes the church bell woke her, other times it was the wind whistling in through the window. Claire always seemed to be awake when Jemma opened her eyes. The woman moved in a slow motion that was soothing to the eyes. She offered Jemma warm broth that didn't tempt her. Her stomach cramped at the idea of any food, so she closed her eyes and escaped back into sleep.

"Ye need the nourishment, lass."

Gordon's voice drew her back to the harsh world with its discomforts. She opened her eyes to discover that the sunlight was gone and only moonlight shone through the open window.

Her husband lifted her up and placed another pillow behind her to keep her head more elevated.

"There's my lass, open yer eyes and share a bit of supper with me."

"The night feels further gone than supper."

He offered her a smile and a nod. "Aye, it is. The sun will rise in another hour." Claire brought him a small bowl that gently steamed. Jemma wrinkled her nose, the scent of food sickening her, but her husband offered her a spoonful in spite of her disgruntled expression.

"Ye can nae expect to recover without food, lass, and I've gone to quite a bit of trouble to share a bit of a meal with ye."

She opened her mouth and swallowed the soup. A cramp seized her belly. It was so painful she gasped. Gordon set the bowl aside and placed a large hand on her stomach to gently massage the tension from her muscles. His fingers forced the knots to loosen, allowing her to draw breath. Sweat dotted her forehead, and she shook her head.

"No more. I cannot stomach it."

Claire stood nearby, unrelenting in her quiet fashion. The companion took only a single step forward and waited until Gordon turned his attention to her.

"She must eat to cleanse the poison from her flesh, else it will fester."

Gordon's fingers tensed where they still worked the tight

muscles of her belly, and his expression hardened. She'd only seen such determination in him when he faced down the English knights who had tried to kill her. Now it was aimed at her. He picked up the bowl and the spoon, but from the look in his eyes, it might as well have been sword and shield.

"Ye will eat, Jemma, because I know that ye are every bit as stubborn as I am and ye will nae allow this foul deed to take yer life away."

The spoon was pressing against her lips, but it was his tone that made her open her mouth and take his offering.

"The sun is going to rise, and I want ye to see how beautiful the day is, lass."

There was no relenting in him. One spoon after the other, he pressed the contents of the bowl into her. But her insides only gave a few more twinges before accepting the soup. It might even be called soothing except that there was dull pain still lingering everywhere within her. She heard the spoon scraping the bottom of the bowl and sighed with relief. Her eyelids closed in weary fatigue.

"Aye, lass, 'tis enough for the moment." He set the bowl aside, sparing her the last bit. She blew out a sigh of relief while her belly balanced on the edge of nausea. She closed her eyes, trying to think of other things besides the discomfort attempting to make her reject the soup.

"I brought ye something, sweet wife. Open yer eyes and look at what ye reduce me to gathering for ye. Me men believe I've gone soft, and that is a fact."

Jemma opened her eyes to see him lifting a small bundle of heather up off the table. This time he'd tied it with a ribbon.

"A bit of an enticement to make ye want to rise from this bed. The world is out there waiting on ye to fill it with mayhem once again. I believe even the laundresses miss ye."

"They do not." She reached for the heather, her eyes drinking in the sight of the tiny flowers so rich with color. Why had she never noticed the brilliant shade before? Each tiny petal was unique but blended together to form a magnificent display of beauty. It was breathtaking. "So kind of you . . ." Her words trailed off, and the hand she raised to reach for his gift never made it. Now that she was full, her strength seemed to be gone. Her eyelids fluttered shut, but she smiled because she took the vision of that bouquet with her and the feeling of tenderness for the man who had picked it for her.

He'd never been so frightened.

Gordon watched his sleeping wife and ground his teeth in frustration. His sword arm was no use here. The urge to have Anyon whipped until she confessed threatened to boil over, past his logical ability to reason. Although the girl was the likely culprit, they had no proof. He'd never been a laird to condemn without evidence. Barras Castle had never once held the reputation as being a place where mercy was absent. There was no rack in the dungeon or any other foul means of torture. At the moment he felt as if that fact was the only thing holding his hand back from ordering something he might regret.

He wanted to hang her.

Or himself for tumbling her. It had been the rash mistake that many a man made when they'd had one or two ales and the night was cool enough to make the idea of pressing up against something warm enticing.

Aye, a mistake, and one that may have risen up to cut far deeper than he believed he might survive. Jemma was too pale, and dark circles ringed her eyes. Lady Justina would not confirm to him that his wife would recover; instead, the lady offered him only the hope that their action ensured—that no further poison would make its way into her body. He reached out and stroked his hand along his wife's face. Her skin felt more delicate than before, more fragile. But her breath teased his knuckle, giving him solid proof that she was still the wildcat he'd labeled her. There was fight in her yet.

But would it be enough?

That question tore at the very fabric of Gordon's soul.

He stood up and left the chamber, moving toward the sanctuary of the church. There had never been a woman who drove him to his knees, but now he knelt willingly in the hope that God might hear him.

For his lament was great and the blessing he sought more precious than he could say. For Jemma, he would fall to his knees.

Gladly, even humbly.

Chapter Eleven

"I am so tired of this bed." Jemma folded her legs and let out a huff. Claire eyed her from across the room.

"You should spend more time being grateful that you are still alive."

"I am grateful." But she did sound like she was whining, and she was very aware of how fortunate she was to be alive. The sunlight looked brighter and the air smelled better than she had ever noticed. Scooting to the edge of the bed, she stood up, but she had to hug the thick banister that held up the curtain to remain on her feet. Weakness still ruled her.

Claire knew her duty well, for the companion was quickly by her side, offering her shoulders to help support Jemma.

"Do you wish to go to the window, my lady?"

"Yes, thank you."

It was a long journey that frustrated Jemma almost to the point of tears. Now that the pain was gone, she was impatient to return to normal, but her body didn't seem to agree. She needed to lean on Claire for every step. Her knees felt wobbly, and the activity demanded that her heart move faster, but it felt like the muscle was too weak to keep up with the simple task of walking. Her blood was sluggish, resisting the command to circulate. Along her legs, her muscles protested having to move, but the sunlight drew her forward.

"There now, the sun must feel good on your face."

"It does."

And the sight of the yard filled her with happiness. The church was in sight, and she could see the nuns tending to the windows. Off to the other side the boys were once more training with their wooden swords. She could see men walking along the curtain wall and hear the blacksmith working on his anvil, the steady hammering drifting up to her window. She could also hear the water beyond the tower in front of her. Her senses wanted to notice everything suddenly, and Jemma drank it in, absorbing it. But she forced herself to be realistic about how much effort it was going to take to return to the bed.

She might be weak, but she was sick of being carried like a babe.

"I should return now."

"Very well, my lady."

Claire lent her strength again on the way back to the bed, and Jemma blew out a tiny sigh of relief when she reached it. Her legs quivered, but satisfaction filled her, too, for being able to do something beyond waiting to be catered to. There was an ache in her legs, but the sort that came from working hard. She felt better, as though the short walk had begun the process of unfreezing her body. Her breathing felt deeper, and she smiled as the increased air cleared up her thoughts even more. The fresh breath banished the haze that seemed to have settled into her for so long. Relief replaced the weakness, and she smiled with satisfaction.

"Shall I read to you, my lady?"

"Umm, that would be thoughtful." And a test of her newly cleared thoughts.

Claire opened up a small book and sat down on a stool near the bed. Her voice was even and soft as she began to read. Jemma reached over to pick up the newest piece of heather Gordon had brought her. Holding it up to her nose, she inhaled the fragrance, allowing it to chase away the depression that was attempting to settle into her.

He hasn't told me he loves me.

Which was not to say that he didn't, but it wasn't to say that he did.

I love him.

She knew it now and even found herself being thankful for the poison because it had forced her to see what she had. When time grew short, everything became dearer. It had been that way with her father, too. She smiled at the memories, able to recall them without sorrow now. She would never regret the years she had spent with him, for that was what made her into the woman she was. It was what had taught her to love. If that was insanity, so be it. She wanted no cure, only time to spend loving the man who was her husband. There was never enough time to love the ones you held dear, but always plenty of days to mourn your mistakes.

A soft knock landed on the door. Claire stopped reading and stood up, but the door opened before she reached it. Jemma turned her head to see one of the nuns standing there in her wool robe. The garment was undyed, only the light cream color of the wool. Her head was covered with another piece of wool; this one had a black band that tightened around her forehead. The black signified that she had taken her final vows. There wasn't a hint of her hair showing, the head wrap tightened down to help her preserve her chastity and modesty vows. She even hid her hands inside the wide cuffs of her sleeve by crossing her arms in front of her body and clasping her own wrists. Jemma wondered if the girl had a true calling, for she appeared to take the duty of being a nun very seriously.

"Forgive me, but the laird wishes to see ye in the church sanctuary."

Claire frowned and looked at Jemma.

"The laird bid me care for his wife while you attend him." The nun was meek and her tone mild. She even lowered herself when she finished speaking.

"I see. Yes. Thank you." Claire walked toward the wall where her length of rust and orange Barras wool was hung. She placed it over her shoulder and belted it at her waist as she had been instructed to do. There was nothing to show that she was anything but another girl brought into the castle to work during the busy harvest season.

"I will return, my lady."

The door opened and closed softly behind Claire. The nun seemed to be frozen in place for a long moment. She stared at her with eyes that were impossible to read. She suddenly stiffened and walked to the window. Reaching out she placed her hands in the opening and rested them on the thick stone of the wall.

"I saw you looking out of the window."

Jemma felt a shiver go down her back. There was something in the tone of her voice that seemed cold. "Yes, the sunlight drew me toward it."

"No, that is not what drew you toward the window." The nun spoke sharply.

Jemma jerked and pushed herself up off the pillows. The nun turned slowly and watched her while shaking her head.

"It was God who drew you to this window. *God*."

"Yes, of course, since God made all things."

The nun had a smile on her lips that looked strange. It was almost as if the woman enjoyed seeing how much Jemma had to strain to sit up. She turned and looked out the window before turning back around to aim her attention at Jemma.

"God sent you to the window so that I might find you and finish the duty that He charged me with."

The chill went down her back again, this time much colder because the nun was moving slowly toward her.

"What duty is that?"

"To help my husband live a pure life." The nun's voice turned sweet. "We shall be blessed in too many ways to count just like Abraham if we remain free of sin. But he doesn't understand, he doesn't trust in the gift that God can grant to those who listen to him."

"Your husband?"

The nun moved closer and nodded. "Gordon, my husband. My father made me swear to wed him in spite of my devotion to God, but I see now that I may serve both God and my husband."

"Imogen?"

"I am Mary Job. Sister Mary Job, and God sent you to that window so that I might know where you were and finish removing ye from tempting my sweet husband away from me."

"Sweet Christ." Jemma scooted across the bed, horror filling her. The woman was mad; Jemma could see the insanity burning brightly in her eyes.

"Yes . . . why yes . . . You understand. I am going to send you to our sweet savior where there shall be no earthly sin."

"Imogen, no! This is not what God wants." Jemma swung her legs over the edge of the bed.

Imogen didn't like hearing her name. She frowned, her face turning red. "It is, and you are naught but a usurper! Trying to take my husband, oh whore! Ye shall not sully him! I shall smother you and remove ye from his path!"

Imogen lunged at her with her hands outstretched like the claws of a wolf. Jemma screamed and stood up. She had strength for enough steps to get to the door and pull it wide, but even the fear of her life was not enough to overcome the weakness that the poison had left. She stumbled into the wall, and Imogen slammed into her. Pain slashed through her as Imogen grabbed her braid and yanked.

"I must smother you in yer bed to show him what lust brings! Nothing but death."

Jemma forced herself to draw enough breath in to scream again. This time the sound echoed down the stairway.

Imogen snarled and tried to drag her back into the chamber, but the door had shut, making it necessary to open it with one hand. Jemma jerked against her hold while it was divided between the door and her hair. Imogen snarled and pulled on her head, but Jemma allowed her legs to crumple, making her body dead weight. Imogen was jerked off her feet and fell over the top of her.

A shriek came from the nun's lips as she began falling down the narrow stairs. Her hand tightened in her hair, pulling Jemma after her.

At least the truth will be known . . .

It was little comfort, and her body tumbled down the steps. Pain tore through her as her spine struck the edge of one step and then her shoulder fell against another, and over she tumbled to strike her cheek. She lacked the strength to stop her fall, and it felt like time was standing still. Jemma heard each one of her heartbeats, listened to them and discovered that the wait between one and the next was very long indeed when you were anticipating the end of your life. They fell for what seemed like an hour before landing on the bottom floor.

"I must kill you!"

Imogen rose up with blood staining her cream-colored robe, the crimson fluid flowing from a cut in her forehead.

Her eyes glowed with insanity, and her fingers were clenched into fists. Jemma tried to rise, but her body refused. Her muscles were useless, the weakness completely laying her at Imogen's mercy.

"I must strike now! Now where God has delivered ye to me."

Jemma rolled over and stumbled away from her a few more precious steps.

"No!" she wailed loud and almost pitifully.

"You interfere in God's work! Stand steady to receive His judgment."

Jemma gritted her teeth and forced her protesting legs to move again. But Imogen was far stronger. The nun jumped onto her, pushing her back onto the stone floor. Her hands locked around her throat, choking the breath from her. Jemma struggled, but Imogen held tight, preventing any breath from reaching her burning lungs.

"Yes . . . yes . . . so simple . . . ye will die now!"

Jemma forced her hands to stop trying to break Imogen's hold on her neck. She clawed at the nun's eyes instead. Imogen snarled but suddenly gasped when men rounded the corner. They were running and skid across the stone floor when they realized the way was blocked.

Jemma gasped for breath now that she could. Kerry reached out and pulled Imogen off her with one jerk of his arm.

"Christ in heaven, what are ye doing to the Mistress?"

"She is not the Mistress! She can never be my husband's wife." Imogen was distraught. She began walking in a circle while she babbled.

"Sweet God." Kerry crossed himself, his face full of horror to hear a nun talk of murder. He went to grab Imogen but couldn't force his hands to close around her arm. He didn't need to. The nun was in shock, hugging herself.

"Why, God? Why wasn't I able to kill her? I have been so close twice, and yet she still draws breath . . . he is my husband, joined to me by yer holy church . . . she is worldly sin and everything ye forbid . . . ye sent me to kill her, why did I fail? I am yer servant, yer most humble servant . . ."

The men who had come with Kerry all backed away from Imogen. Another set of footfalls came around the corner. This time Gordon led the charge, but he stumbled to a halt when he ran into his captain.

"What goes on here?"

The horror on Kerry's face drew a frown from Jemma's husband.

"Yer first wife, Laird."

Gordon froze and turned to look at the nun. His face drained of color while he listened to her continue to babble.

"Imogen?" It was a whisper filled with horror and the desire to have himself proved wrong. His first wife looked up and smiled as innocently as a child. She held her hands open to him in welcome, but her palms were covered in her own bright red blood.

"Dearest husband, we must seek God's favor through rejection of all earthly sin . . . I failed to kill the whore that draws ye away from chastity . . . so ye must help me . . . ye are my husband, my partner in this world . . . together we shall have all of the Lord's blessings if we keep His commandments . . ."

"No, Imogen. Ye are nae me wife, ye chose the Church and I bid ye joy." Gordon shook his head. "Take her away, Kerry."

"But she's a nun."

"I shall take her if you have not the stomach for it." Curan stepped forward with Synclair on his heels. His English accent drew a horrified gasp from Imogen.

"Stay away from me, *Protestant*! Do not touch me. I belong to Holy Mother Church."

Curan slowly walked toward her. "Then you had best walk, madam, for I will gladly fit the noose about your neck myself."

Imogen laughed. She tilted her head back and howled with amusement, her entire body shaking. She opened her arms wide and looked upward.

"Is this the gift ye send me? Release from this earthly body in the form of a Protestant? Oh, yes! Like Jesus being condemned by a Roman!"

"You cannot hang her, Curan. You must not."

Every head turned to look at Jemma. She had her hands pressed against the floor to hold her body up, but she lacked the strength to get to her feet.

"I surely can, Jemma. It is something I do not expect women to understand, but it is a necessary thing. Her crime is grave."

Kerry wiped a hand over his mouth, but the captain nodded as did Gordon.

"She is mad, Gordon. Even the King cannot order the execution of an insane person without special permission."

"No . . . No!" Imogen pointed a finger at her. "You whore! You cannot take yet more from me! Release me from this life! Hang me! That is God's will . . ."

Synclair reached out and hooked her upper arm with his hand. She shrieked and turned to look at him.

"I will take you away from here, madam."

Imogen instantly complied, smiling once more like a child. Synclair looked over her head at his lord. "I will secure her so she can cause no more harm."

"But ye should listen to God's will . . ." Imogen's words trailed off as Synclair pulled her down the hallway.

"Kerry, go and tell the priest."

"Aye, Laird."

The captain left with the youths following him.

Gordon crossed the space between them and scooped Jemma up off the floor. His body was so warm it made her shiver and realize how cold she had become. Her hands reached for him, desperately seeking out his strength. He kissed her forehead gently.

"Easy, lass. 'Tis finished now."

Finished. A beautiful word, one that promised a new beginning. Hope flowed through her, soothing the aches that assaulted her. There was no more reason to struggle, so she let her head rest on the shoulder of the man she loved.

It was astounding the way relief brought peace to a soul.

Jemma slept soundly, truly resting throughout the night because she believed that the threat to her life and her remaining at Gordon's side was indeed over. It was not that she was English, and that left her with the sound belief that the future held acceptance for her as mistress of Barras Castle.

But did it hold love?

That was the thought that she awoke to. The place beside her was empty, but the sheet was wrinkled, hinting that her husband had slept there.

Does that mean he loves me?

She couldn't put the thought from her mind. So she sat up, finding the task much more achievable than it had been yesterday. Her belly only gave the briefest twinge that she couldn't truly label pain. The floor was cool beneath her feet, but she smiled when she stood up and her knees didn't wobble.

Strength felt like it was flowing out from her heart to every inch of her body. She walked to the side of the room in search of her clothing, smiling when she realized she was alone in the chamber. Relief surged through her, and it gave her plenty of strength to dress. A low rumble from her stomach made her giggle.

Hungry—now there was something she had missed.

A riding dress constructed to be simple and useful awaited. She tugged on her hip roll and then lifted her skirts high over her head to put on the dress. Once the waistband was tied securely, she slipped into her stays and laced them up the front like a bodice. The corset fit looser than it had the last time she wore it. Another rumble from within made her reach for her doublet and shrug into it. With how hungry she felt, the few pounds she had lost would not be hard to find.

Once her doublet was buttoned, she reached for the comb and straightened out her hair. She hummed a tune, eagerly anticipating a meal outside her bed. The bells began to ring, announcing the first meal of the day, and Jemma went to join the rest of her household.

"Mistress."

The first maid she passed looked at her in surprise, but the girl smiled. " 'Tis right well to see ye up."

"Thank you."

People were hurrying into the great hall, but several younger retainers skidded to a halt when they noticed her. They jostled one another in an attempt to offer her their hand as escort.

"I believe that is my duty."

Her brother spoke from behind her, his voice deep and rich. "Something that I missed the opportunity to do when you took your wedding vows."

Curan swept her from head to toe with that keen stare that had once annoyed her.

"I am well, Brother."

He tilted his head slightly to one side in question.

"I can see that, Sister." He offered her his arm, and she

placed her hand on it with a smile. "However, I am going to stay a few more days to ensure that everything is settled. You are, after all, my only sister."

"A fortunate fact."

Curan offered her a soft chuckle before escorting her into the hall. Word had already spread of her arrival, and every soul was on their feet. They turned to watch her come down the aisle, and the men tugged on their hats while the girls nodded their heads. Tears stung her eyes because it was the respect that she had dreamed of, longed for, but could only earn.

Somehow, she had.

But her attention settled on the man waiting for her. Gordon stood at the head table, every one of his captains beside him. But they did not sit next to him today. There were two chairs for her and Curan.

The look in Gordon's eyes sent two tears down her cheeks. Joy shimmered there, so much of it that there was no way to mistake it. He pulled the "X" chair back for her, and no one sat down until he had pushed it back toward the table.

The rest of the hall became noisy once more as the meal was served.

"Ye are a fine sight, lass, even if I find myself wanting to carry ye back above stairs because I want to make sure ye are truly rested."

"Really, Gordon, I am not sure that you should declare so boldly that you want to carry me off with my brother listening."

One of his eyebrows arched at the suggestive tone of her voice. A hint of passion flickered in his eyes. Jemma lowered her eyelashes, shielding her own emotions from him. A second later she jumped when his hand landed on top of her thigh and gave it a squeeze.

Curan chuckled once more. "Careful, Barras, I did warn you that my sister is not meek."

"Was that a warning then?" Gordon reached out to pick an apple off the table. He cut into it with a small knife, splitting it with a sharp sound. He placed one-half on her plate before taking a bite out of the firm fruit and chewing it while contemplating her brother. "And here I thought ye were bragging to me. Ye know, polishing up yer sister's image so that I'd be hungry for a match with her."

Gordon's captains laughed, but her husband watched her pick up the apple and take a small bite from it. The flesh was sweet, and the smell filled her nose as she swallowed slowly.

"Maybe I was." Curan answered Gordon, but Jemma discovered that her brother was watching her as well. She took another bite and chewed it faster, shooting both men a warning look.

"I, for one, am grateful that things are settled now and no one shall feel the need to look after me."

The table quieted, several frowns appearing. Jemma looked to Gordon for an explanation.

"It seems that the Church shelters its own. Imogen was smuggled away by her fellow sisters, and none of them will tell me where she is."

"The priest told us to trust the Church and pray for her."

It was a disheartening thought but one that didn't hold up against the greeting that she had received from the castle's inhabitants. Her hope was burning brightly, and it was even balm for her heart to know that she would not have to endure the guilt of Imogen suffering somewhere in a cell, or worse yet, her execution.

"I wish her well."

There were plenty of raised eyebrows in response, but her husband considered her from behind a frown.

"I do."

"Well then, ye may wish Anyon well, too, for she has taken leave of the castle to join her cousin on McIre land."

Jemma swallowed again and noticed everyone at the head table watching her.

"Another bit of glad tidings."

"I agree, wife."

Jemma heard the tone in her husband's voice that often sent her temper to heating. He'd sent Anyon away, and he was not sorry.

She wasn't, either.

Her pride might ache, but her heart applauded the action. She reached beneath the table and pinched his thigh.

His hand captured hers, the feeling of his fingers wrapping around hers awakening more desire in her. She suddenly needed to be touched. It began to take command of her attention as her belly filled. She turned her hand beneath his and began to stroke his fingers, one after the other. Their skin sliding against each other was intoxicating; even the bright sunlight didn't make her shy away from the desire inside her.

It made her feel even more alive, and that was something that she had missed too sorely to feel guilty over.

"Since ye claimed the duty of escorting me wife in, I believe I'll take my chance to have her on my arm now."

They made it halfway down the aisle before Gordon laughed low and deep and scooped her off her feet. Those still eating erupted with amusement. Many of them slapping the tabletop while their laird carried her off.

"You enjoy that too much."

Gordon tossed her into the air and caught her. "Aye, I do, lass." He carried her up the stairs to their chamber, never stopping to catch his breath.

"But I confess that I enjoy being inside ye more." He laid

her down on the bed, his gaze moving over her as though he was attempting to memorize her. "However bold or blunt ye might find that, lass."

"I find it pleasing. Very pleasing."

"Is that so?" He reached out and flipped her skirt up to expose one leg. He clamped his hand around her knee and slid it up to her thigh. "How pleasing?"

"So pleasing that I wouldn't mind if you ripped this dress off me, so long as you lay with me, no clothing between us."

He drew in a stiff breath, a muscle twitching on the side of his jaw. The fingers on her thigh tightened.

"No just yet, lass. Ye need to rest."

Jemma hissed and sat up. She slid her own hand across the sheet and beneath his kilt to smooth along his thigh, but she did not stop there. She continued on until she felt the sac that hung beneath his member and then the hard rod itself.

"I need to feel you inside me, Gordon. I need to be your wife."

"Sweet lass." His voice was hoarse, but he captured the sides of her face between his hands and kissed her. She lost her grip on his cock but happily reached for him as he pushed her back while his lips teased hers. He didn't rush to open her mouth, the tip of his tongue flicking along her lower lip in a slow motion before he pressed a harder kiss against her lips. Slowly, steadily, he increased the pressure until she opened her mouth and allowed his tongue to penetrate. Liquid fire pooled inside her, like molten metal going into a mold. His tongue stabbed down into her mouth, stroking along her own, and she eagerly accepted it, closing her lips around it to suck it.

"Sweet wife."

He released her and stood. She ached for him, rolling up to

follow him until she heard his belt open. He pulled on the thick leather with a hard motion and tossed the open belt aside. His tartan received only enough attention to keep his colors from landing on the floor. He gathered up the loosened pleats and tossed them in a heap on top of a table.

Jemma reached for the top button on her doublet and flicked it open.

"No." He barked the command at her while ripping open the ties at the neck of his shirt.

"I want to undress ye."

His eyes glowed with excitement, and he pulled his shirt up and over his head to finish baring himself. He climbed onto the bed, his knees digging into the soft mattress.

"I want to kiss every inch of ye." His voice was hoarse again and his eyes bright with emotion. He released the buttons on her doublet with soft motions before gently easing the garment down her arms. His touch was the complete opposite of the way he had stripped his own clothing aside. Now he was tender and almost hesitant. He seemed to be savoring every movement, and she moaned softly as he stroked his hands back up her arms with only her chemise interfering.

"I spent too many hours dreading the possibility that I might not ever get to feel yer warm skin next to mine in this life again." He grasped the tie that held her stays closed and pulled the knot loose. Her breasts felt heavy and swollen. Gordon worked the lace free and pushed the corset over her shoulders so that it fell onto the bed behind her.

His hands trailed over the curves of her breasts, unleashing sweet sensation that rippled along her skin. She wanted to fall back onto the bed and simply enjoy being touched.

Gordon slid his hands down to her waistband and opened the tie there. With a few motions of his fingers he had it open and was pulling her skirts up and over her head. Her arms were stretched high above her head, and then the garment was finally free.

"Stay like that, lass."

The position pushed her breasts out, and her chemise fell in soft waves over her thighs. She was kneeling on the bed, and Gordon sent her hip roll onto the floor in one swift motion, leaving her in nothing but the thin linen shift.

He slid his hands down her arms and onto the sides of her body. Moving them inward, he cupped each breast, sending a shiver down her back. His hands kept moving, down across her midsection and then over the curves of her hips and still farther along her thighs until he found the hem of her last garment. He drew it up slowly, and she felt the air touching her bare skin. A soft murmur of delight whispered past her lips as he drew it higher, up until her breasts felt the morning air kiss them. Her nipples tingled, beginning to contract. And the skin on her arms felt the linen brushing over them until it was drawn completely away.

"Ye are a vision, lass. One that I swear I dreamed of every moment that we were separated."

Jemma reached for her hair and began to comb her fingers through the strands. Gordon settled on his knees in front of her, his gaze centered on her fingers as they slid through her hair. His cock stood erect with its ruby head swollen, and her passage felt wet for it, but there was no pressing urgency. Instead there was an enjoyment of the building heat.

Jemma finished freeing her hair, and he reached out to grasp a handful. He allowed the strands to rest in his palm for a long moment before leaning forward to inhale their fragrance.

"I adore the way ye smell, lass."

He pushed her back, nuzzling and kissing the tender skin at her neck.

"Everywhere."

His lips traveled to her collarbone and then down to her chest. His hands smoothed up from her waist to cup her breasts, and his lips captured one nipple. She gasped, stretching out across the bed. Pleasure streamed through her, feeding the heat that flickered in her passage. His tongue flicked across the hard point her nipple had become before he began licking his way toward her opposite point. He didn't hurry, and the hard nipple tightened with excitement as she felt his warm lips nearing it. She whimpered when he closed his lips around her breast, her back arching to offer it to his mouth. He sucked harder, and she gasped when need speared through her.

But he left the tender spot soon and trailed his kisses across her stomach.

Jemma shivered, unable to control the urge to spread her thighs. She craved the pleasure she knew he could give her with his lips. There was no thought given to right or wrong, there was only the yearning burning inside her.

"Ah, and the sweetest place of all."

Gordon pushed her thighs farther apart, the folds of her sex opening to expose her clitoris. His thumb brushed across the little point, drawing a sharp sound from her lips. The next contact was slightly firmer and longer, his thumb rubbing in several tiny circles before it traced the center of her sex down to the opening of her passage. He toyed with it, inserting his thumb for several long seconds and sending need racing through her.

"I could spend hours listening to the sound ye make when I'm pleasuring ye."

Her cheeks pinkened slightly, and he chuckled because he was watching her from between her open thighs. He moved his thumb back up to her clitoris and began rubbing it again.

"I confess that I could listen to ye whimper like that for hours."

Jemma hissed at him. His lips twitched up into a mischievous grin.

"But I agree that what we both crave isn't exactly this."

He rose up from between her legs, and her attention lowered to the length of his member. Her passage craved it, the walls feeling empty and needy. She lifted her arms in invitation, and his lips thinned, his expression becoming intense.

"I've dreamed of seeing ye issue that invitation, sweet lass." He settled his weight over her, the head of his cock pressing against the opening to her passage. "But the reality is far better than anything my mind teased me with."

His mouth claimed hers in a hard kiss. Urgency fueled his lips, and she met him with equal longing. His hips pressed forward, his hard flesh tunneling into her sheath. She clasped her hands around his neck, whimpering again with the sheer amount of sensation that filled her. He pushed deeply into her passage, and her hips lifted to meet him. They worked together perfectly, passion commanding them both. Pleasure was building inside her, tightening and threatening to release far too soon. She could see the passion on his face, too, and she watched his eyes battle to hold it back, but to no avail. His thrusts became harder and faster, and she kept pace with him, as eager for the release as he. The pleasure built until it broke, and the moment that it took control of her she felt his cock begin spurting its hot seed against the mouth of her womb.

Her lungs froze between breaths, and every muscle drew taut while the pleasure ruled her. It ran from her belly out to her toes and fingertips and then back to her belly without stopping. Only when it landed deep inside her did she draw breath again, gasping to fill her burning lungs. Gordon shuddered on top of her, his arms holding just enough of his weight to keep her from being crushed.

"Too fast."

He rolled over and pulled her along with him. " 'Twas too quickly done, lass."

He gathered her close, and she laid her head on his shoulder, listening to his heartbeat.

"We have plenty of time to perfect our timing."

But did they have enough time for love to grow? Many men never loved; it was a cruel fact. Tears stung her eyes and he shifted, placing a finger beneath her chin to raise it when he felt the wetness against his chest. Jemma resisted, keeping her head lowered.

"Why do ye cry, lass?" There was emotion in his voice, such deep caring that more tears spilled from her eyes and she felt guilty for them, but that did not grant her the ability to contain them.

He cupped her chin and raised it. "For I can nae bear it, those tears. Nae from the woman I love."

She stiffened, sitting up to slap a hand over her mouth to contain the sound that erupted from her lips. Gordon followed her, reaching out to grasp her with one solid arm around her waist. Her temper suddenly lit, and she balled up one fist and hit him. But she was so close she did little damage to his shoulder, so she lifted her hand and hit him again.

"You never spoke of love, not when I declared myself to you." She struggled, but he held her tight. "Beast. Was three words so much to ask for when my life might have ended before I heard them from your lips?"

"That is why I didna tell ye."

"Ohh . . . Toad! Release me."

He rolled onto his back, his amusement bouncing off the canopy above the bed. His hands captured her and pulled her down on top of him. But he rolled over to pin her down where he could clasp the sides of her head and keep her face where his gaze might connect with hers.

"I didna tell ye because I could nae bear the thought that ye might consider yer life complete. I wanted ye to have something to fight for, something to wake up for, lass. Ye have a spirit that refuses to surrender, and I was willing to use that to gain ye back."

She hit him again, but he only smiled.

"But 'twas the sweetest thing that I ever heard, those words from yer lips."

"I may never repeat them. It would be your just reward for allowing me to worry about your feelings. You miserable toad."

"I was miserable." Deep emotion flickered in his eyes, and it touched her heart. There was no missing the tenderness there, looking straight into her eyes like a bolt of lightning between them. It was warm and impossible not to love.

"So damn miserable that I believe I would have died if ye did. I never thought it possible that one woman might bring a man to his knees, but ye did, lass. I prayed in the church for hours on my knees, and I'd do it again for ye because I love ye more than I even like myself."

"Oh, Gordon, you are a fine man." She reached up to place her hands on his cheeks and he closed his eyes with a soft sound of male enjoyment. "You are the man I love, love so much I cry with it."

He opened his eyes, and they shimmered with unshed tears, betraying just how sincere he was.

"So are ye saying that ye love toads, lass? Well now, I've nae heard that before."

Jemma scoffed at him. "Good. I like knowing that I am the only woman who loves you."

"Well I can nae swear to that—" He snorted when she moved her knee and knocked his cock with it. He rolled over and tucked her along his body once again, pressing her head onto his shoulder with a tender hand.

"But I can swear that ye are the only woman that I love."

A week later . . .

"You look much better." Justina spoke the words, but her heart was not in them. The woman's eyes kept shifting to the windows and the clouds darkening the horizon.

"And you appear unhappy." Jemma stood up and walked across the room. She swore that she was never going to take such a thing for granted again. A week of rest and eating was restoring her strength quite rapidly.

"The last time I was happy was years ago, when I was with my son." Justina's blue eyes filled with joy, but she nibbled on her lip when she looked at the dark sky. "Brandon is seven now."

And it had been a long time since the lady had set eyes upon her child, much less held him.

"Do not pity me. I have spent all of my time in your company with that pity lurking in your eyes. There is nothing perfect about this life. Except for our children. You do not yet know the gift that feeling a life growing inside you is. It is even more precious to know that I can keep my son away from the worries of this world. There is nothing more that I may expect or ask for."

"There can be." Jemma walked toward the other woman

and placed a hand on her arm. "I have discovered happiness that I never believed could be. You need to open your heart to the possibilities that surround you."

"You mean Synclair? Oh, yes, that is the worst kept secret at Amber Hill."

"Must it remain a secret?"

Justina shook off her hand and folded her hands in front of her. It was a perfect pose, one that could have been an oil portrait instead of a living person. Justina reminded her too often of a painting with her delicate motions and polished manners. It was impossible to see into her feelings because she hid them behind a serene expression that never betrayed what she was truly thinking.

"My son enjoys a simple life now. On his father's estate because I obey Chancellor Wriothesley. If I do not, my son will be brought to court." Justina's face drained of color. "With its poisons and lusts. Such a fate would destroy everything good inside him."

Jemma felt her heart ache. Curan had refused to allow Justina to depart from Amber Hill, hoping to draw out the man who had sent her to betray him. Her brother was a man of strategy, but at the moment, Jemma discovered that she felt more kinship with Justina because they were women who sought to survive in a male-dominated world.

"I need to return to court, Jemma. Curan is married with a child on the way. He cannot shelter me, and I do not want him to. Can you understand that?" She looked out the window again. "Winter is creeping down from the north and I feel like it is strangling my ability to protect Brandon."

"I am not sure I can understand it."

Justina drew in a stiff breath, but Jemma continued. "You told me not to pity you, Justina, but it is a truth that when I do, I notice how unfair it is for you to be kept here."

Justina stood silent for a long moment, her gaze returning to the windows.

"Then pity me, but force your brother to give me my freedom."

Her voice was low and rough, betraying how little liking she had for the manner in which she might gain what she desired.

"That would achieve naught."

Justina turned an angry look toward her. "Are you playing with me?"

"Nay, merely stating what we both know, even if you are asking for me to try reasoning with my brother because you are desperate."

"I am desperate." Justina sounded hollow now, and she laid a hand on the glass, looking as though she might actually will herself to where her son was.

"I only know of one way to offer you something different from what Curan plans for you, but you would have to be desperate to attempt it."

Justina turned to stare at her. The look was full of longing and need so strong, Jemma felt it. Jemma cast a look toward the doors of the chamber to ensure that no one was there but them.

"If you still have the boy clothing that you came here in, my mare is in the back of the stable. My brother would never listen to me when it comes to something he considers a point of honor, and I doubt my husband will allow you to risk yourself on the road with the English knights, but I will give my mare to you, Justina."

Justina's eyes lit with joy. She clasped her hands together and pressed them against her lips to remain silent. For a moment she appeared as though she might burst with her happiness.

"It is more risk than any person should take."

"But I will and gladly so." She reached out and clasped one of Jemma's hands. "Never regret what you do for me, for I consider it the finest of gifts, no matter what befalls me."

"Are you certain, Justina? Life is a precious thing as I have learned recently."

Justina shook her head. "But you have also noticed that being without a place is no true life."

Jemma nodded for it was a truth if ever she had heard one. "I will pray for you."

And herself because her husband was very much like her brother when it came to his honor. However, she would not take back the gift of the mare for one simple reason. She trusted Gordon to understand why she did it and not hate her for it.

Jemma awoke early, and her husband was already gone. She rubbed her eyes and sought out her clothing. Dawn was turning the edge of the horizon pink when she made her way down the steps to discover her brother and her husband frowning. Kerry stood with one hand stroking his chin, but Synclair offered the most fierce expression. The knight looked ready to kill, with his bare hands, no less.

They all turned when she came into sight. Her brother looked pensive, and she knew what that meant.

He knew. It was as simple as that. Justina must have taken her chance immediately.

"You are correct, Brother. Lady Justina did leave on my mare."

Curan drew in a stiff breath, but it was Synclair who scowled at her. Jemma leveled a firm look back at the knight.

"She asked for my help in convincing you to release her, but I knew that would not happen, so I gave her the only thing I had. My mare."

"She needed protection." Synclair growled out the words before lowering his head in apology for the outburst. "I feel that she still needs it."

"Well I can nae hold with any woman riding out at night. 'Twas foolish when ye did it, my wife, and it is still so." There was hard reprimand in her husband's voice, some of it deserved, but Jemma kept her chin steady.

"There is no member of your household here, so I shall speak my mind."

Gordon stiffened, his expression becoming tight.

"I know you do not agree with me giving her the mare, but it was my horse and I wanted to help her. She did me a great service by coming here and placing herself at risk for me. Besides, none of us can truly understand the torment it is for her to be kept from seeing to the welfare of her son. I gave her the mare, and I only pray that she makes good use of the animal."

"Which means she has stolen nothing except clothing." It was Synclair who spoke again, the knight appearing to lose interest in everyone in the room while he glanced toward the window. "I understand why she left the armor behind now."

Jemma felt her eyes rounding.

Of course Justina had left the armor behind. Armor was very expensive, and to steal it was a high crime.

"Then she is away and that is the end of it." Curan spoke in an oddly light tone considering his past position on keeping Justina under his protection. "I will not begrudge her the clothing. Synclair, ready the men. We shall return to Amber Hill."

"Yes, my lord."

The knight spoke through clenched teeth but not from anger. He seemed abnormally pleased with his lord's order and turned in a quick motion before moving out of the tower at a fast pace.

Her brother actually chuckled, drawing her attention. Curan lifted one dark eyebrow.

"Ah, perhaps you do not realize that Synclair has only this day left of his service to me."

Jemma felt her eyes round. "This day?"

"Indeed, and then he shall have completed his service as his father made him swear to do. I will miss him, of course, but he has an estate to take in hand as well as the title that his father inherited from his uncle. The Baron Harrow died recently without issue. Synclair has much to do at court."

"At court." Jemma nibbled on her lower lip, contemplating what Lady Justina was about to have surprising her.

Curan offered her one of his rare grins. "Yes, Sister, recently I have become more tolerant of fate and her need to insist on gaining her way."

"So have I." She took a deep breath and allowed her worry to subside. Maybe Justina needed fate just as much as she had. In fact, Jemma was more sure of it when she considered the way the lady had looked the last time she saw her. She needed Synclair, and it appeared that fate was about to thrust them together again.

Her brother shared a long look with her and then aimed another at her husband. He offered his hand, and Gordon took it, clasping his hand around Curan's wrist in a gesture that was considered as binding as written contract between knights.

"I place my trust in you, Barras. Take care of my sister, for the times are soon to become more turbulent."

"Aye, that's for sure with two children on the thrones of both our countries. In a way, 'tis a pity that they can nae be allowed to rule. There would be less bloodshed for they'd spend their time ordering their armies on adventures through the woods."

"A charming thought, Brother. I can see you dancing with fairies and forest sprites even now."

Curan offered her a frown, but it did not reach his eyes. "You have a husband now, Jemma, to deal with that tongue."

He turned and walked through the doors that led to the yard. His men waited, the sound of horses and leather filling the morning air. Eagerness floated on the breeze, and a man brought her brother's horse to him the moment he appeared. They were Englishmen who longed to return to England, but beneath that they were men who wanted to lay their heads beside their families. That wasn't unique to Scot or English; it was a desire all men had.

Curan gained the saddle and placed his helmet on his head before raising one fist into the air.

"Ride!"

The group surged forward in a symphony of motion. Their action gave testimony to the years of training every man down to the squires had taken in the art of being who they were. A knight was not trained in a week; he began his toil at a young age and faced many years of obstacles before gaining the golden chain that would declare his rank. The days were long and the tasks too many to count, but they forged a man who was unbendable in spirit.

Jemma spotted Sinclair; the helmet he wore sported two white feathers. The morning light shone off his knight chain that was perfectly polished in spite of the many things that he did to serve her brother. The reason was simple; it represented what he had dedicated his life to.

"Will ye miss yer brother very much, lass?"

Gordon stepped up beside her, standing just enough away from her body to maintain his position as head of the house. She turned and lowered herself, making the appearance of the perfect wife, but she lifted her eyes and shot him a look that was full of passion.

"Only if you prove to be boring, toad."

His lips parted to show her a flash of his teeth a moment before he spread his arms wide and captured her. He tossed her up and over his shoulder and turned toward the stairs that led to their chamber.

"I swear to do my toady best, lass."

IMPROPER GENTLEMEN are a lot more fun!
Go get this sexy anthology from Diane Whiteside,
Mia Marlowe, and Maggie Robinson,
available now. Turn the page for a sample
of Diane's story, "Talbot's Ace" . . .

Wolf Laurel, Colorado,
High Rockies, September 1875

Silver and black spun through the man's fingers in deadly pinwheels of steel under the lead-grey skies.

Charlotte Moreland froze in front of the Silver King Hotel, unable to take another step even though the young man was more than a dozen paces away.

Three years of playing poker in the West's worst gambling dens had taught her much about the narrow margin between great shootists and the dead. She had no desire to join the latter in front of an establishment named Hair Trigger Palace.

Handsome and harsh as a Renaissance angel, he was utterly absorbed in weaving patterns of light as he spun his revolvers. His black broadcloth frockcoat, black trousers, and black boots were as finely made as if they too bore homage to the death-dealing implements he worshipped.

Her fellow stagecoach passengers streamed into the closest saloon to warm themselves with beer or whiskey. One headed swiftly into the hotel to claim his clean lodging, more priceless than a good meal in this hastily built town. A few pedestrians glanced at the effortless display of gun tricks, then walked swiftly past.

He flipped the heavy guns between his hands and they smacked into his palms like a warrior's salute. He immediately tossed them high and spun them back into the holsters at his hips.

Last spring in Denver, she'd seen a shootist testing his pistols. He'd shot a can of peaches until it had exploded its innards across a wall, just like a person would. She'd been wretchedly sick in her hotel room afterward.

He slapped the leather holsters and, an instant later on a ragged beat, death looked out of the guns' barrels.

His expression hardened to that of an angry fallen angel leading armies of destruction. He shoved his guns back into place, clearly ready to teach them another lesson.

Charlotte gave a little squeak and trotted onto the boardwalk in front of the hotel. No matter how flimsy its roof and planks were, it still offered more protection than the open street. Men, equipped with guns and a temper, were dangerous to both themselves and everyone nearby.

The shootist whirled to face her and his gaze drilled into her.

Heaven help her, it was the same man she'd seen in Denver—Justin Talbot, the fastest gun in Colorado.

Recognition flashed across his face. But not greed, thank God. Perhaps he hadn't recognized her photo, flaunted by those skulking Pinkerton's men throughout the mining towns.

Why had she dreamed about him for so many months?

He bowed to her with a flourish and she froze. Her heart drummed in her throat, too fast to let her breathe or think.

How should she acknowledge him—formally, with a bow or a curtsy? Heartily, with a wave inviting affection or perhaps intimacy? Or coldly, with an averted shoulder and gaze, as befitted such an experienced death-dealer, no matter what living in this town required?

He frowned and anguish slipped into his eyes. A man whistled from behind him.

Talbot's mouth tightened and he bowed to her again, far more coldly. She gave him the barest of nods in return, all her drumming pulse would support.

He disappeared into the Hair Trigger Palace an instant later, his expression still harsher than an ice-etched granite mountain.

Truly, she should not feel bereft, as if she'd lost a potential friend.

Don't miss DEAD ALERT
by Bianca D'Arc,
new this month from Brava.

Fort Bragg, North Carolina

"I've got a special project for you, Sam." The commander, a former Navy SEAL named Matt Sykes, began talking before Sam was through the door to Matt's private office. "Sit down and shut the door."

Sam sat in a wooden chair across the cluttered desk from his commanding officer. Lt. Sam Archer, US Army Green Beret, was currently assigned to a top secret, mixed team of Special Forces soldiers and elite scientists. There were also a few others from different organizations, including one former cop and a CIA black ops guy. It was an extremely specialized group, recruited to work on a classified project of the highest order.

"I understand you're a pilot." Matt flipped through a file as he spoke.

"Yes, sir." Sam could have said more but he didn't doubt Matt had access to every last bit of Sam's file, even the top secret parts. He had probably known before even sending for him that Sam could fly anything with wings. Another member of his old unit was a blade pilot who flew all kinds of choppers, but fixed wing aircraft were Sam's specialty.

"How do you like the idea of going undercover as a charter pilot?"

"Sir?" Sam sat forward in the chair, intrigued.

"The name of a certain charter airline keeps popping up." Matt put down the file and faced Sam as his gaze hardened. "Too often for my comfort. Ever heard of a company called Praxis Air?"

"Can't say that I have."

"It's a small outfit, based out of Wichita—at least that's where they repair and maintain their aircraft in a company-owned hangar. They have branch offices at most of the major airports and cater mostly to an elite business clientele. They do the odd private cargo flight and who knows what else. They keep their business very hush-hush, 'providing the ultimate in privacy for their corporate clients,' or so their brochure advertises." Matt pushed a glossy tri-fold across the desk toward Sam.

"Looks pretty slick."

"That they are," Matt agreed. "So slick that even John Petit, with his multitude of CIA connections, can't get a bead on exactly what they've been up to of late. I've been piecing together bits here and there. Admiral Chester, the traitor, accepted more than a few free flights from them in the past few months, as did Ensign Bartles, who it turns out, was killed in a Praxis Air jet that crashed the night we took down Dr. Rodriguez and his friends. She wasn't listed on the manifest and only the pilot was claimed by the company, but on a hunch I asked a friend on the National Transportation Safety Board to allow us to do some DNA testing. Sure enough, we found remnants of Beverly Bartles's DNA at the crash site, though her body had to have been moved sometime prior to the NTSB getting there. The locals were either paid off or preempted. Either option is troubling, to say the least."

"You think they're mixed up with our undead friends?" They were still seeking members of the science team that had created the formula that killed and then turned its victims into the walking dead. Nobody had figured out exactly how they were traveling so freely around the country when they were on every watch list possible.

"It's a very real possibility. Which is why I want to send you in undercover. I don't need to remind you, time is of the essence. We have a narrow window to stuff this genie back into its bottle. The longer this goes on, the more likely it is the technology will be sold to the highest bidder and then, God help us."

Sam shivered. The idea of the zombie technology in the hands of a hostile government or psycho terrorists—especially after seeing what he'd seen of these past months—was unthinkable.

"If my going undercover will help end this, I'm your man." He'd do anything to stop the contagion from killing any more people.

Sam opened the flyer and noted the different kinds of jets the company offered. The majority of the planes looked like Lear 35's in different configurations. Some were equipped for cargo. Some had all the bells and whistles any corporate executive could wish for and a few were basically miniature luxury liners set up for spoiled celebrities and their friends.

"I hoped you'd say that. I've arranged a little extra training for you at Flight Safety in Houston. They've got Level D flight simulators that have full motion and full visual. They can give you the Type Rating you'll need on your license to work for Praxis Air legitimately."

"I've been to Flight Safety before. It's a good outfit." Sam put the brochure back on Matt's desk.

"We'll give you a suitable job history and cover, which you will commit to memory. You'll also have regular check-ins while in the field, but for the most part you'll be on your own.

I want you to discover who, if any, of their personnel are involved and to what extent." Matt paused briefly before continuing. "Just to be clear, this isn't a regular job I'm asking you to do, Sam. It's not even close to what you signed on for when we were assigned as zombie hunters. I won't order you to do this. It's a total immersion mission. Chances are, there will be no immediate backup if you get into trouble. You'll be completely on your own most of the time."

"Understood, sir. I'm still up for it. I like a challenge."

Matt cracked a smile. "I hear that. And I appreciate the enthusiasm. Here's the preliminary packet to get you started." He handed a bulging envelope across the desk. "We'll get the rest set up while you're in flight training. It'll be ready by the time you are. You leave tomorrow for Houston."

"Yes, sir." Sam stood, hearing the tone of dismissal in the commander's voice.

"You can call this whole thing off up until the end of your flight training. After that, wheels will have been set in motion and can't be easily stopped. If you change your mind, let me know as soon as possible."

"Thank you, sir." Unspoken was the certainty that Sam wouldn't be changing his mind any time soon.

And keep an eye out for
SEVEN YEARS TO SIN by Sylvia Day,
coming next month!

Alistair Caulfield's back was to the door of his warehouse shipping office when it opened. A salt-tinged gust blew through the space, snatching the manifest he was about to file right out of his hand.

He caught it deftly, then looked over his shoulder. Startled recognition moved through him. "Michael."

The new Lord Tarley's eyes widened with equal surprise, then a weary half-smile curved his mouth. "Alistair, you scoundrel. You didn't tell me you were in Town."

"I've only just returned." He slid the parchment into the appropriate folder and pushed the drawer closed. "How are you, my lord?"

Michael removed his hat and ran a hand through his dark brown hair. The assumption of the Tarley title appeared to weigh heavily on his broad shoulders, grounding him in a way Alistair had never seen before. He was dressed somberly in shades of brown, and he flexed his left hand, which bore the Tarley signet ring, as if he could not accustom himself to having it there. "As well as can be expected under the circumstances."

"My condolences to you and your family. Did you receive my letter?"

"I did. Thank you. I meant to reply, but time is stretched so thin. The last year has raced by so quickly; I've yet to catch my breath."

"I understand."

Michael nodded. "I'm pleased to see you again, my friend. You have been gone far too long."

"The life of a merchant." He could have delegated more, but staying in England meant crossing paths with both his father and Jessica. His father complained about Alistair's success as a tradesman with as much virulence as he'd once complained about Alistair's lack of purpose. It was a great stressor for his mother, which he was only able to alleviate by being absent as much as possible.

As for Jessica, she'd been careful to avoid him whenever they were in proximity. He had learned to reciprocate when he saw how marriage to Tarley changed her. While she remained as cool in deportment as ever, he'd seen the blossoming of her sensual nature in the languid way she moved and the knowledge in those big, gray eyes. Other men coveted the mystery of her, but Alistair had seen behind the veil and *that* was the woman he lusted for. Forever beyond his reach in reality, but a fixture in his mind. She was burned into his memory by the raging hungers and impressionableness of youth, and the years hadn't lessened the vivid recollection one whit.

"I find myself grateful for your enterprising sensibilities," Michael said. "Your captains are the only ones I would entrust with the safe passage of my sister-in-law to Jamaica."

Alistair kept his face impassive by considerable practice, but the sudden awareness gripping him tensed his frame. "Lady Tarley intends to travel to Calypso?"

"Yes. This very morning, which is why I'm here. I intend to speak to the captain myself and see he looks after her until they arrive."

"Who travels with her?"

"Only her maid. I should like to accompany her, but I can't leave now."

"And she will not delay?"

"No." Michael's mouth curved wryly. "And I cannot dissuade her."

"You cannot say no to her," Alistair corrected, moving to the window through which he could view the West India docks. Ships entered the Northern Dock to unload their precious imports, then sailed around to the Southern Dock to reload with cargo for export. Around the perimeter, a high brick wall deterred the rampant theft plaguing the London wharves, which increased his shipping company's appeal to West Indian landowners requiring secure carriage of goods.

"Neither can Hester—forgive me, *Lady Regmont.*"

The last was said with difficulty. Alistair had long suspected his friend nursed deeper feelings for Jessica's younger sister and had assumed Michael would pay his addresses. Instead, Hester had been presented at court then immediately betrothed, breaking the hearts of many hopeful would-be swains. "Why is she so determined to go?"

"Benedict bequeathed the property to her. She claims she must see to its sale personally. I fear the loss of my brother has affected her deeply and she seeks a purpose. I've attempted to anchor her, but duty has me stretched to wit's end."

Alistair's reply was carefully neutral. "I can assist her in that endeavor. I can make the necessary introductions, as well as relay information it would take her months to find."

"A generous offer." Michael's gaze was searching. "But you just returned. I can't ask you to depart again so soon."

Turning, Alistair said, "My plantation borders Calypso, and I could use the expansion. It's my hope to position myself as the best purchaser of the property. I will pay her handsomely, of course."

Relief swept over Michael's expressive features. "That would ease my mind considerably. I'll speak to her at once."

"Perhaps you should leave that to me. If, as you say, she needs a purpose, then she'll want to maintain control of the matter in all ways. She should be allowed to set the terms and pace of our association to suit her. I have all the time in the world, but you do not. See to your most pressing affairs, and entrust Lady Tarley to me."

"You've always been a good friend," Michael said. "I pray you return to England swiftly and settle for a time. I could use your ear and head for business. In the interim, please encourage Jessica to write often and keep me abreast of the situation. I should like to see her return before we retire to the country for the winter."

"I'll do my best."

Alistair waited several minutes after Michael departed, then moved to the desk. He began a list of new provisions for the journey, determined to create the best possible captive environment. He also made some quick but costly adjustments to the passenger list, moving two additional travelers to another of his ships.

He and Jessica would be the only non-crewmen aboard the *Acheron*.

She would be within close proximity for weeks—it was an extraordinary opportunity Alistair was determined not to waste.